THE EXCURSION TRAIN

As a bustling crowd clambers aboard the Great Western Railway excursion train taking them to an illegal prize-fight, the guard fears for the safety of his rolling stock. Little does he expect, however, the murder of one of his passengers, public executioner Jake Bransby. Detective Inspector Robert Colbeck and his assistant Sergeant Victor Leeming are sent to the scene and are intrigued by the murder weapon – a noose. When a second man is strangled by a noose on a train, Colbeck must act quickly to catch the murderer before more lives are lost?

THE EXCURSION TRAIN

THE EXCURSION TRAIN

by

Edward Marston

Magna Large Print Books
Long Preston, North Yorkshire,
BD23 4ND, England.

British Library Cataloguing in Publication Data.

Marston, Edward
    The excursion train.

    A catalogue record of this book is
    available from the British Library

    ISBN   0-7505-2405-7

First published in Great Britain in 2005 by Allison & Busby Ltd.

Published in Large Print 2005 by arrangement with
Allison & Busby Ltd.

Magna Large Print is an imprint of Library Magna Books Ltd.

Printed and bound in Great Britain by
T.J. (International) Ltd., Cornwall, PL28 8RW

On the appointed day about five hundred passengers filled some twenty or twenty-five open carriages – they were called 'tubs' in those days – and the party rode the enormous distance of eleven miles and back for a shilling, children half-price. We carried music with us and music met us at the Loughborough station. The people crowded the streets, filled windows, covered the house-tops, and cheered us all along the line, with the heartiest welcome. All went off in the best style and in perfect safety we returned to Leicester; and thus was struck the keynote of my excursions, and the social idea grew upon me.

Leisure Hour – Thomas Cook, 1860

Chapter One

London, 1852

They came in droves, converging on Paddington Station from all parts of the capital. Coster-mongers, coal-heavers, dustmen, dock labourers, coachmen, cab drivers, grooms, glaziers, lamplighters, weavers, tinkers, carpenters, bricklayers, watermen, and street sellers of everything from rat poison to pickled whelks, joined the human torrent that was surging towards the excursion train. Inevitably, the crowd also had its share of thieves, pickpockets, cardsharps, thimble riggers and prostitutes. A prizefight of such quality was an increasingly rare event. It was too good an opportunity for the low life of London to miss.

There was money to be made.

Extra ticket collectors were on duty to make sure that nobody got past the barrier without paying, and additional railway policemen had been engaged to maintain a degree of order. Two locomotives stood ready to pull the twenty-three carriages that were soon being filled by rowdy spectators. The excitement in the air was almost tangible.

Sam Horlock looked on with a mixture of interest and envy.

'Lucky devils!' he said.

'All I see is danger,' complained Tod Galway,

the guard of the train. 'Look how many there are, Sam – all of them as drunk as bleedin' lords. There'll be trouble, mark my words. Big trouble. We should never have laid on an excursion train for this rabble.'

'They seem good-natured enough to me.'

'Things could turn ugly in a flash.'

'No,' said Horlock, tolerantly. 'They'll behave themselves. We'll make sure of that. I just wish that I could join them at the ringside. I've a soft spot for milling. Nothing to compare with the sight of two game fighters, trying to knock the daylights out of each other. It's uplifting.'

Sam Horlock was one of the railway policemen deputed to travel on the train. Like his colleagues, he wore the official uniform of dark, high-necked frock coat, pale trousers and a stovepipe hat. He was a jovial man in his forties, short, solid and clean-shaven. Tod Galway, by contrast, was tall, thin to the point of emaciation, and wearing a long, bushy, grey beard that made him look like a minor prophet. A decade older than his companion, he had none of Horlock's love of the prize ring.

'The Fancy!' he said with disgust, spitting out the words. 'That's what they calls 'em. The bleedin' Fancy! There's nothing fancy about this load of ragamuffins. They stink to 'igh 'eaven. We're carryin' the dregs of London today and no mistake.'

'Be fair, Tod,' said Horlock. 'They're not all riff-raff, crammed into the third-class carriages. We've respectable passengers aboard as well in first and second class. Everyone likes the noble art.'

'What's noble about beatin' a man to a pulp?'

'There's skill involved.'

'Pah!'

'There is. There's tactics and guile and raw courage. It's not just a trial of brute strength.'

'I still don't 'old with it, Sam.'

'But it's manly.'

'It's against the bleedin' law, that's what it is.'

'More's the pity!'

'The magistrates ought to stop it.'

'By rights, they should,' agreed Horlock with a grin, 'but they got too much respect for the sport. My guess is that half the magistrates of Berkshire will be there in disguise to watch the contest.'

'Shame on them!'

'They don't want to miss the fun, Tod. Last time we had a fight like this was six or seven years ago when Caunt lost to Bendigo. Now *that* was milling of the highest order. They went toe to toe for over ninety gruelling rounds, the pair of them, drooping from exhaustion and dripping with blood.'

'Yes – and what did that do to the spectators?'

'It set them on fire, good and proper.'

'That's my worry,' admitted Galway, watching a trio of boisterous navvies strut past. 'These buggers are bad enough *before* the fight. Imagine what they'll be like afterwards when their blood is racing and their passions is stoked up. I fear for my train, Sam.'

'There's no need.'

'Think of the damage they could cause to railway property.'

'Not while we're around.'

'We're carryin' over a thousand passengers. What can an 'andful of policemen do against that lot?'

'Ever seen a sheepdog at work?' asked Horlock, hands on hips. 'If it knows its job, one dog can keep a flock of fifty under control. That's what we are, Tod. Sheepdogs of the Great Western Railway.'

'There's only one problem.'

'What's that?'

'You're dealing with wild animals – not with bleedin' sheep.'

When, the excursion train pulled out of Paddington in a riot of hissing steam and clanking wheels, it was packed to capacity with eager boxing fans. There were two first class carriages and three second class but the vast majority of passengers were squeezed tightly into the open-topped third class carriages, seated on hard wooden benches yet as happy as if they were travelling in complete luxury. As soon as the train hit open country, rolling landscape began to appear on both sides but it attracted little attention. All that the hordes could see in their mind's eye was the stirring spectacle that lay ahead of them. Isaac Rosen was to take on Bill Hignett in a championship contest.

In prospect, the fight had everything. It was a match between two undefeated boxers at the height of their powers. Rosen worked in a Bradford slaughterhouse where his ferocity had earned him his nickname. Hignett was a giant Negro who toiled on a Thames barge. It was a case of Mad Isaac versus the Bargeman. North versus South. White versus Black. And – to add some real piquancy – Jew versus Christian. Nobody could

12

remain impartial. The London mob was going to cheer on Bill Hignett and they were baying for blood. As flagons of beer were passed around thirsty mouths, tongues were loosened and predictions became ever more vivid.

'The Bargeman will tap his claret with his first punch.'

'Then knock his teeth down his Jewish throat.'

''E'll 'it Mad Isaac all the way back to Bradford.'

'And slaughter the Yid!'

Such were the universally held opinions of the experts who occupied every carriage. In praising Bill Hignett, they denigrated his opponent, swiftly descending into a virulent anti-semitism that grew nastier with each mile they passed. By the time they reached their destination, they were so certain of the outcome of the fight that they indulged in premature celebrations, punching the air in delight or clasping each other in loving embraces. Anxious to be on their way, they poured out of the excursion train as if their lives depended on it.

There was still some way to go. The field in which the fight was being held was over three miles away from Twyford Station but the fans made no complaint about the long walk. Guides were waiting to conduct them to the site and they fell gratefully in behind them. Some began to sing obscene ditties, others took part in drunken horseplay and one lusty young sailor slipped into the bushes to copulate vigorously with a buxom dolly-mop. There was a prevailing mood of optimism. Expectations were high. The long column of tumult began to wend its way through the Berkshire countryside.

Tod Galway was pleased to have got rid of his troublesome cargo but his relief was tempered by the thought that they would have to take the passengers back to London when they were in a more uncontrollable state. As it was, he found a man who was too inebriated to move from one of the third-class carriages, a second who was urinating on to the floor and a third who was being violently sick over a seat. He plucked at his beard with desperation.

'They've got no respect for company property,' he wailed.

'We're bound to have a few accidents, Tod,' said Sam Horlock, ambling across to him. 'Take no notice.'

'I got to take notice, Sam. I'm *responsible*.'

'So am I – worse luck. I'd give anything to be able to see the Bargeman kick seven barrels of shit out of Mad Isaac. Do you think anyone would notice if I sneak off?'

'Yes,' said Galway, 'and that means you'd lose your job.'

'Be almost worth it.'

The guard was incredulous. 'You taken leave of your senses?'

'This fight is for the championship, Tod.'

'I don't care if it's for that Kohinoor Bleedin' Diamond what was give to Queen Victoria. Think of your family, man. You got mouths to feed. What would your wife and children say if you got sacked for watchin' a prizefight?' Horlock looked chastened. 'I know what my Annie'd say and I

14

know what she'd do. If I threw my job away like that, my life wouldn't be worth livin'.'

'It was only a thought.'

'Forget it. I'll give you three good reasons why you ought to 'ang on to a job with the Great Western Railway. First of all–'

But the guard got no further. Before he could begin to enumerate the advantages of employment by the company, he was interrupted by a shout from the other end of the train. A young railway policeman was beckoning them with frantic semaphore.

Galway was alarmed. 'Somethin' is up.'

'Just another drunk, I expect. We'll throw him out.'

'It's more serious than that, Sam. I can tell.'

'Wait for me,' said Horlock as the guard scurried off. 'What's the hurry?' He fell in beside the older man. 'Anybody would think that one of the engines was on fire.'

The policeman who was gesticulating at them was standing beside a second class carriage near the front of the train. His mouth was agape and his cheeks were ashen. Sweat was moistening his brow. As the others approached, he began to jabber.

'I thought he was asleep at first,' he said.

'Who?' asked the guard.

'Him – in there.'

'What's up?' asked Horlock, reaching the carriage.

The policeman pointed. 'See for yourself, Sam.'

He stood back so that Horlock and Galway could peer in through the door. Propped up in the far corner was a stout middle-aged man in non-descript clothing with his hat at a rakish angle. His eyes were open and there was an expression of disbelief on his face. A noisome stench confirmed that he had soiled himself. Galway was outraged. Horlock stepped quickly into the carriage and shook the passenger by the shoulder so that his hat fell off.

'Time to get out now, sir,' he said, firmly.

But the man was in no position to go anywhere. His body fell sideward and his head lolled back, exposing a thin crimson ring around his throat. The blood had seeped on to his collar and down the inside of his shirt. When he set out from London, the passenger was looking forward to witnessing a memorable event. Somewhere along the line, he had become a murder victim.

'This is dreadful!' cried Tod Galway, recoiling in horror.

'Yes,' said Horlock, a wealth of sympathy in his voice. 'The poor devil will never know who won that fight now.'

Chapter Two

When the summons came, Inspector Robert Colbeck was at Scotland Yard, studying the report he had just written about his last case. He abandoned it at once and hurried along the corridor. Superintendent Tallis was a not a man who liked to be kept waiting. He demanded an instant response from his detectives. Colbeck found him in his office, seated behind his desk, smoking a cigar and poring over a sheet of paper. Tallis spoke to his visitor without even looking up.

'Don't sit down, Inspector. You're not staying long.'

'Oh?'

'You'll be catching a train to Twyford.'

'In Berkshire?'

'I know of no other,' said Tallis, raising his eyes. 'Do you?'

'No, sir.'

'Then do me the courtesy of listening to what I have to say instead of distracting me with questions about geography. This,' he went on, holding up the sheet of paper, 'is an example of the value of the electric telegraph, a priceless tool in the fight against crime. Details of the murder have been sent to us while the body is still warm.'

Colbeck's ears pricked up. 'There's been a murder at Twyford?'

'In a railway carriage, Inspector.'

'Ah.'

'It was an excursion train on the Great Western Railway.'

'Then I suspect I know where it was going, sir,' said Colbeck.

He also knew why the assignment was being handed to him. Ever since his success in solving a train robbery and its associated crimes in the previous year, Robert Colbeck had become known as the Railway Detective. It was a name bestowed upon him by newspapers that had, in the past, mocked the Detective Department of the Metro-

17

politan Police for its apparent slowness in securing convictions. Thanks largely to Colbeck, the reporters at last had reason to praise the activities of Scotland Yard. He had masterminded the capture of a ruthless gang, responsible for armed robbery, blackmail, abduction, criminal damage and murder. Colbeck's reputation had been firmly established by the case. It meant that whenever a serious crime was committed on a railway, the respective company tended to seek his assistance.

Colbeck was, as usual, immaculately dressed in a black frock coat with rounded edges and high neck, a pair of well-cut fawn trousers and an Ascot cravat. His black shoes sparkled. Tall, lean and conventionally handsome, he cut a fine figure and always looked slightly out of place among his more workaday colleagues. None of them could challenge his position as the resident dandy. Edward Tallis would not even have cared to try. As a military man, he believed implicitly in smartness and he was always neatly, if soberly, dressed. But he deplored what he saw as Colbeck's vanity. It was one of the reasons that there was so much latent tension between the two of them. The Superintendent was a stocky, red-faced man in his fifties with a shock of grey hair and a small moustache. A chevron of concern was cut deep into his brow.

'You say that you knew where the train was going, Inspector?'

'Yes, sir,' replied Colbeck. 'It was taking interested parties to the scene of a prizefight.'

'Prizefights are illegal. They should be stopped.'

'This one, it seems, was allowed to go ahead.'

18

'*Allowed?*' repeated Tallis, bristling. 'A flagrant breach of the law was consciously allowed? That's intolerable. The magistracy is there to enforce the statute book not to flout it.' His eyelids narrowed. 'How did you come to hear about this?'

'It's common knowledge, Superintendent.'

'Did you not think to report it?'

'The fight is outside our jurisdiction,' said Colbeck, reasonably, 'so there was no point in bringing it to your attention. All that I picked up was tavern gossip about the contest. But,' he continued, 'that's quite irrelevant now. If a murder investigation is to be launched, I must be on the next train to Twyford.'

'You'll need this,' Tallis told him, rising from his seat and handing him the sheet of paper. 'It contains the few details that I possess.'

'Thank you, sir. I take it that Victor Leeming will come with me?'

'The Sergeant will meet you at Paddington Station. I sent him on an errand to C Division so I've dispatched a constable to overtake him with fresh orders.'

'Because of the speed of this message,' said Colbeck, indicating the piece of paper, 'we might even get there before the fight finishes. It can't be much more than thirty miles to Twyford.'

'Report back to me as soon as you can.'

'Of course, sir.'

'And find me the name of the man who sanctioned the running of this excursion train. If he knowingly conveyed people to an illegal prizefight, then he was committing an offence and should be called to account. We must come down

19

hard on malefactors.'

'Railway companies are there to serve the needs of their customers, Superintendent,' Colbeck pointed out. 'They simply carry passengers from one place to another. It's unfair to blame them for any activities that those passengers may get up to at their destination.'

Tallis stuck out his jaw. 'Are you arguing with me, Inspector?'

'Heaven forbid!'

'That makes a change.'

'I would never question your judgement, sir.'

'You do it out of sheer force of habit.'

'That's a gross exaggeration. I was merely trying to represent the position of the Great Western Railway.'

'Then permit me to represent *my* position,' said the other, tapping his chest with a stubby fore-finger. 'I want prompt action. A murder has been committed and we have received an urgent call for assistance. Instead of debating the issue, be kind enough to vacate the premises with all due speed and do the job for which you're paid.'

'I'll take a cab to Paddington immediately,' said Colbeck, moving to the door. 'By the way,' he added with a teasing smile, 'do you wish to be informed of the result of the fight?'

'No!' roared Tallis.

'I thought not, sir.'

And he was gone.

There was a fairground atmosphere at the scene of the prizefight. Descending on it after their trudge across the fields, the high-spirited crowd

20

from London saw that the ring had been set up and that it was encircled by a number of booths and stalls. Pies, sandwiches, fruit and other food-stuffs were on sale and there was a ready supply of beer. A pig was being roasted on a spit. One tent was occupied by a gypsy fortune-teller, who, having first discovered which man each of her clients was supporting, was able to predict the outcome of the contest to his complete satisfaction. A painted sign over another booth – THE GARDEN OF EDEN – left nobody in any doubt what they would find inside, especially as the artist had added a naked lady, with a large red apple and an inviting smile. A group of negro serenaders was touting for custom under an awning. There was even a Punch and Judy show to entertain the visitors with some make-believe violence before they were offered the real thing.

The Londoners were the last to arrive. Excursion trains from other parts of the country had already brought in a massive audience. Members of the gentry chose to watch the festivities from the comfort of their coaches, carriages and gigs. Farmers had come in carts or on horseback. But the overwhelming number of people would either clamber onto the makeshift stands or search for a good vantage point on the grass. Meanwhile, they could place their bets with bookmakers, play cards, watch the jugglers and tumblers, visit some of the freaks on show or enjoy an improvised dog fight. With beer flowing freely, it all served to whip them up into a frenzy of anticipation.

The inner ring, where the fight would take place, was protected by an outer ring so that

21

spectators could not get close enough to interfere in the contest. The space between the two sets of ropes was patrolled by a number of brawny figures, waddling around like so many bulldogs, ageing pugs with scarred faces, swollen ears and missing teeth, muscular sentries with fists like hams, there to ensure the safety of Mad Isaac and the Bargeman. Veterans of the sport themselves, their advice was eagerly sought by punters who were still unsure on whom to place their money.

By way of introduction, an exhibition bout was staged between two young fighters, still in their teens, talented novices who wore padded gloves to lessen the injuries they could inflict on each other's faces. Later, when they graduated to the bareknuckle breed, they would pickle their hands to harden them and do their utmost to open deep cuts, close an opponent's eye, break his ribs or cover his body with dark bruising. The preliminary contest lacked any real sense of danger but it was lively enough to thrill the onlookers and to give them an opportunity both to jostle for a position around the ring and to test the power of their lungs. After six rounds, the fight came to an end amid ear-splitting cheers. Between the two fighters, honours were even.

With the spectators suitably warmed up, it was time for the main contest of the afternoon. Everyone pushed in closer for a first glimpse of the two men. The Bargeman led the way, a veritable mountain of muscle, striding purposefully towards the ring with a face of doom. His fans were quick to offer their sage counsel.

'Knock 'im to from 'ere to kingdom come, Bargeman!'

'Split the lousy Jew in 'alf!'

'Circumcise 'im!'

'Flay the bugger alive!'

The Negro raised both arms in acknowledgement, cheered and booed with equal volume by rival supporters. Isaac Rosen was the next to appear, strolling nonchalantly along as he chewed on an apple and tossed the core to a woman in the throng. He was every bit as tall as Hignett but had nothing like his sheer bulk. Dark-haired and dark-eyed, Rosen grinned happily as if he were on his way to a picnic rather than to an extended ordeal in the ring. It was the turn of the Bradford crowd to offer a few suggestions.

'Come on, Mad Isaac! Teach 'im a lesson.'

'Smash 'im to the ground!'

'Crack 'is 'ead open!'

'Kill the black bastard!'

Both sides were in good voice. As the fighters stripped off their shirts, the cheers and the taunts reached a pitch of hysteria. Wearing cotton drawers and woollen stockings, the boxers confronted each other and exchanged a few ripe insults. Each was in prime condition, having trained for months for this confrontation. Hignett had the clear weight advantage but Rosen had the more eye-catching torso with rippling muscles built up by hard years in the slaughterhouse. A coin was tossed to see who would have choice of corners, a crucial advantage on a day when the sun was blazing down. Fortune favoured the Jew and he elected to have his back to the sun so that it dazzled his opponent's eyes as he came out of his corner.

With two seconds apiece – a bottleman and a kneeman – they took up their positions. The bottleman was there to revive his charge with a wet sponge or a cold drink while the kneeman provided a rickety stool on which the boxer could sit between rounds. All four seconds were retired fighters, seasoned warriors who knew all the tricks of the trade and who could, in the event of trouble, act as additional bodyguards. On a signal from the referee, the Bargeman moved swiftly up to the scratch in the middle of the ring, but Mad Isaac kept him waiting for a moment before he deigned to leave his corner. As they shook hands, there was another barrage of insults between them before the first punches were thrown with vicious intent. Pandemonium broke out among the spectators. They were watching the two finest boxers in the world, both unbeaten, slugging it out until one of them was pounded into oblivion. In an ecstasy of blood-lust, they urged the boxers on with full-throated glee.

'Who discovered the body?' asked Colbeck, coming out of the carriage.

'I did, Inspector,' replied Ernest Radd, stepping forward.

'When was this?'

'Immediately after the passengers had left the train.'

'Could you give me some idea of the time?'

'Not long after noon, Inspector.'

'I knew that it was a mistake to run this train,'

said Tod Galway, wringing his hands. 'Something like this was bound to happen.'

'I disagree,' said Colbeck, turning to him. 'This is a very singular occurrence. It's the first murder that I've encountered on a train. One might expect a little over-excitement from the Fancy but not this.'

The detectives had reached the scene of the crime while the fight was still in progress. To clear the line for use by other traffic, the excursion train had been driven into a siding. Inspector Robert Colbeck was accompanied by Sergeant Victor Leeming, a heavyset man in his late thirties with an unprepossessing appearance. One eye squinted at a bulbous nose that had been battered during an arrest and his chin was unduly prominent. Beside his elegant companion, he looked scruffy and faintly villainous. After examining the dead body with Colbeck, the Sergeant remained in the doorway of the carriage, blocking the view of the group of railway policemen who had come to stare.

'I knew he was gone as soon as I saw him,' explained Radd, a chubby young man whose cheeks were still whitened by the shock of what he had found. 'But it was Sam here who went into the carriage.'

'That's right,' Horlock chimed in, relishing the opportunity to get some attention at last. 'Horlock's the name, Inspector. Samuel Horlock. Ernie called us to the carriage and, as the more experienced policeman,' he boasted, 'I took over. The man was stuck in the corner. I shook him by the shoulder and he keeled over, losing his hat.

25

That's when we saw them marks around his neck, Inspector. Someone must have used a rope to strangle him.'

'A piece of wire, I think,' said Colbeck. 'Rope would never have bitten into the flesh like that. It would simply have left a red weal where the neck had been chafed. This man was garrotted with something much thinner and sharper.'

'Then we know one thing about the killer,' volunteered Leeming. 'He must have been a strong man. The victim would not have been easy to overpower. Judging by the size of him, there would have been resistance.'

'I found these in his pockets, Inspector,' said Horlock, handing over a wallet and a slip of paper, 'so at least we know his name.'

'You should have left it to us to search him, Mr Horlock.'

'I was only trying to help.'

'In tramping around the carriage, you might unwittingly have destroyed valuable clues.' He looked at the other railway policemen. 'How many of you went in there to gawp at him once the alarm was raised?' Half-a-dozen of them looked shamefaced and turned away. 'It was not a freak show, gentlemen,' scolded Colbeck.

'We was curious, that's all,' said Horlock, defensively.

'If you'd shown some curiosity during the train journey, the murder might not have occurred. Why did none of you travel in this particular carriage?'

'We never expected trouble in first and second class. Leastways, not on the ride here. It'll be different on the way back,' warned Horlock. 'There's bound to be some drunken idiots with third class tickets trying to travel back to London in comfort.'

'Nobody can use *this* carriage,' said Galway, anxiously. 'Not with a corpse lyin' there like that. I mean, it's unwelcomin'.'

'The body will travel back in the guard's van,' declared Colbeck.

'I'm not 'avin' that bleedin' thing in my van, Inspector!' protested the other. 'Gives me the shakes just to look at 'im.'

'Don't worry Sergeant Leeming and I will be there to protect you.' Colbeck turned to the others. 'Some of you might find a means of carrying the murder victim along the track. There may be a board of some kind at the station or even a wheelbarrow. We need to move him before the passengers return, and to get this carriage cleaned up.'

Four of the railway policemen shuffled off. The rest of them stared resentfully at Colbeck, annoyed that he had taken over the investigation and relegated them to the position of bystanders. Colbeck's refinement, educated voice and sense of authority aroused a muted hostility. They did not like being given orders by this peacock from Scotland Yard. Aware of their antagonism, Colbeck chose to ignore it.

'Sergeant Leeming.'

'Yes, Inspector?' said his colleague.

'Take a full statement from Mr Horlock, if you will,' instructed Colbeck, 'and from Mr Radd. Meanwhile,' he added, pointedly, 'if the rest of

27

you would be good enough to give us some breathing space, I'll make a more thorough examination of the body.'

Blaspheming under their breath, the knot of railway policemen drifted away, leaving only Sam Horlock, Ernest Radd and Tod Galway beside the carriage. Leeming jumped down on to the ground and took out his notebook so that he could question two of the men. Colbeck hauled himself into the carriage and took the opportunity to look at the two items that Horlock had given him. The wallet contained nothing more than a five-pound note and a ticket for the excursion train, but the piece of paper was far more useful. It was a bill for a supply of leather and it contained the name and address of the person to whom it had been sent.

'So,' said Colbeck with compassion, 'you are Mr Jacob Bransby, are you? I'm sorry that your journey had to end this way, sir.'

Putting the wallet and bill into his pocket, he looked more closely at the injury to the man's neck, trying to work out where the killer must have been standing when he struck. Colbeck then studied the broad shoulders and felt the solid biceps. Bransby might have a paunch but he must have been a powerful man. Evidently, he was no stranger to manual work. His hands were rough, his fingernails dirty. A livid scar ran across the knuckles of one hand. His clothing was serviceable rather than smart and Colbeck noticed that his coat had been darned in two places. The hat was shabby.

But it was the face that interested the detective most. Though contorted by an agonising death, it still had much to reveal about the character of the man. There was a stubbornness in the set of his jaw and protective quality about the thick over-hanging brows. Mutton-chop whiskers hid even more of his face and the walrus moustache reached out to meet them. Colbeck sensed that he was looking at a secretive individual, covert, tight-lipped, taciturn, unsure of himself, a lonely crea-ture who travelled without any friends because they would otherwise have been on hand to save his life instead of rushing out of the carriage, leaving him to the mercy of his executioner.

Wishing that the man did not smell so much of excrement, Colbeck searched him thoroughly. Sam Horlock had already been through the pockets so the Inspector concentrated on other parts of his clothing. If Bransby had been as fur-tive by nature as the detective believed, he might have hidden pockets about his person. He soon found the first, a pouch that had been attached to the inside of the waist of his trousers to safeguard coins from the nimble fingers of pickpockets. Horlock had missed the second hiding place as well. Ingeniously sewn into the waistcoat below the left arm, the other pouch contained a large and expensive gold watch.

It was the third find, however, that intrigued Colbeck. As he felt down the right trouser-leg, his hand made contact with a hard, metal object that, on investigation, turned out to be a dagger strapped above the ankle. Colbeck removed it from the leg, unsheathed the weapon and inspected it. He glanced down at the murder victim.

'Well, Mr Bransby,' he said, raising an eyebrow, 'you're full of surprises, aren't you?'

He put the dagger in its sheath and concealed them in his coat. After completing his search, he left the carriage and dropped to the ground, relieved to be able to inhale fresh air again. Colbeck said nothing about what he had found, unwilling to humiliate Horlock in front the others and, in any case, not wishing to share information with railway employees. The four policemen who had walked off to the station came down the track, carrying a large table between them. Colbeck supervised the transfer of the dead body from the carriage to the guard's van. Tod Galway was not happy about the arrangement.

'I don't want 'im in there, Inspector,' he moaned, waving his arms. 'The dirty dog shit 'imself.'

'That was purely involuntary,' said Colbeck. 'If *you* had been killed in that way, I daresay that your own bowels would have betrayed you. Death plays cruel tricks on all of us.'

'But why did this 'ave to 'appen on *my* train?'

'Only the killer can tell us that.'

Leaving him there, Colbeck strolled back towards the front of the train. He was pleased to see that Leeming had finished taking statements from the two men. It allowed him to confide in the Sergeant.

Leeming was astonished. 'A gold watch and a dagger?'

'Both cunningly hidden, Victor.'

'Is that why he carried the weapon, sir? To protect the watch?'

30

'No,' decided Colbeck, 'I fancy that it was there for self-defence and with good cause. Mr Bransby feared an attack of some kind. He did not strike me as a man who slept easily at nights.'

'A guilty conscience, perhaps?'

'He certainly had something to hide. How, for instance, could a man who plied his trade afford such a costly watch? I venture to suggest that you'll find very few cobblers with the requisite income.'

'How do you know that he was a cobbler?'

'Who else would order that amount of leather?' asked Colbeck. 'And there was what could well be cobbler's wax under his fingernails. Not that he was the most dexterous craftsman, mind you. It looked as if a knife slipped at some stage and slit his knuckles open.'

'I see.' Leeming shrugged. 'What do we do now, sir?'

'All that we can do, Victor – wait until the passengers come back. Only a relatively small number travelled here in these second-class carriages. We need to find someone who might remember Jacob Bransby.'

'One of them will remember him extremely well – the killer!'

'Yes, but I doubt if he'll oblige us by turning up so that we can question him. My guess is that he's already slipped away.'

'And miss the chance of seeing a fight like that?' said Leeming in amazement. 'More fool him, I say.' He brightened as an idea struck him. 'I'd love to watch the Bargeman hit lumps out of Mad Isaac. One of the policemen knows where

31

the fight is taking place, sir. Why don't I rush over there to keep an eye on things?'

'Because you'd be too late, Victor.'

'Too late?'

'Look up there.'

Glancing up at the sky, Leeming saw a flock of birds flying in the general direction of London. He sighed as he realized that the fight must be over. The carrier pigeons were carrying word of the result. Several, he knew, would be winging their way to Bradford.

Leeming cupped his hands to shout up at the birds.

'Who *won?*' he yelled. 'Was it the Bargeman?'

The trouble had begun when the fight was only an hour old. Supporters of Mad Isaac had been inflamed by what they felt were unfair tactics on the part of his opponent. When they grappled in the middle of the ring, the Bargeman used his forehead to crack down on the bridge of the other man's nose and uncorked the blood. As the fighters swung round crazily in an impromptu dance, the men from Bradford thought that they saw the Negro inflict a bite on their man's neck. They shrieked with rage. Rosen was quick to take revenge. Seized by a madness that turned him into a howling wolf, he lifted the Bargeman bodily and flung him to the ground with a force that winded him. What infuriated the London mob was that he seemed to get in a sly kick to the Negro's groin.

Demands for a disqualification rang out on all sides and a few private fights started on the fringes. The Bargeman, however, had great powers of recovery. Helped back to his corner by his seconds, he needed only a swig of water and a brief rest on a wooden stool before he was able to fight again. When the contest restarted, his arms were flailing like black windmills. And so it went on for another forty arduous rounds, advantage swinging first one way, then the other, the audience keeping up such hullabaloo that it was like watching a brawl in Bedlam. When the rowdier element began to take over, brandishing staves and cudgels, the gentry began to withdraw, worried for the safety of their vehicles and their horses in the seething morass of danger.

The end finally came. It was disputed belligerently by almost half of the spectators. Both men had taken severe punishment and were tottering on the edge of complete fatigue. The Bargeman then found the energy to launch one more savage attack, sending his opponent reeling back against the ropes. Moving in for the kill, he tried to get the Jew in a bear hug to crush the last vestiges of resistance but he suddenly backed away with his hands to his eyes. Nobody had seen Mad Isaac use his fingers yet the Bargeman was temporarily blinded. He was then hit with a relay of punches that sent him staggering backwards and, as he was in the act of dropping to one knee to gain quarter, he was caught with a thunderous uppercut that laid him out flat. It was all over.

Cries of 'Foul!' from the Londoners mingled with roars of delight from the Bradford contingent. The noise was deafening. Every one of the Bargeman's fans believed that he had been hit unfairly though, in truth, few had actually witnessed the blow. Most were in no position to see over the ranks of hats in front of them or they were so befuddled with drink that their vision was impaired. Partisans to a man, they nevertheless took up the chant for retribution. The umpires claimed that they had not seen anything under-hand and the referee, sensing that a disqualification would put his life at risk, declared Mad Isaac to be the winner. At that precise moment, thousands of pounds were won and lost in bets.

The more sporting members of the Fancy immediately contributed to a purse for the gallant loser, who was carried back to his corner by his seconds. Because the Bargeman had given a good account of himself in the ring, coins were tossed into the hat with generosity. But there were hundreds of people who disputed the decision and sought to advance their argument with fists, whip handles, sticks, stones, clubs and hammers. The two fighters were not the only ones to shed copious blood that afternoon in Berkshire.

At the point when the whole scene was about to descend into utter chaos, someone fired a warning pistol in the air. A magistrate was on his way to stop the event with a detachment of dragoons at his back. It was time to disappear. Brawls were abandoned in mid-punch and everyone took to their heels. Hustled onto separate carts, the Barge-man and Mad Isaac were driven off in opposite directions by their backers, determined that two brave men would not feel the wrath of the law. Hurt, angry and consumed with righteous in-dignation, the London mob headed towards their excursion train, licking their wounds and cursing their fate. Having invested time, money and high emotion into the contest, they were going home empty-handed. It made them burn with frustration. They had come with high hopes of victory but were slinking away like a beaten army.

'The Bargeman lost,' said Leeming in dismay as the first of them came in sight. 'I can tell from the look of them.'

'Inquire about the fight at a later stage,' ordered Colbeck. 'All that concerns us now are the passengers who were in the same carriage as Jacob Bransby on their way here.'

'Yes, sir.'

'And don't expect me to share your sorrow, Victor. You may as well know that I put a sovereign on Mad Isaac to win.'

Leeming groaned. 'I had two on the Bargeman.'

When the crowd reached the train, all that most of them wanted to do was to tumble into their seats and nurse their grievances. Some were in an aggressive mood and others tried to sneak into first- and second-class carriages without the appropriate tickets. Railway policemen were on hand to prevent them. Those who had been in the same carriage as Jacob Bransby were taken aside for questioning, but only one of them had actually spoken to the man whom Inspector Colbeck described.

'Yes,' said Felix Pritchard. 'I remember him, sir, though he didn't give me his name. Sat next to him, I did – shoulder to shoulder.'

'Did you talk to him?' asked Colbeck.

35

'I tried to but he didn't have very much to say for himself.'

'What was your impression of the man?'

'Well, now, let me see.'

Felix Pritchard was a tall, rangy young man with a coat that had been torn in the course of the afternoon and a hat that was badly scuffed. A bank clerk by profession, he had pleaded illness so that he could go to the fight but he was now having second thoughts about the wisdom of doing so. Apart from having backed the wrong man and lost money that he could not afford, he had drunk far too much beer and was feeling sick. As a witness, he was less than ideal. Colbeck was patient with him. Pritchard was all that he had.

'Start with his voice,' suggested the Inspector. 'Did it tell you where he came from?'

'Oh, yes, he was a true Cockney, just like me, sir.'

'Did he say what he did for a living?'

'That never came up in conversation,' said Pritchard, wishing that his stomach were not so rebellious. 'All we talked about was the fight.'

'And what did Mr Bransby have to say?'

'That, barring accidents, the Bargeman was bound to win.'

'Did he bet money on the result?'

'Of course. We all had.'

'Had he ever seen Bill Hignett fight before?'

'Yes,' said the other. 'He was a real disciple of the sport. Told me that he'd been all over the country to see fights. It was his hobby.'

'What else did he say?'

'Very little beyond the fact that he did a bit of

milling in his youth. I think he was handy with his fists at one time but he didn't brag about it. He was one of those quiet types, who keep themselves to themselves.'

'Tell me about the people in the carriage.'

'We were jammed in there like sardines.'

'How many of them did you know?'

'Only one,' replied Pritchard. 'My brother. That's him, sitting in the corner,' he went on, pointing into the carriage at a youth whose face and coat were spattered with blood. 'Cecil chanced his arm against one of those Bradford cullies and came off worst.'

'Did he speak to Jacob Bransby at any point?'

'No, sir. He was sat on the other side of me. Couldn't take his eyes off the woman who was opposite him.'

'A woman?' echoed Colbeck with interest, looking around. 'I've not seen any women getting back into the second class carriages.'

'She must be making her way back home by other means.'

'What sort of woman was she, Mr Pritchard?'

'*That* sort, sir,' returned the bank clerk.

'Age?'

'Anything from thirty upward,' said Pritchard. 'Too old for my brother, I know that, and too pricey in any case.'

'Why do you say that?'

'She wasn't a common trull you might see walking the streets, sir. I mean, she was almost respectable. Except that a respectable woman wouldn't be going on an excursion train to a fight, would she? She could only have been there for one thing.'

'Did you see her at the contest?'

'In that crowd?' Pritchard gave a derisive laugh. 'Not a chance! Besides, I didn't look. I was too busy cheering on the Bargeman.'

'Apart from Jacob Bransby, your brother and this woman, can you recall anyone else who was in that carriage with you?'

'Not really, sir. They were all strangers to me. To be honest, I've had so much to drink that I wouldn't recognise any of them if they stood in front of me.' He gave a sudden belch. 'Pardon me, Inspector.'

'What happened when the train reached Twyford?'

'We all got out.'

'Did you see Mr Bransby leave his seat?'

'I didn't notice,' admitted Pritchard. 'There was a mad dash for the door because we were so keen to get out.'

'Did the woman leave before you?'

'Oh, no. She had to take her chances with the rest of us. Cecil and me pushed past her in the rush. That was the last we saw of her.'

'So she could have held back deliberately?'

'Who knows, Inspector? If she did, it wasn't because she'd taken a fancy to Mr Bransby. He was an ugly devil,' said Pritchard, 'and he was so miserable. You'd never have thought he was on his way to a championship fight.'

'No?'

'No, sir. He looked as if he was going to a funeral.'

Colbeck made no comment.

Chapter Three

The excursion train reached Paddington that evening without any undue incident. There were some heated arguments in the third-class carriages and a few minor scuffles but the railway policemen soon brought them under control. Most of the passengers were still too numbed by the defeat of their hero, the Bargeman, to cause any mayhem themselves and they were noticeably quieter on their way back. Those in the second class carriage that had brought Jacob Bransby to Twyford were quite unaware of the fact a murder had taken place there. When he interviewed Felix Pritchard earlier, Inspector Colbeck had been careful to say nothing about the crime, explaining that he was simply making routine inquiries about a missing person. Unbeknown to the excursionists, a corpse travelled back to London in the guard's van with two detectives from the Metropolitan Police and an irate Tod Galway.

'It ain't decent, Inspector,' asserted the guard.

'The body could hardly be left where it was,' said Colbeck.

'You should 'ave sent it back by other means.'

'What other means?'

'Any way but on my train.'

'Mr Bransby had a return ticket in his pocket. That entitles him to be on this particular train and here he will be.'

'Bleedin' liberty, that's what it is!'

'Show some respect for the dead. And to us,' added Colbeck, sternly. 'Do you think we *want* to ride back to London in the company of a murder victim and a grumbling railwayman?'

Galway lapsed into a sullen silence until the train shuddered to a halt in the station. Victor Leeming was given the job of organising the transfer of the dead body to the police morgue, first waiting until the train had been emptied of passengers so that a degree of privacy could be ensured. Colbeck, meanwhile, took a Hansom cab back to Scotland Yard and delivered his report to Superintendent Tallis. The latter listened to the recital with mounting irritation.

'Nobody saw a thing?' he asked, shaking his head in wonder. 'A man is throttled aboard a crowded train and not a single pair of eyes witnesses the event?'

'No, sir.'

'I find that hard to believe.'

'Everyone rushed out of the train in order to get to the fight.'

'Then why didn't this Mr Bransby join them?'

'I have a theory about that, Superintendent.'

'Ah,' sighed Tallis, rolling his eyes. 'Another of your famous theories, eh? I prefer to work with hard facts and clear evidence. They are much more reliable guides. Very well,' he conceded, flicking a wrist, 'let's hear this latest wild guess of yours.'

'I believe that the woman was involved.'

'A female assassin? Isn't that stretching supposition too far?'

'She was no assassin,' argued Colbeck. 'The woman was there as an accomplice to distract the victim. While she delayed him, the killer attacked from behind.'

'What put that notion into your head, Inspector?'

'The fact that she was in that carriage at all.'

'There's no mystery in that,' said Tallis, darkly. 'We both know why she was there. Such creatures always follow a crowd. Clearly, she was looking for a better class of customer than she'd find among the ruffians in third class.'

'I've only Mr Pritchard's word that the woman was, in fact, a prostitute. He could well have been mistaken. He confessed that he'd been drinking before he boarded the train so his judgement may not be altogether sound. What interests me,' Colbeck continued, 'was that the woman did not return to the train at Twyford.'

'Perhaps she went astray.'

'Deliberately.'

'You've no means of knowing that.'

'I have this instinct, sir.'

'We need more than theory and instinct to solve this murder, Inspector. We need definite clues. So far you seem to have drawn a complete blank.' He glowered at Colbeck. 'What's your next move?'

'To visit the home of the deceased. He wore a wedding ring so he must have a wife and family. They deserve to know what has happened to him. I intend to go to Hoxton at once.'

'What about Sergeant Leeming?'

'He's on his way to the morgue with Mr Bransby, sir. I told him to stay there until the doctor had examined the body in case any important new details came to light. Victor and I will confer later on.'

'For an exchange of theories?' said Tallis with gruff sarcasm.

'Useful information can always be picked up from the doctor even before a full autopsy is carried out. He may, for instance, give us a more accurate idea of what murder weapon was used.'

'Bring me news of any progress that you make.'

'Of course, sir.'

'*Soon.*'

'We'll do our best.'

'I trust that you will. I've already had the railway company on to me, demanding an early arrest. A murder on one of their trains is a bad advertisement for them. It deters other passengers from travelling. The crime must be solved quickly. But they must bear some responsibility,' said Tallis, wagging a finger. 'If the Great Western Railway hadn't condoned an illegal fight and transported the sweepings of the slums to it, this murder would never have been committed.'

'It would, Superintendent,' said Colbeck, firmly, 'albeit at another time and in another place. Theft was not the motive or the man's wallet would have been taken. No,' he insisted, 'this was not an opportunist crime. It was a calculated homicide. Jacob Bransby was being stalked.'

At the time when the Domesday Book had been compiled, Hoxton was a manor of three hides, held by the Canons of St. Paul's. It had been a tranquil place with green pastures and open meadows intersected by the river along which mills were conveniently sited. There was not the tiniest hint of its former rural beauty now. A part of Shoreditch, it belonged to a community of well over 100,000 souls in an unsightly urban sprawl. It was one of the worst parts of London with poverty and overcrowding as the salient features of its dark, narrow, filthy, cluttered streets. As the cab took him to the address on the tradesman's bill, Robert Colbeck reflected that Hoxton was hardly the district in which to find a man who carried a gold watch and a five pound note on his person. The dagger, however, was a more understandable accessory. In many parts of the area, a weapon of some sort was almost obligatory

Colbeck was well-acquainted with Hoxton, having been assigned a beat there during his days in uniform. He was wearily familiar with its brothels, gambling dens, penny gaffs, music halls, seedy public houses and ordinaries. He knew the rat-infested tenements where whole families were crammed into a single room and where disease ran amok in the insanitary conditions. He remembered the distinctive smell of Hoxton with its blend of menace, despair and rotting food. What had always struck him was not how many criminals gravitated to the place to form a thriving underworld but how many decent, hardworking, law-abiding people also lived there and managed to rise above their joyless surroundings.

After picking its way through the busy streets, the cab turned a corner and slowed down before stopping outside a terraced house. It was in one of the better parts of Hoxton but there was still a distinct whiff of decay about it. Children were playing with a ball in the fading light or watching an ancient man struggling to coax music out of his barrel organ. When they saw the cab, some of the younger ones scampered across to pat the horse and to ask the driver for a ride. Colbeck got out, paid his fare and knocked on the door of Jacob Bransby's house. There was a long wait before a curtain was twitched in the window. Moments later, the door opened and the curious face of a middle-aged woman peered around it.

'Can I help you, sir?'

'Mrs Bransby?'

'Yes,' she said after a considered pause.

'My name is Detective Inspector Colbeck,' he explained, displaying his warrant card. 'I wonder if I might have a word with you?'

Alarm sounded. 'Why? Has something happened to my husband? I expected him back before now.'

'Perhaps I could come in, Mrs Bransby,' he said, softly. 'This is not something that we should be discussing on your doorstep.'

She nodded and moved back to admit him. Removing his top hat, he stepped into a small passageway and waited until she shut the door behind them. Louise Bransby led him into the front room that was better furnished than he had expected. A lighted oil lamp bathed it in a warm glow. Over the mantelpiece was a picture of the Virgin Mary. On the opposite wall was a crucifix. The carpet had a new feel to it.

'Why don't you sit down?' he suggested.

'If you say so, Inspector.'

'Is there anyone else in the house?'

'No,' she said, lowering herself into an arm-chair. 'Jake and I live here alone. Our son has a home of his own now.'

'Is there a friend or a neighbour you'd like to call in?'

'Why?'

'You might need some company, Mrs Bransby.'

'Not from anyone round here,' she said, sharply. 'We have no friends in Hoxton.' She took a deep breath and steeled herself. 'I'm ready, Inspector. Tell me what brought you here.'

Louise Bransby was a plump woman in a blue dress that had been worn once too often. She had curly brown hair and an oval face that was dis-figured by a frown. Colbeck sensed a quiet tough-ness about her that would make his task slightly easier. Whatever else she did, Louise Bransby seemed unlikely to collapse in hysterics or simply pass out.

'I'm afraid that I have some bad news for you,' he began.

'It's not his heart again, is it?' she asked with concern. 'The doctor warned him against getting too excited but Jake just had to go to that fight. He loved boxing. It gave him so much pleasure. He'd go anywhere to watch it.' She leaned forward. 'Has he been taken ill?'

'It's worse than that,' said Colbeck, sitting on the upright chair beside her. 'Your husband is dead.' As she convulsed momentarily, he put a sympathetic hand on her shoulder. 'I'm so sorry, Mrs Bransby. I hate to be the bearer of such sad tidings.'

She bit her lip. 'It was bound to happen sooner or later,' she said, wiping away a tear with her hand. 'I knew that. Jake would drive himself so. And I was afraid that it would all end once we came here. Moving to Hoxton was a bad mistake.'

'How long have you been in the house?'

'A couple of months.'

'Where were you before?'

'Clerkenwell.'

'Why did you come here?'

'That's private, sir,' she said, evasively. 'Not that it matters any more, I suppose. If my husband has died, I can get away from this place.' She clutched her hands to her breast. 'If only Jake had listened to that doctor! He was told to take it easy.' She read the look in Colbeck's eyes and stiffened. 'There's something you haven't told me, isn't there?' she asked, warily. 'It wasn't his heart, after all.'

'No, Mrs Bransby,' he said, gently. 'There's no way to hide the truth, I fear. Your husband was killed this afternoon.'

'Killed?' she gasped. 'There's been an accident?'

'Unfortunately not. At some time around noon today, Mr Bransby was murdered on an excursion train.'

'Holy Mary!' she exclaimed.

She looked up at the picture of the Virgin, crossed herself then brought both hands up to her face. Louise Bransby was too stunned to say anything. Lost in a world of her own, she needed several minutes to recover her composure. Colbeck waited beside her, ready to offer physical support if need be, relieved that she did not burst

46

into tears or howl with anguish as other women had done in similar circumstances. Imparting news of a tragedy to a wife was a duty that had fallen to him more than once in Hoxton and it had always been an uncomfortable task.

When she eventually lowered her hands, her eyes were moist but there was no overt display of grief. Louise Bransby was a woman who had learned to keep her emotions under control in difficult situations and Colbeck suspected that she had had a lot of experience in doing so. There was an innate strength about her that he admired, a practical streak, a capacity for dealing with things as they were instead of clinging on pointlessly to how they had been. He offered her a handkerchief but she shook her head.

'Is there anything that I can get you, Mrs Bransby?' he inquired.

'No, Inspector.'

'A glass of water, perhaps?'

'I'll be well in a moment.'

'Are you sure there isn't a friend I could invite in?'

'Yes,' she said with sudden contempt. 'Quite sure. I don't want anyone here knowing my business. I can manage on my own.' She made an effort to pull herself together. 'How did it happen?'

'This may not be the time to go into details,' he said, trying to keep the full horror from her at this stage. 'Suffice it to say that it was a quick death. Your husband would not have lingered in agony.'

'Where was he killed?'

'At Twyford station. When the train stopped,

everyone rushed to get off. Evidently, someone took advantage of the commotion to attack Mr Bransby.' Hands clasped in her lap, she gazed down at them. 'We found a bill for some leather on him. Was your husband a cobbler?'

'Yes, Inspector.'

'Did he work from home?'

'He has a shed in the yard at the back of the house.'

'The bill is your property now,' he said, reaching inside his coat, 'and so is his wallet.' Colbeck extracted them and set them on a small table close to her. 'There were also a few coins in a secret pocket,' he went on, fishing them out to place beside the other items. 'That was not all that we found on your husband, Mrs Bransby.' She glanced up. 'Do you know what I'm talking about?'

'His watch.'

'It's a very expensive one.'

'But paid for, Inspector,' she declared, 'like everything else in this house. Jake *earned* that watch, he did. He worked hard for it. That's why he took such good care of it. I sewed the pouch into his waistcoat for him. That watch was got honestly, I swear it.'

'I'm sure that it was,' said Colbeck, producing the watch from a pocket and giving it to her. 'But it was a rather unexpected thing to find on your husband.' He brought out the dagger. 'And so was this. Do you know why he carried it?'

'This is a dangerous place to live.'

'I know that. I walked the beat in Hoxton as a constable.'

'Jake never felt safe here.'

'Then why did you move to this part of London?'

'We had to go somewhere,' she said with an air of resignation. 'And we'd tried three or four other places.'

'Couldn't you settle anywhere?' he probed.

'My husband was a restless man.'

'But a cobbler depends on building up local trade,' he noted. 'Every time you moved, he must have had to search for new customers.'

'We got by.'

'Obviously.'

'And we never borrowed a penny – unlike some around here.'

'That's very much to your credit, Mrs Bransby.'

'We had too much pride, Inspector. We *cared*. That's why I dislike the neighbours. They have no pride. No self-respect.'

There was edge of defiance in her voice that puzzled him. Minutes ago, she had learned of the murder of her husband yet she seemed to have set that aside. Louise Bransby was more concerned with correcting any false impression that he might have formed about a humble cobbler who lived in an unwholesome part of the city. Colbeck did not sense any deep love for the dead man but his wife was showing a loyalty towards him that verged on the combative.

'How long were you married, Mrs Bransby?' he asked.

'Twenty-eight years.'

'And you have a son, you say?'

'Yes. His name is Michael.'

'Any other children?'

'No, Inspector,' she replied, crisply. 'The Lord only saw fit to allow us one son and we would never question His wisdom.' After glancing down wistfully at the gold watch, she turned back to Colbeck. 'Do you have any idea who did this terrible thing to Jake?'

'Not at the moment. I was hoping that *you* might be able to help.'

'Me?'

'You knew your husband better than anybody, Mrs Bransby. Did he have any particular enemies?'

'Jake was a good man, Inspector. He was a true believer.'

'I don't doubt that,' said Colbeck, 'but the fact remains that someone had a reason to kill him. This was no random act of murder. Mr Bransby was carefully singled out. Can you think of anyone who might have had a grudge against him?'

'No, Inspector,' she replied, avoiding his gaze.

'Are you quite certain?' he pressed.

'Yes.'

'Did he have arguments with anyone? Or a feud with a rival cobbler, perhaps? To take a man's life like that requires a very strong motive. Who might have had that motive, Mrs Bransby?'

'How would I know?' she said, rising to her feet as if flustered. 'Excuse me, Inspector, this terrible news changes everything. I've a lot of thinking to do. If you don't mind, I'd like to be left alone now.'

'Of course,' he agreed, getting up immediately, 'but there is one request that I have to make of you, I fear.'

'What's that?'

'The body will need to be formally identified.'

'But you know that it was Jake. You found those things on him.'

'All the same, we do need confirmation from a family member.'

'I want to remember my husband as he was,' she said. 'I'd hate to see him...' Her voice trailed off and there was a long pause. She became more assertive. 'I'm sorry but I can't do it.'

'Then perhaps your son would replace you. He'll have to be told about his father's death. Does he live close by? I'll pay him a visit this evening and apprise him of the situation.'

'No, no, you mustn't do that.'

'Why not?'

'You keep Michael out of this.'

'One of you has to identify the body,' Colbeck told her. 'The doctor is unable to put the correct name on the death certificate until we are absolutely sure who the man is.'

She bit her lip. 'I *know* it's my husband. Take my word for it.'

'We need more than that, Mrs Bransby.'

'Why?'

'There are procedures to follow. I appreciate that you might find it too distressing to visit the morgue yourself so I'll have to ask your son to come in your place. Where can I find him?'

A hunted look came into her eyes. Her lips were pursed and the muscles in her face twitched visibly. Wrestling with her conscience, she turned for help to the Virgin Mary, only to be met with

51

apparent reproof. It made her start. After swallowing hard, she blurted out the truth.

'I didn't mean to lie to you, Inspector,' she confessed. 'I was brought up to believe in honesty but that was not always possible. You must understand the position we were in.'

'I'm not blaming you for anything,' he promised, trying to calm her. 'And I do sympathise with your position. It can't have been easy for either of you to be on the move all the time, pulling up roots, finding new accommodation, living among strangers. You told me that your husband was restless. I believe that he also lived in fear.'

'He did – we both did.'

'Is that why you never stayed long in one place?'

'Yes, Inspector.'

'What kept you on the run?'

'They did,' she said, bitterly. 'That's why we had to hide behind a lie. But sooner or later, someone always found out and our lives were made a misery. It was so painful. I mean, someone has to do it, Inspector, and Jake felt that he was called. We prayed together for a sign and we believed that it was given to us.'

'A sign?'

'Jake would never have taken the job without guidance.'

'I don't quite follow, Mrs Bransby.'

'Guttridge,' she corrected. 'My name is Mrs Guttridge. Bransby was my maiden name. We only used it as a disguise. As a policeman, you must have heard of my husband – he was Jacob Guttridge.'

Colbeck was taken aback. 'The public executioner?'

'Yes, sir. Jake was not only a cobbler – he was a hangman as well.'

Victor Leeming did not like visiting the police morgue. The place was cold, cheerless and unsettling. He could not understand how some of those who worked there could exchange happy banter and even whistle at their work. He found it worryingly inappropriate. To the detective, it was an ordeal to spend any time in such an oppressive atmosphere. Robust, direct and fearless in most situations, Leeming was oddly sensitive in the presence of the deceased, reminded all too keenly of his own mortality. He hoped that he would not have to stay there long.

The doctor took time to arrive but, once he did, he was briskly professional as he examined a body that had been stripped and cleaned in readiness. After washing his hands, Leonard Keyworth joined the other man in the vestibule. Short, squat and bearded, the doctor was a bustling man in his late forties. Leeming stood by with his notebook.

'Well, Doctor?' he prompted.

'Death by asphyxiation,' said Keyworth, staring at him over the top of his *pince-nez*, 'but I daresay that you worked that out for yourself. It was a very unpleasant way to die. The garrotte was pulled so tight that it almost severed his windpipe.'

'Inspector Colbeck thought a piece of wire was used.'

'Almost certainly. The kind used to cut cheese,

53

for instance.'

'How long would it have taken?'

'Not as long as you might suppose,' said the doctor. 'I can't be sure until I carry out a post mortem but my guess is that he was not a healthy man. Cheeks and nose of that colour usually indicate heavy drinking and he was decidedly overweight. There were other telltale symptoms as well. I suspect that he may well have been a man with a heart condition, short of breath at the best of times. That might have hastened his death.'

'A heart attack brought on by the assault?'

'Possibly. I'll stay with my initial diagnosis for the time being. The prime cause of death was asphyxiation.'

'Right,' said Leeming, wishing that he could spell the word.

'This time, it seems, someone finally succeeded.'

'In what way?'

'It was not the first attempt on his life, Sergeant.'

Leeming blinked. 'How do you know?'

'When a man has a wound like that on his back,' said the doctor, removing his *pince nez*, 'it was not put there by accident. There's an even larger scar on his stomach. He's been attacked before.'

'No wonder he carried a weapon of his own.'

'A weapon?'

'He had a dagger strapped to his leg,' explained Leeming.

'Then he was obviously unable to reach it. The killer had the advantage of surprise, taking him

54

from behind when he least expected it. Do you have any notion of the victim's identity?'

'According to a bill in his pocket, his name was Jacob Bransby.'

'A manual worker of some kind, I'd say.'

'The Inspector is fairly certain that he's a cobbler.'

'Not a very good one, it appears.'

'Why not?'

'Because he has too many discontented customers,' said Keyworth with a mirthless laugh. 'Three of them at least didn't like the way that he mended their shoes.'

Robert Colbeck did not linger in Hoxton. Having learned the dead man's real name and discovered his other occupation, the Inspector decided that revenge was the most likely motive for the murder. However, since Louise Guttridge knew nothing whatsoever of her husband's activities as a public executioner – a deliberate choice on her part – there was no point in tarrying. After warning her that details of the case would have to be released to the press and that her anonymity would soon be broken, he managed to prise the address of her son out of her, wondering why she was so reluctant to give it to him. Colbeck took his leave and walked through the drab streets until he could find a cab. It took him at a steady clatter to Thames Street.

Michael Guttridge lived in a small but spotlessly clean house that was cheek by jowl with the river. He was a fleshy man in his twenties who bore almost no facial resemblance to his father.

His wife, Rebecca, was younger, shorter and very much thinner than her husband, her youthful prettiness already starting to fade in the drudgery of domestic life. Surprised by a visit from a Detective Inspector, they invited Colbeck in and were told about events on the excursion train. Their reaction was not at all what the visitor had anticipated.

'My father is *dead?*' asked Guttridge with an unmistakable note of relief in his voice. 'Is this true, Inspector?'

'Yes, sir. I went to the scene of the crime myself.'

'Then it's no more than he deserved.' He put an arm around his wife. 'It's over, Becky,' he said, excitedly. 'Do you see that? It's all over.'

'Thank God!' she cried.

'We don't have to care about it ever again.'

'That's wonderful!'

'Excuse me,' said Colbeck, letting his displeasure show, 'but I don't think that this is an occasion for celebration. A man has been brutally murdered. At least, have the grace to express some sorrow.'

Guttridge was blunt. 'We can't show what we don't feel.'

'So there's no use in pretending, is there?' said his wife, hands on hips in a challenging pose. 'I had no time for Michael's father.'

'No, and you had no time for me while I lived under the same roof with my parents. I had to make a choice – you or them.' Guttridge smiled fondly. 'I'm glad that I picked the right one.'

'Were you so ashamed of your father?' asked Colbeck.

'Wouldn't *you* be, Inspector? He was a common hangman. He lived by blood money. You can't get any lower than that.'

'I think you're doing him an injustice.'

'Am I?' retorted Guttridge, angrily. 'You didn't have to put up with the sneers and jibes. Once people knew what my father did, they turned on my mother and me as well. You'd have thought it was us who put the nooses around people's necks.'

'If your father had had his way,' his wife reminded him, 'you would have.' Rebecca Guttridge swung round to face Colbeck. 'He tried to turn Michael into his assistant. Going to prisons and killing people with a rope. It was disgusting!' Her eyes flashed back to her husband. 'I could never marry a man who did something like that.'

'I know, Becky. That's why I left home.'

'What trade *do* you follow?' said Colbeck.

'An honest one, Inspector. I'm a carpenter.'

'When were you estranged from your parents?'

'Three years ago.'

'I made him,' said Rebecca Guttridge. 'We've had nothing to do with them since. We've tried to live down the shame.'

'It should not have affected you,' maintained Colbeck.

'It did, Inspector. It was like a disease. Tell him, Michael.'

'Rebecca is right,' said her husband. 'When I lived with my parents in Southwark, I'd served my apprenticeship and was working for a builder. I was getting on well. Then my father applied for a job as a hangman. My life changed immediately

57

When the word got round, they treated me as if I was a leper. I was sacked outright and the only way I could find work was to use a false name – Michael Eames.'

'It's my maiden name,' volunteered Rebecca. 'I took Michael's name at the altar but we find it easier to live under mine. There's no stain on it.'

'I'm sorry that you see it that way,' said Colbeck. 'I can't expect either of you to admire Mr Guttridge for what he did, but you should have respected his right to do it. According to his wife, he only undertook the job because of religious conviction.'

'Ha!' snorted the carpenter. 'He always used that excuse.'

'What do you mean?'

'When he beat me as a child, he used to claim that it was God's wish. When he locked me in a room for days on end, he said the same thing. My father wouldn't go to the privy unless it was by religious conviction.'

'Michael!' exclaimed his wife.

'I'm sorry, Becky. I don't mean to be crude.'

'He's gone now. Just try to forget him.'

'Oh, I will.'

'We're free of him at last. We can lead proper lives.'

Michael Guttridge gave her an affectionate squeeze and Colbeck looked on with disapproval. During his interview with Louise Guttridge, he had realised that some kind of rift had opened up between the parents and their son but he had no idea of its full extent. Because of their family connection with a public executioner, the carpenter and his wife had endured a twilight existence, bitter, resentful, always on guard, unable to outrun the long shadow of the gallows. They were almost gleeful now, sharing a mutual pleasure that made their faces light up. It seemed to Colbeck to be a strange and reprehensible way to respond to the news of a foul murder.

'What about your mother?' he asked.

'She always took my father's part,' said Guttridge with rancour. 'Mother was even more religious than him. She kept looking for signs from above. We had to be guided, she'd say.'

'Mrs Guttridge had no time for me,' Rebecca put in.

'She tried to turn me away from Becky. Mother told me that she was not right for me. It was not proper. Yes,' he went on, wincing at the memory, 'that was the word she used – proper. It was one of my father's favourite words as well. You can see why we never invited them to the wedding.'

'They wouldn't have come in any case,' observed Rebecca. 'They never thought I was good enough for their son.'

'Becky was brought up as a Methodist,' explained her husband. 'I came from a strict Roman Catholic family.'

'I gathered that,' said Colbeck, recalling his encounter with the widow, 'but, when I asked about your mother, I was not talking about the past. I was referring to the present – and to the future.'

'The future?'

'Your mother has lost everything, Mr Guttridge. She and your father were obviously very close. To lose him in such a cruel way has been a dreadful blow for her. Can't you see that?'

'Mother will get by,' said the other with a shrug. 'Somehow or other. She's as hard as nails.'

'It sounds to me as if you've inherited that trait from her.'

'Don't say that about Michael,' chided Rebecca.

'I speak as I find.'

'My husband is the kindest man in the world.'

'Then perhaps he can show some of that kindness to his mother. Mrs Guttridge is in great distress. She's alone, confused, frightened. She's living in a house she dislikes among people she detests and the most important thing in her life has just been snatched from her.' Colbeck looked from one to the other. 'Don't you have the slightest feeling of pity for her?'

'None at all,' snapped Rebecca.

'Put yourself in her position. How would *you* cope if it had been your husband who had been murdered on a train.'

'I won't even think such a horrid thought!'

'Inspector Colbeck has a point,' admitted Guttridge as family ties exerted their pull. 'It's unfair to blame Mother for what happened. It was my father who took on that rotten job and who made me hate my name. And he's gone now – for good.' He gave a wan smile. 'Maybe it is time to let bygones be bygones.'

'No, Michael,' urged Rebecca. 'I won't let you do that.'

'She's my mother, Becky.'

'A woman who looked down on me and said that I was not fit to be your wife. She insulted me.'

'Only because she didn't know you properly.'

'She didn't *want* to know me.'

'I can't turn my back on her,' he said, earnestly.

'You managed to do it before.'

'That was because of my father.'

There was a long, silent battle between them and Colbeck did not interfere. Michael Guttridge was at last afflicted by a modicum of guilt. His wife remained cold and unforgiving. At length, however, she did consent to take his hand and receive a conciliatory kiss on the cheek. Colbeck chose the moment to speak up again.

'I came to ask you a favour, Mr Guttridge,' he said.

'Eames,' attested his wife. 'Everyone knows us under that name.'

'Listen to what the Inspector has to say,' said her husband.

'Someone has to identify the body,' explained Colbeck, 'and your mother is not able to do that. It will only take a few moments but it has to be done for legal reasons. Would you consent to come to the morgue to make that identification?'

Guttridge was uncertain. 'I don't know.'

'Let *her* go,' said Rebecca. 'It's not your place.'

'In the absence of the wife, an only son is the obvious person,' remarked Colbeck. 'It's crucial that we have the right name on the death certificate. A false one will not suffice. We don't want to compel a family member to perform this duty,' he cautioned, 'but it may come to that.'

The young carpenter walked to the window and looked out into the darkness. His wife stood at his shoulder and whispered something in his ear but he shook his head. Guttridge eventually turned round.

'I'll do it, Inspector.'

'Thank you, sir,' said Colbeck, glad to have wrested the concession from him. 'It can wait until morning, if you prefer.'

'No, I need to get it over with as soon as possible.'

'Wait until tomorrow,' advised Rebecca. 'That will give us time to talk about it. I don't want you to go at all.'

'The decision has been made,' said Colbeck, anxious to separate husband and wife. 'We'll take a cab there immediately.'

Guttridge nodded. 'I'm ready, Inspector.'

'Michael!' protested his wife.

'It has to be done, Becky.'

'Have you forgotten everything that he *did* to us?'

'No, I haven't,' said Guttridge, grimly. 'I'm only doing this to spare Mother the trouble and to give myself some pleasure.'

'Pleasure?' reiterated Colbeck in surprise. 'I can't promise that you'll find much pleasure in the police morgue, sir.'

'Oh, but I will, Inspector.'

'How?'

'I'll enjoy something that I've wanted for over twenty years.' He was triumphant. 'I'll be able to see for certain that my father is dead.'

Chapter Four

Because of its proximity to Scotland Yard, one of the pubs frequented by members of the Detective Department was the Lamb and Flag, a well-run establishment with a friendly atmosphere, a cheery landlord and excellent beer. While he waited for Colbeck to arrive, Victor Leeming nursed a tankard of bitter, taking only occasional sips so that he could make it last. Seated alone at a table on the far side of the bar, the Sergeant consulted his watch. The lateness of the hour worried him. He was still wondering what had kept the Inspector when Colbeck came in through the door, exchanged greetings with other police colleagues and made his way across the bar through the swirling cigarette smoke.

'I'm sorry to keep you waiting, Victor,' said Colbeck, joining him. 'Can I get you something else to drink?'

'No, thank you, sir. One is all that I dare touch. If I'm late back, as I will be, I can tell my wife that it's because of my work. Estelle accepts that. Let her think that I've been drinking heavily, however, and all hell will break loose. She'll call me names that I wouldn't care to repeat.'

'I'm glad you brought up the subject of names.'

'Are you, sir?'

'Yes, I've a tale to tell you on that score. Excuse me a moment.'

63

Colbeck went across to the counter and ordered a whisky and soda for himself. When he returned to the table, he took off his hat and sat opposite Leeming, who was in his customary sombre mood. Colbeck raised his glass to his companion.

'Good health, Victor!'

'I could do with it and all, sir,' admitted Leeming. 'Five minutes in that morgue and I feel as if I'm ready for the slab myself. It fair turns my stomach to go in there. How can anyone *work* in a place like that?'

'It takes special qualities.'

'Well, I don't have them. I know that. It's eerie.'

'I didn't find it so when I was there earlier,' said Colbeck, tasting his drink. 'Nor should you, Victor. By now, you should have got used to the sight of dead bodies. Over the years, we've seen enough of them and the one certain thing about policing this city is that we'll be forced to look at many more before we retire.'

'That's what depresses me, Inspector.'

'Learn to take it in your stride, man.'

'If only I could,' said Leeming, solemnly. 'But did you say that you'd been to the morgue as well?'

'I was accompanying the son of the murder victim. He made a positive identification of the body – all too positive, as it happens.'

'What do you mean?'

'That I've never seen anyone laugh in those circumstances before. And that's what Michael Guttridge did. When he looked at his father, he seemed to think it an occasion for hilarity.'

Leeming was nonplussed. 'Michael Guttridge?' he said. 'How could he be the son? The dead man's name was Bransby.'

'It was and it wasn't, Victor.'

'Well, it can't have been both.'

'As a matter of fact, it can.'

Colbeck told him about the visit to Hoxton and drew a gasp of amazement from the other when he revealed that the man who had been killed on the excursion train was none other than a public hangman. The Sergeant was even more surprised to learn of the way that Michael Guttridge and his wife had behaved on receipt of the news of the murder.

'That's disgraceful,' he said. 'It's downright indecent.'

'I made that point very forcefully to the young man.'

'And he actually laughed over the corpse?'

'I took him to task for that as well.'

'What did he say?'

'That he couldn't help himself,' said Colbeck. 'In fairness, once we left the building, he did apologise for his unseemly conduct in the morgue. I suppose that I should be grateful that his wife was not with us. Given her intransigent attitude to her father-in-law, she might have stood over the body and applauded.'

'Has she no feelings at all?'

'Far too many of them, Victor.'

Colbeck explained about her relationship with the Guttridge family and how it had made the iron enter her soul. A father himself, Leeming could not believe what he was hearing.

'My children would never treat me like that,' he said, indignantly.

'You'd never give them cause.'

'They love me as their father and do as they're told – some of the time, anyway. If I was to die, they'd be heart-broken. So would Estelle.'

'What if you were to become a public executioner?'

'That would never happen!'

'But supposing it did, Victor. Let me put it to you as a hypothetical question. In that event, would your children stand by you?'

'Of course.'

'How can you be so sure?'

'Because we're a real *family*,' said Leeming with passion. 'That's all that counts, sir. Blood is thicker than water, you know. Well, we see it every day in our work, don't we? We've met some of the most evil villains in London and they always have wives and children who dote on them.'

'True.'

'Murderers, rapists, screevers, palmers, patterers, kidnappers, blackmailers – they can do no wrong in the eyes of their nearest and dearest.'

'That's a fair point.'

'Look at that man we arrested last month on a charge of beating a pimp to death with an iron bar. His wife swore that he didn't have a violent bone in his body. She never even asked what he was doing in that brothel in the first place.'

'Guttridge's case is somewhat different.'

'It all comes back to family loyalty,' insisted Leeming. 'Most people have got it. If he had nothing to do with his father for three years, this

Michael Guttridge was the odd man out. How could he turn his back on his parents like that? I mean, how could he look at himself in the shaving mirror of a morning?'

'Very easily, Victor. He'd had a miserable childhood.'

'It makes no difference, sir. There are *obligations*.'

'You were clearly a more dutiful son than Michael Guttridge. The pity of it is,' said Colbeck, drinking some more whisky, 'that it robs us of a valuable line of inquiry. Since he shunned his father all that time, Michael was unable to give me the names of any possible suspects. Come to that, nor was the dead man's wife.'

'We're in the dark, then.'

'Not necessarily. One thing is self-evident. If you supplement your income as a cobbler by hanging people, you are not going to make many friends. Jacob Guttridge must have aroused undying hatred among the families of his various victims.'

'Lots of them will have wanted to strike back at him.'

'Exactly,' said Colbeck with a sigh. 'Our problem is that we may well end up with far too many suspects. Still, you've heard *my* story. What did you discover at the morgue?'

'Very little beyond the fact that the place scares me.'

'Whom did you speak to?'

'Doctor Keyworth.'

'Leonard's a good man. He knows his job.'

'What he told me,' said Leeming, flicking open the pages of his pad in search of the relevant place, 'was very interesting.'

He gave a halting account of his talk with the doctor, struggling to read his own writing by the light of the gas lamp. Colbeck was not surprised to learn that there had been two earlier attacks on Guttridge. It accounted for the fact that he was armed when he went out in public.

'Doctor Keyworth will have more to tell us when he's finished cutting him up,' said Leeming, closing his book. He opened it again at once. 'By the way, sir, how do you spell asphyxiation?'

Colbeck chuckled. 'Differently from you, I expect.'

'I wrote in "strangling" just to be on the safe side.'

'An admirable compromise, Victor.'

'So where do we go from here?'

'You must go home to your wife and family while I have the more forbidding task of placating the Superintendent. Because it's bound to attract a lot of publicity, Mr Tallis wants a bulletin about this case every five minutes. That's why I suggested that we meet here,' said Colbeck, lifting his glass. 'I felt that I needed a dram before facing him.'

'I'd need a whole bottle of whisky.'

'His bark is far worse than his bite.'

'Both frighten me. Will Mr Tallis still be in his office this late?'

'The rumour is that he never leaves it. Give the man his due – his dedication is exemplary. Mr Tallis is married to his job.'

'I'd prefer to be married to a woman,' confided Leeming with a rare smile. 'When I get back,

Estelle will make me a nice cup of tea and tell me what she and the children have been up to all day. Then we'll climb into a warm bed together. Who does all that for the Superintendent?'

'He has his own rewards, Victor.' Colbeck became businesslike. 'Tomorrow, we start the hunt for the killer. You can begin by reviewing the executions that involved Jacob Guttridge. Start with the most recent ones and work backward.'

'That could take me ages.'

'Not really. He was only an occasional hangman, taking over the work that others were unable to tackle. If he'd had a regular income from the noose, Guttridge wouldn't have had to keep working as a cobbler – or to live in such a small house.'

'I'll get in touch with the Home Office. They should have details.'

'All they will tell you is who was sentenced to be hanged, the nature of the crime and the place of execution. You must dig deeper than that. Find out everything you can about the individual cases. I'm convinced that that's where we'll track down our man.'

'And woman, sir.'

'What?'

'You thought he had a female accomplice.'

'It's a strong possibility.' Colbeck drained his glass. 'Get a good night's sleep, Victor. You need to be up at the crack of dawn tomorrow to make a start.'

'What will you be doing, sir?'

'Learning more about the mysterious Jacob Guttridge.'

'And how will you do that?'

'By talking to the man who has been the hangman for London and Middlesex for over twenty years.'

'William Cathcart?'

'He's the only person really qualified to talk about Guttridge in his professional capacity. Hangmen are an exclusive breed. They cling together. Cathcart will tell me all I need to know about the technique of executing a condemned prisoner.' Colbeck's eyes twinkled. 'Unless you'd rather talk to him, that is.'

'No, thank you,' replied Leeming with a shiver.

'It might be an education for you, Victor.'

'That's what I'm afraid of, sir.'

'In a sense, he is a colleague of ours. We provide his customers.'

'I wouldn't want to get within a mile of a man like that. Think how much blood he's got on his hands. He's topped dozens and dozens. No, Inspector, I'll leave Mr Cathcart to you.'

Word of any disaster travelled with amazing speed among railwaymen. Whenever the boiler of a locomotive burst, or a train came off the track or someone was inadvertently crushed to death between the buffers, news of the event soon reached those who worked in the industry. Caleb Andrews was employed by the London and North Western Railway, one of the fiercest rivals of the GWR, but he had heard about the murder at Twyford by mid-evening. It was the main topic of discussion among the drivers and fireman at Euston. To learn more about what had occurred, he was up even earlier than usual so that he could walk to the newsagent's to collect a morning paper. When he got back home, he found breakfast waiting for him on the table. His daughter, Madeleine, who lived alone with her father and who ran the household, was as anxious for detail as he was.

'What does it say, Father?' she asked.

'I haven't had time to read it yet,' said Andrews, taking a leather case from his inside pocket. 'Let me put my glasses on first.'

'A murder on a train! It's terrifying.'

'First one I've ever come across, Maddy.'

'Do they tell you who the victim was?'

Sitting at the table, Andrews put on his spectacles and squinted through the lenses at the front page of the newspaper. His eyebrows shot up and he released a whistle of surprise through his teeth.

'Well,' pressed Madeleine, looking over his shoulder. 'What was the man's name?'

'Jacob Guttridge,' he replied. '*The* Jacob Guttridge.'

'Am I supposed to have heard of him?'

'Every criminal in London has, Maddy. He's a Jack Ketch.'

'A *hangman?*'

'Not any more. He's not as famous as Mr Cathcart, of course, but he's put the noose around lots of guilty necks, that much I do know. It says here,' he went on, scanning the opening paragraph, 'that he was on an excursion train taking passengers to a prize fight.'

'I thought they were banned.'

'There are always ways of getting around that

71

particular law. I tell you this, Maddy, I'd have been tempted to watch that fight myself if I'd been given the chance. The Bargeman was up against Mad Isaac.'

Andrews put his face closer to the small print so that he could read it more easily. A diminutive figure in his early fifties, he had a fringe beard that was salted with grey and thinning hair that curled around a face lined by a lifetime on the railway. Renowned among his colleagues for his blistering tongue and forthright opinions, Andrews had a softer side to him as well. The death of a beloved wife had all but broken his spirit. What helped him to go on and regain a sense of purpose was the presence and devotion of his only child, Madeleine, an alert, handsome, spirited young woman, who knew how to cope with his sudden changes of mood and his many idiosyncrasies. She had undoubtedly been her father's salvation.

When he got to the end of a column, Andrews let out a cackle.

'What is it?' she said.

'Nothing, nothing,' he replied, airily.

'You can't fool me. I know you better than that.'

'I came across another name I recognised, that's all, Maddy. It would have no interest for you.' He gave her a wicked smile. 'Or would it, I wonder?'

Her face ignited. 'Robert?'

'Inspector Colbeck's been put in charge of the case.'

'Let me see,' said Madeleine, excitedly, almost snatching the paper from him. Her eye fell on the

72

name she sought. 'It's true. Robert is leading the investigation. The murder will soon be solved.'

'The only crime I want to solve is the theft of my paper,' he complained, extending a hand. 'Give it here, Maddy.'

'When I've finished with it.'

'Who went to the shop to buy it?'

'Eat your breakfast, Father. You don't want to be late.'

'There's plenty of time yet.'

She surrendered the newspaper reluctantly and sat opposite him. Madeleine was delighted to see that the Railway Detective was involved in the case. When the mail train had been robbed the previous year, her father had been the driver and he was badly injured by one of the men who had ambushed him. Robert Colbeck had not only hunted down and arrested the gang responsible for the crime, he had rescued Madeleine when she was abducted and used as a hostage. As a result of it all, the two of them had been drawn together into a friendship that had grown steadily over the intervening months without ever quite blossoming into a romance. Colbeck was always a welcome visitor at the little house in Camden.

Andrews remained buried in the newspaper article.

'We should be seeing the Inspector very soon,' he observed.

'I hope so.'

'Whenever he's dealing with a crime on the railway, he drops in for my advice. I know that you like to think he comes to see you,' teased Andrews, 'but I'm the person that he really wants to talk to, Maddy. I've taught him all he knows about trains.'

'That's not true, Father,' she responded, loyally. 'Be fair to him. Robert has always taken a special interest in trains. When you first met him, you couldn't believe that he knew the difference between a Bury and a Crampton locomotive.'

But she was talking to herself. Andrews was so engrossed in the newspaper account that he did not hear her. It was only when he had read every word about the murder on the excursion train three times that he set the paper aside and picked up his spoon. He attacked his breakfast with relish.

'One thing, anyway,' he said as he ate his porridge.

'What's that?'

'You'll have a chance to wear that new dress of yours, Maddy.'

'Father!' she rebuked.

'Be honest. You always make a special effort for the Inspector.'

'All I want is for this dreadful crime to be solved as soon as possible.' She could not hide her joy. 'But, yes, it will be nice if Robert finds the time to call on us.'

Once he had set his mind on a course of action, Inspector Colbeck was not easily deflected. The search for William Cathcart took him to four separate locations but that did not trouble him. He simply pressed on until he finally ran the man to earth at Newgate. He did not have to ask for Cathcart this time because the hangman was clearly visible on the scaffold outside the prison, testing the apparatus in preparation for an execution that was due to take place the next day. Colbeck understood why extra care was being taken on this occasion. Cathcart had bungled his last execution at Newgate, leaving the prisoner dangling in agony until the hangman had dispatched him by swinging on his feet to break his neck. Reviled by the huge crowd attending the event, Cathcart had also been pilloried in the press.

Colbeck waited until the grisly rehearsal was over then introduced himself and asked for a word with Cathcart. Seeing the opportunity for a free drink, the latter immediately took the detective across the road to the public house that would be turned into a grandstand on the following day, giving those that could afford the high prices a privileged view of the execution. Colbeck bought his companion a glass of brandy but had no alcohol himself. They found a settle in a quiet corner.

'I can guess why you've come, Inspector,' said Cathcart, slyly. 'The murder of Jake Guttridge.'

'You've obviously seen the newspapers.'

'Never read the blessed things. They always print such lies about me. Criminal, what they say. Deserves 'angin' in my opinion. I'd like to string them reporters up in line, so I would.'

'I'm sure.'

'Then cut out their 'earts and livers for good measure.'

'I can see why you're not popular with the gentlemen of the press.'

75

William Cathcart was an unappealing individual. One of eleven children, he had been raised in poverty by parents who struggled to get by and who were unable to provide him with any real education. The boy's life had been unremittingly hard. Cathcart was in his late twenties when he secured the post of public executioner for London and Middlesex, and the capital provided him with plenty of practice at first. Notwithstanding this, he showed very little improvement in his chosen craft. Coarse, ugly and bearded, he was now in his fifties, a portly man in black frock coat and black trousers, proud of what he did and quick to defend himself against his critics with the foulest of language. Conscious of the man's reputation, Colbeck did not look forward to the interview with any pleasure.

'How well did you know Jacob Guttridge?' he began.

'Too well!' snarled the other.

'In what way?'

'Jake was my blinkin' shadow, weren't 'e? Always tryin' to copy wor I did. 'Cos I was an 'angman, Jake takes it up. 'Cos I earned a crust as a shoemaker, Jake 'as to be a cobbler. Everythin' I did, Jake manages to do as well.' He smacked the table with the flat of his hand. 'The bugger even moved after me to 'Oxton, though 'e couldn't afford to live in Poole Street where I do. I'd never 'ave stood for that, Inspector.'

'I get the impression that you didn't altogether like the man,' said Colbeck with mild irony. 'You must have worked together at some point.'

'Oh, we did. Jake begged me to let 'im act as my

assistant a couple of times. Watched me like an 'awk to see 'ow it was done. Then 'e 'as the gall to say that 'e can do it better. Better!' cried Cathcart. 'You're lookin' at a man who's topped some of the worst rogues that ever crawled on this earth. It was me who 'anged that Swiss villain, Kervoyseay.'

'Courvoisier,' said Colbeck, pronouncing the name correctly. 'He was the butler who murdered his employer, Lord William Russell.'

'Then there was Fred Mannin' and 'is wife, Marie,' boasted the other. 'I strung the pair of 'em up at 'Orsemonger Lane a few years back. They danced a jig at the end of my rope 'cos they killed 'er fancy man, Marie Mannin', that is. Nasty pair, they were.'

Colbeck recalled the event well. He also remembered the letter of protest that was published in *The Times* on the following day, written by no less a person than Charles Dickens. An execution that Cathcart obviously listed among his successes had, in fact, provoked widespread disapproval. There was a gruesome smugness about the man that Colbeck found very distasteful but his personal feelings had to be put aside. He probed for information.

'Does it worry you to be a figure who inspires hatred?' he asked.

'Not at all,' returned Cathcart with a chuckle. 'I thrives on it. In any case, most of the cullies who come to goggle at an 'angin' looks up to me really. They're always ready to buy me a drink afterwards and listen to my adventures. Yes, and I never 'ave any trouble sellin' the rope wot done the job. I cuts it up into slices, Inspector. You've no idea 'ow much some people will pay for six inches of 'emp when it's been round the neck of a murderer.'

'Let's get back to Jacob Guttridge, shall we?'

'Then there's another way to make extra money,' said Cathcart, warming to his theme. 'You lets people touch the 'and of the dead man, see, 'cos it's supposed to cure wens and that. Don't believe it myself,' he added with a throaty chuckle, 'but I makes a pretty penny out of it.'

'Some of which you give to your mother, I understand.'

As Colbeck had intended it to do, the comment stopped Cathcart in his tracks. Two years earlier, the hangman had been taken to court for refusing to support his elderly mother, who was in a workhouse. Though he earned a regular wage from Newgate, and supplemented it by performing executions elsewhere in the country, he had had the effrontery to plead poverty and was sharply reprimanded by the magistrate. In the end, as Colbeck knew, the man sitting opposite him had been forced to pay a weekly amount to his mother, who, though almost eighty, preferred to remain in a country work-house. It was a case that reflected very badly on the public executioner.

'I'm a dutiful son,' he attested. 'I done right by my mother.'

'It's reassuring to hear that,' said Colbeck, 'but it's Mr Guttridge that I came to talk about. You claimed just now that you don't mind if people hate you because of what you do. Jacob Guttridge did. He was so nervous about it that he used a false name.'

'That's why 'e'd never be another Bill Cathcart.'

'He obviously tried to be.'

'Jealousy, that's wor it was. Jake knew, in his 'eart, that I was the master. But did 'e take my advice? Nah!' said Cathcart with contempt. 'I told 'im to use a short drop like me but 'e always used too much rope. Know wor 'appened at 'is first go?'

'No,' said Colbeck. 'Tell me.'

'Jake allowed such a long drop that 'e took orff the prisoner's 'ead, clean as a whistle. They never let 'im work at Norwich again.'

'Were there other instances where mistakes were made?'

'Dozens of 'em, Inspector.'

'Recently, perhaps?'

'There was talk of some trouble in Ireland, I think.'

'What kind of trouble?'

'Who knows? I don't follow Jake's career. But I can tell this,' said Cathcart, slipping his thumbs into his waistcoat pockets. 'If I was in the salt-box, waitin' to be took to the gallows, I'd much rather 'ave someone like me to do the necessary than Jake Guttridge.'

'Why do you say that, Mr Cathcart?'

'Because I tries to give 'em a quick, clean, merciful death and put 'em out of their misery right way. It's not 'ow Jake did it.'

'No?'

'That psalm-singin' fool made their sufferin'

worse before they got anywhere near the scaffold. A condemned man needs peace and quiet to fit 'is mind for the awful day. Last thing 'e wants is someone like Jake, givin' 'im religious bloody tracts or readin' poetry and such like at 'im. All that a public 'angman is there to do,' announced Cathcart with the air of unassailable authority, 'is to 'ang the poor devil who's in the condemned cell. Not try to save 'is blinkin' soul when the likelihood is that 'e ain't got one to save. Follow me, Inspector?'

Even allowing for natural prejudice, Colbeck could see that the portrait painted of Jacob Guttridge was very unflattering. Driven to take on the job by a combination of need and religious mania, he had proved less than success-ful as a public executioner. Yet he still had regular commissions from various parts of the country.

'Have you never been afraid, Mr Cathcart?' he asked.

'No, Inspector. Why should I be?'

'A man in your line of work must have had death threats.'

'Dozens of 'em,' confessed the other with a broad grin. 'Took 'em as a compliment. Never stopped me from sleepin' soundly at nights. I been swore at, spat at, punched at, kicked at, and 'ad all kinds of things thrown at me in the 'eat of the moment, but I just got on with my work.'

'Do you carry any weapons?'

'I've no need.'

'Mr Guttridge did. He had a dagger strapped to his leg. You and he are as different as chalk and cheese,' said Colbeck, stroking his chin. 'Both of

80

you did the same office yet it affected you in contrasting ways. You walk abroad without a care in the world while Jake Guttridge sneaked around under a false name. Why did he do that?'

'Cowardice.'

'He was certainly afraid of something – or of someone.'

'Then the idiot should never 'ave taken on the job in the first place. A man should be 'appy in 'is work – like me. Then 'e's got good reason to do it properly, see?' He held up his glass. 'Another brandy wouldn't come amiss, Inspector. Pay up and I'll tell you about 'ow I topped Esther 'Ibner, the murderess, 'ere at Newgate. My first execution.'

'Another time,' said Colbeck, getting up. 'Solving a heinous crime like this takes precedence over everything else. But thank you for your help, Mr Cathcart. Your comments have been illuminating.'

'Will you be 'ere tomorrow, Inspector?'

'Here?'

'For the entertainment,' said Cathcart, merrily. 'I always work best when there's a big audience. Maybe Jake will be lookin' down at me from a front row seat in 'eaven. I'll be able to show 'im wor a proper execution looks like, won't I?'

His raucous laughter filled the bar.

Louise Guttridge had been unfair to her neighbours. Because she shut them out of her life, she never really got to know any of them. She was therefore taken aback by the spontaneous acts of kindness shown by unnamed people in her street.

81

All that most of them knew was that her husband had died. Posies of flowers appeared on her doorstep and condolences were scrawled on pieces of paper. Those who could not write simply slipped a card under her door. Louise Guttridge was deeply moved though she feared that more hostile messages might be delivered when the nature of her husband's work became common knowledge.

As in all periods of crisis, she turned to her religion for succour. With the blinds drawn down, she sat in the front room, playing with her rosary beads and reciting prayers she had learned by heart, trying to fill her mind with holy thoughts so that she could block out the horror that had devastated her life. She was dressed in black taffeta, her widow's weeds, inherited from her mother, giving off a fearsome smell of mothballs. Her faith was a great comfort to her but it did not still her apprehensions completely. She was now alone. The death of her husband had cut her off from the only regular human contact she had enjoyed. She had now been delivered up to strangers.

Closing her eyes, she offered up a prayer for the soul of the deceased and coupled it with a plea that his killer should soon be caught, convicted and hanged. In her mind, one life had to be paid for with another. Until that happened, she could never rest. While the murderer remained at liberty, she would forever be tortured by thoughts of who and where he might be, and why he had committed the hideous crime.

Hoxton was to blame. She was fervent in that

belief. Disliking and distrusting the area, she wished that they had never moved there. The tragedy that, from the very start, she felt was imminent had now taken place. The irony was that it had prompted a display of sympathy and generosity among her neighbours that she had never realised was there. In losing a husband, she had gained unlikely friends.

She was still lost in prayer when she heard a knock on her door. The sudden intrusion alarmed her. It was as if she had been shaken roughly awake and she required a moment to gather herself together. A second knock made her move towards the front door. Then she hesitated. What if it were someone who had discovered she was the wife of Jacob Guttridge and come to confront her? Should she lie low and ignore the summons? Or should she answer the door and simply brazen it out? A third knock – much firmer than the others - helped her to make her decision. She could hide no longer behind her maiden name. It was time to behave like the woman she really was – the widow of a hangman. Gathering up her skirt, she hurried to the door and opened it wide.

Louise Guttridge was so astonished to find her son standing there that she was struck dumb. He, too, was palpably unable to speak, seeing his mother for the first time in three years and unsure how his visit would be received. Michael Guttridge looked nervous rather than penitent, but the very fact that he was there touched her. Louise's feelings were ambivalent. Trying to smile, all that she could contrive was a grimace. He cleared his throat before speaking tentatively.

'Hello, Mother.'

'What do you want?' she asked, suspiciously. 'Have you come here to gloat?'

'Of course not.' He sounded hurt. 'May I come in?'

'I don't know, Michael.'

'But I'm your *son*.'

'You were – once.'

And she scrutinised him as if trying to convince herself of the fact.

'I knew that you'd need my advice,' said Caleb Andrews, nudging his elbow. 'Whenever there's a crime on the railway, bring it to me.'

'Thank you for the kind offer,' said Colbeck, amused.

'How can I help you this time, Inspector?'

'Actually, it was Madeleine I came to see.'

'But *I'm* the railwayman.'

'Stop playing games, Father,' said his daughter. 'You know quite well that Robert would not discuss a case with you.'

'All right, all right,' said Andrews, pretending to be offended. 'I know when I'm not wanted. I'll get out of your way.'

And with a wink at Madeleine, he went off upstairs to change out of his driver's uniform. Left alone with her, Colbeck was able to greet her properly by taking both hands and squeezing them affectionately. For her part, Madeleine was thrilled to see him again, glad that she had taken the precaution of wearing her new dress that evening. Colbeck stood back to admire it and gave her a smile of approval.

'We saw your name in the newspaper,' she said. 'I can see why the Great Western Railway asked for you.'

'It's a double-edged compliment. It means that the investigation falls into my lap, which is gratifying, but – if I fail – it also means that I take the full blame for letting a killer escape justice.'

'You won't fail, Robert. You never fail.'

'That's not true,' he admitted. 'I've made my share of mistakes since I joined the Metropolitan Police. Fortunately, I've been able to hide them behind my occasional successes. Detection is not a perfectible art, Madeleine – if only it were! All that we can do is to follow certain procedures and rely on instinct.'

'Your instinct solved the train robbery last year.'

'I did have a special incentive with regard to that case.'

'Thank you,' she said, returning his smile. 'But I don't think that I was your only inspiration. I'd never seen anyone so determined to track down the men responsible for a crime. Father was very impressed and it takes a lot to earn a word of praise from him.'

'He's so spry for his age.'

'Yes, he's fully recovered from his injuries now.'

'He's looking better than ever. And so are you,' he added, standing back to admire her. 'That dress is quite charming.'

'Oh, it's an old one that you just haven't seen before,' she lied.

'Everything in your wardrobe becomes you, Madeleine.'

'From someone like you, that's a real tribute.'

'It was intended to be.' They shared another warm smile. 'But I haven't asked how your own career is coming along.'

'It's hardly a career, Robert.'

'It could be, if you persist. You have genuine artistic talent.'

'I'm not so sure about that,' she said, modestly.

'You have, Madeleine. When you showed me those sketches you did, I could see their potential at once. That's why I introduced you to Mr Gostelow and he agreed with me. If you can learn the technique of lithography, then your work could reach a wider audience.'

'Who on earth would want to buy prints of mine?'

'I would for a start,' he promised her. 'What other woman could create such accurate pictures of locomotives? Most female artists content themselves with family portraits or gentle landscapes. None of them seem to have noticed that this is the railway age.'

'From the time when I was a small girl,' she said, 'I've always done drawings of trains. I suppose that it was to please Father.'

'It would please a lot of other people as well, Madeleine. However,' he went on, 'I didn't only come here for the pleasure of seeing you and talking about your future as an artist. I wanted to ask a favour.'

'Oh?'

'It concerns this murder on the excursion train.'

'How can I possibly help?'

'By being exactly what you are.'

86

'The daughter of an engine driver?'

'A kind and compassionate young woman,' he said. 'It fell to me to break the news of her husband's death to his widow, and I did so as gently as I could. In the circumstances, Mrs Guttridge bore up extremely well, almost as if she'd been preparing for such an appalling event. One can understand why. Her husband had been attacked twice before.'

'Was he injured?'

'Quite seriously.'

'I still don't see where I come in, Robert.'

'Let me tell you,' he said, taking her arm to move her to the sofa and sitting beside her. 'I had the distinct feeling that Mrs Guttridge was holding something back from me, something that could actually help the investigation. I don't think that she was deliberately trying to impede me but I was certain that she did not tell me all that she could.'

'The poor woman must have been in a state of shock.'

'It's the reason that I didn't press her too hard.'

'What do you want me to do?'

'Relate to her in a way that I can't, Madeleine. She sees me as a detective, a figure of authority and, most obvious of all, as a man. Mrs Guttridge could not confide in me. I could sense her resistance.'

'Is she any more likely to confide in someone like me?' asked Madeleine, guessing what he wanted her to do. 'You're trained to cope with these situations, Robert. I am not.'

'It doesn't require any previous experience.

Your presence alone would be enough. It would make her feel less uneasy. With luck,' he said, 'it might break down that resistance I mentioned.'

'What exactly do you want me to do?'

'First of all, I want to assure you that you're under no compulsion at all. If you'd rather stay clear of the whole thing...'

'Don't be silly,' she interrupted, relishing the opportunity of working alongside him. 'I'll do anything that you ask. Coming from a railway family, I have a particular interest in solving this crime.'

'Thank you.'

'Just give me my instructions.'

'The first thing I must do is to swear you to secrecy,' he warned her. 'What I'm asking is highly irregular and my Superintendent would tear me to pieces if he were to find out. I won't even breathe a word of this to Victor Leeming, my Sergeant. He'd frown on the whole notion.'

'I won't tell a soul – not even Father.'

'Then welcome to the Detective Department,' he said, shaking her hand. 'You're the first woman at Scotland Yard and I could not imagine a better person to act as a pioneer.'

'You might think differently when you see me in action.'

'I doubt that, Madeleine. I have every confidence in you.'

'It will be an education to watch the Railway Detective at work.'

'That may be,' he said, enjoying her proximity, 'but I fancy that you're the one who'll achieve the breakthrough that we need. In this case, it may be a woman's touch that will be decisive.'

Chapter Five

No matter how early he arrived at work, Victor Leeming could never get there before Edward Tallis. Having made a special effort to reach Scotland Yard by seven o'clock that morning, Leeming was dismayed to see the Superintendent coming out of his office and pounding down the corridor towards him like an army on the march.

'Good morning, sir,' said the Sergeant.

'What time do you call this, man? We've been here for hours.'

'*We*, Superintendent?'

'Inspector Colbeck and I,' growled Tallis. 'At least, I have one person who understands the importance of punctuality, even if deficient in other respects. While you sleep, the criminal underworld is about its nefarious business. What kept you?' A note of censure came into his voice. 'Family matters, no doubt.'

'It was my wife who got me out of bed so early, sir.'

'Indeed?'

'Yes,' said Leeming, thrown on the defensive. 'As soon as we'd had breakfast with the children, I made my way here.'

'You know my opinion of marriage. It gets in the way.'

'We can't be on duty all the time, Superintendent.'

'We should be, Sergeant – metaphorically speaking, that is. Admit a distraction into your life and you weaken your effectiveness.'

'Estelle is no distraction – nor are my children.'

'I dispute that.'

'We're human beings, sir,' argued Leeming, stung by the attack on his family, 'not monks. What do you want – a celibate police force?'

'I want men beneath me who put their work first.'

'That's what I've always tried to do. And so has Inspector Colbeck.'

'While awaiting your arrival,' said Tallis, pointedly, 'he and I have been studying the research that you did into Jacob Guttridge's record as a hangman. Though I have to admit, that I'm not entirely sure that we're looking in the right place.'

'Why not, sir?'

'The killer may have no connection whatsoever with the man's former occupation. He might not even have known who Guttridge was.'

'Then what was his motive?'

'Villains of that stripe need no motive,' said the Superintendent, corrugating his brow until his eyebrows met in the middle. 'They have a destructive urge that is set off by drink or simply by an argument.'

'Inspector Colbeck believes that–'

'I am fully aware of what the Inspector believes,' snapped the other, cutting him off, 'but I prefer to keep an open mind. Make a wrong assumption at the start of an investigation and you find yourself going in circles.'

'We know that, sir. Here, however, we have a

significant clue.'

'Do we?'

'The Inspector saw it immediately,' said Leeming. 'The manner of the victim's death is critical. It would have been easier to stab him and much quicker to shoot him or bludgeon him to death. Instead, a piece of wire was used to strangle him.'

'I'm familiar with the details.'

'A man who made his living by the noose died in the same way. The killer carefully chose the means by which he took revenge.'

'Did he?'

'I think so, sir.'

'I wonder.'

'The Inspector's argument is very convincing.'

'Not to me,' said Tallis, inflating his chest, 'because it is unproven. We've had killers before who favour the garrotte. Foreigners, usually. And there are footpads who like to disable their victims that way. This could be the work of someone quite unrelated to Guttridge's activities on the scaffold. A murderous Italian, for instance.'

'The train was full of them, sir,' said Leeming, attempting humour.

Tallis glared at him. 'Are you being facetious, Sergeant?'

'No, no. I meant that there would have been villains on board.'

'Then I'll let it pass.'

'Thank you, Superintendent.'

'Now that you're finally here, let's have some work out of you.'

'I plan to spend the entire day sifting through

all the information that I gathered about various executions.'

'You'll find that the Inspector has saved you some of the trouble.'

'How?'

'By getting here at the crack of dawn and applying himself to the task in hand.' He stepped in closer to the Sergeant. 'Do you see how efficient a man can be when he's not hampered by a wife and children?'

'Only a family can make life worthwhile, sir,' contended Leeming.

'Tell that to Inspector Colbeck. But you had better be quick about it. He'll be leaving soon to pay a second visit to Mrs Guttridge.'

Robert Colbeck offered his hand to help her up into the Hansom cab. When he and Madeleine Andrews were safely ensconced inside, they were taken on a noisy, twisting, jolt-filled journey from Camden to Hoxton. They were driven down crowded streets, past busy markets, through heavy horse-drawn traffic and beneath a railway bridge over which a train decided to pass at that precise moment. The pungent smells of London were all around them. While Madeleine savoured the pleasure of being shoulder to shoulder with him, Colbeck patiently instructed her in what she had to do when they reached their destination.

'The most important thing is to win her confidence,' he told her. 'Don't ask her anything at all at first. Let her volunteer any information that she wishes to give us.'

'Yes, Robert.'

'If she has the feeling that you are there solely to interrogate her, we'll get no response at all. Let her come to you, Madeleine.'

'How will you introduce me?'

'As a friend. Someone travelling with me.'

'Not as a detective?' she teased.

'That would rather give the game away. Besides,' he said, 'you're not there to search for anything. All you have to do is to listen.'

She laughed. 'I'm used to doing that at home.'

'Was your father always so garrulous?'

'Not when my mother was alive,' she replied. 'In fact, the two of them were remarkably quiet. They'd just sit together happily of an evening without exchanging a word while I got on with my sketching. It's only since her death that Father became so talkative.'

'I can understand that, Madeleine.'

The coach eventually deposited them outside the house in Hoxton and they alighted to discover a fine drizzle starting to fall. An inquisitive dog was sniffing the petals of some flowers that had been left on the doorstep by a caring neighbour. At the approach of the visitors, the animal ran away and Colbeck was able to retrieve the posy. His gaze was then drawn to the noose that had been crudely painted on the front door of the house, clear evidence that Jacob Bransby's true identity had been revealed to the people of Hoxton.

'Don't go in there, sir,' cautioned a boy. 'It's an 'angman's 'ouse.'

'Really?' said Colbeck.

'It'll probbly be 'aunted.'

'Thank you for the warning.'

The boy ran off to join some friends at the end of the street. Before Colbeck could knock on the door, it opened of its own accord and Louise Guttridge appeared with an elderly Roman Catholic priest, his face a mask of benignity. When she recognised the detective, she introduced Father Cleary and the two of them were introduced in turn to Madeleine. After an exchange of niceties, the clergyman left. The visitors were invited into the house and shown into the front room. Since the blinds were down, it was very gloomy but the Virgin Mary caught what little light was left and seemed to glow in appreciation.

'These were outside,' said Colbeck, handing the flowers to Louise Guttridge. 'A kind gesture from a neighbour.'

'Did you see what was on the front door?' she asked.

'Yes,' he replied. 'When was that put there?'

'Some time in the night.'

'Has there been anything else? Warning letters? Broken windows? Unpleasant items being pushed through the letterbox?'

'Not so far, Inspector.'

'I'll call in at the police station later on and make sure that the officers on this beat pass much more often than usual.'

'Thank you.'

'Although the sensible option would be for you to move out.'

The woman shrugged helplessly. 'Where can I go?'

'We have a spare room at our house,' offered

Madeleine, taking pity on her. 'You could come to us for a while.'

'That's very kind of you, Miss Andrews, but I couldn't. I'll stay here till I can sell the house and get out for good.'

Her pallor was accentuated by the black dress and there were bags under her eyes that showed how little sleep she had had since receiving news of her husband's murder. But she was not in distress and the visit of her parish priest had undoubtedly bolstered her.

'I came to tell you that the body has been identified,' said Colbeck. 'Your son was prevailed upon to come to the morgue with me.'

'Yes, Inspector. He told me.'

Colbeck was startled. 'You've *seen* him?'

'He called here yesterday.'

'What did he say, Mrs Guttridge?'

'Very little,' she replied. 'Michael said all that he needed to say three years ago when he married that spiteful creature against our will. Rebecca Eames turned our son against us.'

'Yet he does appear to have made the effort to come here.'

'Yes.' There was a long pause before she remembered the rules of hospitality. 'But do sit down, please. May I get you something?'

'A cup of tea would be welcome,' said Colbeck. 'Miss Andrews?'

'Yes, please.'

The other woman indicated the chairs. 'Take a seat while I get it.'

'Let me help you,' said Madeleine, following her out to the kitchen.

95

Left alone, Colbeck was able to study the room more carefully than he had been able to do on his first visit. Whatever her shortcomings as a mother, Louise Guttridge was a fastidious housekeeper. There was not a hint of dust to be seen anywhere. The mirror on one wall had been polished to a high sheen, the tiles around the fireplace gleamed, and the picture rail looked as if it had been painted that morning. She had even run a vigorous duster around the pot holding the aspidistra and over the blackleading on the grate. Trapped in a false identity and confined largely to the house, she had made it as habitable as possible.

Nor had her spiritual cleanliness been neglected. The crucifix and the Virgin Mary looked down on a well-thumbed Bible and a Catholic missal, side by side on the small table. Colbeck could all but smell the incense in the air. The two women seemed to be taking their time in the kitchen but he did not worry about that. The longer they were alone together, the more likely it was that Madeleine could learn something of consequence. He was especially pleased with the way that she had offered the older woman shelter at her own home, a truly sympathetic response to the predicament in which Louise Guttridge found herself.

Colbeck sat down and waited, noting that there was virtually no sign of anything in the room that had been put there by the deceased. A man who was so passionate about prizefighting might be expected to have a few sporting prints on the wall. His twin occupations of cobbler and hangman had also been excluded but that was understand-

96

able. It was pre-eminently his wife's domain, leading Colbeck to wonder just how much time the husband had spent in there with her. While Guttridge had also been religious, his regular consumption of alcohol – confirmed by the post mortem – had pointed to someone with all too human failings. The former hangman might pray with his wife for guidance but, Colbeck was certain, he did not take her to a public house with him, still less to a boxing match.

The others finally came in from the kitchen and it was Madeleine who was carrying the tray. It was a promising sign. The older woman moved the Bible and the missal so that the tray could be set down on the table. Louise Guttridge stood beside it, ready to pour the tea.

'Mrs Guttridge has just told me about her husband's collection,' said Madeleine, sitting opposite Colbeck. 'It's in the spare room.'

'A collection?' he repeated. 'Of what kind?'

'To do with his work,' explained the widow, removing the tea cosy so that she could take hold of the handle. 'Jacob liked to keep souvenirs. A cup of tea, Miss Andrews?'

'Yes, please,' said Madeleine.

'Help yourself to milk and sugar.'

'Thank you, Mrs Guttridge.'

Colbeck bided his time until his own cup had been poured and he had added a splash of milk. The revelation about the spare room filled him with hope. He stirred his tea.

'Why didn't you mention this collection before?' he wondered.

'Because it was nothing to do with me,' said

97

Louise Guttridge, taking a seat with her own cup of tea. 'Jacob never let me in there – not that I would have cared to see such horrible things, mind you. He kept the room locked.'

'Do you have the key?'

'Yes, Inspector. I found it when I was going through my husband's things last night. But I couldn't bring myself to go into the room.'

'Somebody will have to do so,' said Madeleine, casually. 'Would you like Inspector Colbeck to spare you the trouble? I'm sure that he will have no qualms about what he might find.'

'None at all,' he added, grateful for the ease with which she had made the suggestion. 'I'd be only too glad to help.'

'The decision is yours, Mrs Guttridge.'

The other woman hesitated. Tempted to accept the offer, she felt that it would be an invasion of her privacy and that – at such a vulnerable moment for her – was deeply troubling. In her eyes, there was another drawback. The detective might relieve her of a repellent task but, in the process, he might discover things that she did not wish to know about her late husband. Colbeck was quick to point out a more positive result of any search.

'My job is to catch your husband's killer,' he reminded her. 'It may well be that your spare room contains clues that will lead me to him. It's imperative that I be given access to it.'

'It was Jacob's room. Nobody else was allowed in there.'

'I think that I should find out why, don't you?'

Louise Guttridge agonised over the decision for

a full minute.

'I'll get the key,' she said at length.

When he got to the top of the stairs, Colbeck took the opportunity to peer into the main bedroom at the front of the house. Immaculately clean, it contained a dressing table, an upright chair, a wardrobe with mirrors and a bed over which another crucifix kept guard. The room was small but uncluttered and he saw the hand of the wife at work once again. He went across to the back room and slipped the key into the lock, wondering what he would find on the other side of the varnished timber. Opening the door, he stepped into another world.

The contrast could not have been greater. The tiny, cramped room was the complete antithesis of the other parts of the house. Where they had been spick and span, Jacob Guttridge's den was in total disarray. In place of the odour of sanctity there was a lingering smell of decay. Instead of looking up to heaven, the hangman preferred to stare down into the mouth of hell. The only pieces of furniture in the room were a long table and a single bed, both littered with newspapers, pieces of rope, advertisements for executions and other grim mementos of his craft. Most ghoulish of all were items of clothing that had been worn by condemned men and, more particularly, by women, their names written on scraps of paper that had been pinned to the material.

The walls, too, were covered in drawings, warrants, newspaper articles and curling advertisements, haphazardly arranged but all the more striking as a result. Amid the hideous catalogue of death, Colbeck noticed prints of prizefighters – one of them was The Bargeman – but the overwhelming impression was of a black museum in which Jacob Guttridge had gloried with almost necrophiliac pleasure. Had the law permitted it, the detective mused, the hangman would have parboiled the heads of his victims and had them dangling from the ceiling like so many Chinese lanterns. Guttridge had relished his work.

Below in the front room, Louise Guttridge was being distracted by Madeleine, sublimely unaware of the essential character of the man with whom she had slept for so many years in the shadow of a crucifix. The house that bore her clear imprint was really a façade behind which she could hide as Mrs Bransby. It was the back bedroom that told the truth about the building and its owner. Colbeck resolved that the wife should not be subjected to the discovery that he had just made. Even with the aid of Father Cleary, he was not sure that she would survive the ordeal.

He began a slow, methodical search, first stripping the walls and sorting the various items into piles. Some of the fading newspaper cuttings referred to executions that he had carried out years before. Any periodical in which Guttridge had been mentioned had been saved, even if the comments about him were unfavourable. Under a collection of death warrants on the table, Colbeck found the hangman's invoice book. Each page was neatly printed in italics with spaces left for him to fill in the date, his current address and details of the execution that he was agreeing to undertake. Sent to the High Sheriff of the relevant county, it was signed by 'Your obedient Servant, Jacob Guttridge.'

The hangman had been ubiquitous. Colbeck found a record of his work in places as far apart as Aberdeen, Bodmin, Lancaster, Cambridge, Taunton, Glasgow, Swansea, Bury St Edmunds and Ireland. A tattered account book listed his various fees, copied out laboriously in a spidery hand. There was also a series of squiggly notes about the technique of hanging, complete with rough sketches that showed comparative lengths of the drop, relative to the weight of the condemned person. But it was the last discovery that excited Colbeck the most and made his search worthwhile. Concealed under a ballad about the execution of a man in Devizes was something that Guttridge had not put on display. It was a note, scribbled on a piece of brown paper in bold capitals.

N IS INERCENT. IF YOU HANGS HIM, WEEL KILL YOU.

The warning message was unsigned.

'What took you so long up there, Robert?' asked Madeleine Andrews.

'There was a lot to see in that room.'

'You seem to have brought most of it with you.'

She indicated the bundle that lay between his feet. The two of them were in a cab, on their way back to Camden via the local police station, and they had taken some cargo on board. With the permission of Louise Guttridge, Colbeck had

101

gathered up everything that he felt would distress her and wrapped it all in a cloak that had once belonged to a certain Eleanor Fawcett, hanged at Ipswich the previous summer for poisoning both her husband and her lover. Colbeck could only guess at the impulse that had made the hangman keep it as a treasured souvenir. He was grateful that the widow would never know just how depraved her husband had been. When the two of them had knelt before their Maker, they were sending their supplications in opposite directions.

'What exactly is in there?' said Madeleine.

'Evidence.'

'Of what sort?'

'That's confidential,' he said, not wishing to upset her with details of what he had found upstairs. 'But I haven't thanked you properly yet, Madeleine,' he continued, touching her arm. 'Because of you, I have some vital new information. I'm deeply grateful.'

'I was only too glad to help.'

'I'm sorry to have placed such a burden on you.'

'That was not how I saw it, Robert.'

'Good. What did you make of Mrs Guttridge?'

'I felt sorry for her,' said Madeleine with a sigh. 'She's in such desperate straits. Yet you would hardly have known it from the way that she was bearing up. When my mother died, I was helpless with grief for weeks and Father was even worse. We walked around in a complete daze. That's not what Mrs Guttridge is doing and her husband didn't die of natural causes, as Mother did. He was murdered only a few days ago.'

'She's a very unusual woman.'

'I've never met anyone like her, Robert. Somehow, she's managing to keep everything bottled up inside her.'

'Mrs Guttridge has been doing that since her husband first took on the job as a public hangman. She convinced herself that she should support his choice of occupation yet it cost her both her identity and her peace of mind. It also meant that she had no real friends.'

'Her life was snatched away from her.'

'Yes, Madeleine,' he noted, sadly. 'In a sense, she was another of his victims. That rope of his effectively destroyed Louise Guttridge by turning her into someone she did not really wish to be.'

'Perhaps that's why she's unable to mourn him properly.'

'It was a strange marriage, that much is apparent.'

'What will happen to her?'

'Who knows? All that I can do is to offer her some protection by making sure that her street is patrolled regularly. The one thing that will be of real benefit for her, of course, is the arrest and conviction of the man who committed this crime.'

'And you say that you found new evidence?'

'Yes, Madeleine.'

'So my visit was not a waste of time.'

'I could not have achieved any progress without you.'

'Does that mean you'll ask your Superintendent to take me on?'

Colbeck grinned. 'Even I would not be brave

enough to do that,' he confessed. 'No, your sterling assistance must go unreported but by no means unappreciated.' He squeezed her hand. 'Thank you again.'

'Call on me any time, Robert. It was exciting.'

'It's one of the reasons that I became a policeman. There's nothing quite as stimulating as taking a giant step forward in an investigation,' he said, smiling, 'and that's what I feel we did this morning.'

Still smarting from the rebuke he had received on his arrival, Victor Leeming spent the whole morning at Scotland Yard trying to finish the work that Colbeck had started and assimilate the mass of material that had been assembled. As well as a list of executions carried out by Guttridge over the past two years, Leeming had also found descriptions of the man's career in back copies of various London newspapers. One even contained an artist's impression of the execution of a woman in Chelmsford who, too weak to stand, had been strapped into a chair before being hanged. Leeming felt his stomach lurch. He moved quickly on to the next case he had listed.

Brisk footsteps could be heard in the corridor outside and he steeled himself for yet another abrasive encounter with Superintendent Tallis. Instead, it was Inspector Colbeck who came in through the door with a large bundle under his arm. Leeming got to his feet with relief.

'I'm so glad to see you, Inspector,' he said.

'It's always pleasing to receive a cordial welcome.'

104

'I've been studying Jacob Guttridge's work and it does not make happy reading.' He shuffled some sheets of paper. 'I know that you made a start on all this but I've more or less finished it off.'

'Well done, Victor,' said Colbeck, dropping the bundle on his desk.

'What have you got there, sir?'

'The contents of a private museum. Most of it, anyway. I had to leave the bottles of brandy that were hidden under the bed. The fact that her husband was a secret drinker is one shock that I can't keep from Mrs Guttridge. The items in here, however,' he said, undoing the knot in the cloak so that it fell open to display its contents, 'would have caused her a lot of unnecessary suffering.'

'Why?'

'Judge for yourself, Victor.'

'What *are* all these things?'

'Trophies.'

'Saints preserve us!' exclaimed Leeming as he saw the lengths of rope that had been used in various executions and tagged accordingly. 'There's everything here but the dead bodies themselves.'

'Wait until you come to the religious tracts and the poems.'

'Poems?'

'Written by Jacob Guttridge.'

While the Sergeant sifted his way through the relics, Colbeck told him about the visit to Hoxton, omitting only the fact that Madeleine Andrews had been with him. He then showed him the threatening note that he had found at the house.

Leeming studied it. 'Who is N, sir?'

'That's what we have to determine.'

'It could be Noonan,' said the other, snapping his fingers. 'I was looking at the case just before you came in. Sean Noonan was hanged for murder in Dublin a year ago.'

'Then he's unlikely to be our man.'

'N stands for Noonan, doesn't it?'

'Yes,' agreed Colbeck, 'but it's unlikely that a surname would be used. In all probability, that note was sent to Mr Guttridge by a family member or by a close friend of the condemned man, and they would surely refer to him by his Christian name. We should be looking for a Neil, Nigel or Norman.'

'None of those spring to mind, sir.'

'Where's that list?'

'Wait!' said Leeming. 'There was a Nairn McCracken from Perth.'

'Too long ago,' decided Colbeck, picking up the paper from the table and studying it. 'I'm convinced that we want a more recent case. According to this, McCracken was executed in 1849. I don't think that someone would wait three years to wreak revenge on his behalf.'

'Maybe they'd already had two attempts. Doctor Keyworth told us that there were scars on the body of the deceased.'

'Put there in separate incidents, that much is clear. According to the post mortem, the stomach wound was several years old, inflicted long before Guttridge went anywhere near Perth.' He tapped

106

the list. 'Now this is much more promising.'

'Who is he, sir?'

'Nathan Hawkshaw. Executed less than a month ago.'

'I remember him. It was in Maidstone.'

'What do we know about the case?'

'Precious little. He murdered someone called Joseph Dykes. That's all I can tell you, Inspector. I could find no details.'

'Then I'll have to go in search of them.'

'To Kent?'

'It's not far by train.' He smiled as Leeming pulled a face. 'Yes, I know that you hate rail travel, Victor, so I won't subject you to the ordeal just yet. I've a more attractive assignment for you.'

'I won't find searching through this lot very attractive,' complained Leeming, gazing down at the items in the cloak. 'What sort of man would want to keep things like this?'

'One with a rather macabre outlook on life – and on death, for that matter. Have no fear. We'll lock all this away for the time being.' He tied the cloak into a knot again. 'What I need you to do for me is to find the answer to something that's puzzled me from the start.'

'And what's that, sir?'

'How did the killer know that Jacob Guttridge would be on that excursion train and in that particular carriage?'

'He must have followed him.'

'Granted,' said Colbeck, 'but how did he find him in the first place? You've seen the lengths that Guttridge went to in order to preserve his anonymity. He changed his name, moved house

107

often and never got too friendly with his neighbours.'

'So?'

'Whoever tracked him down went to enormous trouble.'

'Then bided his time until Guttridge caught that excursion rain.'

'No, Victor. The killer could not possibly have watched that house in Hoxton day and night. It's dangerous enough for those who live there. A stranger would be taking serious risks if he lurked in those streets.'

'What's the explanation then?'

'I'm not sure,' said Colbeck, removing his hat and running a hand through his dark, wavy hair. 'At least, not entirely sure.'

'But you have a theory, I can tell.'

'Perhaps.'

'Come on, sir. I know that look in your eye.'

'The Superintendent calls my theories misbegotten brainstorms.'

'Who cares what he calls them? They usually turn out to be right in the long run. You have a gift for putting yourself into the mind of the criminal and Mr Tallis can't understand that. Neither can I, if truth be told,' he said, cheerfully. 'What's your theory, sir?'

'Most of Jacob Guttridge's time was spent at home, working as a cobbler in his shed. His wife confirms that. Now, what would get him out of the house?'

'An execution.'

'What else?'

'Going to Mass every Sunday. We know that he

108

was devout.'

'In every way,' observed Colbeck with a glance at the bundle on his desk. 'He worshipped at more than one altar. But where else might he have gone, Victor?'

'I don't know.'

'Yes, you do. Think. Where was he killed?'

'On an excursion train.'

'Why was he there?'

'He was on his way to a prizefight.'

'Then *that* may be how he was tracked.'

'Was it, sir?'

'Mr Guttridge was one of the Fancy. He idolised those bareknuckle boxers and couldn't miss an opportunity to see a championship contest.'

'But a fight like that comes around once in a blue moon.'

'A public contest might,' said Colbeck, 'but there are exhibition bouts being staged all the time for real followers of the sport. And I can guess where Mr Guttridge went to watch them.'

'Where?'

'Bethnal Green. His hero was Bill Hignett.'

'The Bargeman? How do you know that, sir?'

'Because there was a signed print of him at the house. If he wanted to see Hignett in action, all that he had to do was to go to the Seven Stars in Bethnal Green and watch him spar. There's a room at the back of the inn where the Bargeman trains and passes on his skills to a lot of younger boxers.'

'And you think that Mr Guttridge went there?'

'Almost certainly. It allowed him to do two

things that were very important to him – enjoy some milling and drink his fill.'

'He could get his beer much closer to home than that.'

'Not in Hoxton,' reasoned Colbeck. 'That was on his doorstep and he was careful to keep his neighbours at arm's length in case he let slip his guilty secret. He'd feel safer in Bethnal Green as part of a crowd that cheered on Bill Hignett.'

'How does the killer fit into your theory?'

'Rather hazily at the moment,' admitted Colbeck, thinking it through. 'Somehow, he discovered that Mr Guttridge had a passion for boxing, followed him to Bethnal Green and established that he would be going to the fight near Twyford on that day. All that he had to do then,' he concluded, taking a handkerchief from his pocket by way of demonstration, 'was to wait at Paddington Station until his victim arrived, stay on his heels and get into the same second-class carriage. When the excursion train stopped at Twyford and the hordes charged off,' he went on, using the handkerchief like a garrotte, 'he choked the life out of his victim.'

Leeming fingered his throat uneasily. 'Put that away, sir.'

'I was just trying to illustrate a point.'

'So what do you wish me to do?'

'Go to the Seven Stars and mix with the regular patrons. Ask if any of them recall a Jake Bransby – don't use his real name because we can be certain that *he* didn't do so. And be discreet, Victor. Someone may have realised that Bransby was really Jacob Guttridge, the hangman.

110

Choose your words carefully.'

'I will.'

'You may even get a chance to meet the Barge-man, if he's recovered from the fight.'

'What about the killer?'

'If he *did* trail Mr Guttridge there,' said Colbeck, tucking his handkerchief into his pocket, 'it should be possible to find out. Only the true disciples of pugilism would stand for ages around that boxing ring in Bethnal Green. A stranger would be noticed immediately. Make your way there, Victor. See if any outsider drifted into the Seven Stars in recent weeks. If at all possible, get a description of him.'

'Right, sir,' said Leeming, pleased with his instructions. 'If nothing else, this will get me out from under the Superintendent's big feet. I'll go immediately. What about you, sir?'

'I'll be on a train to Maidstone,' replied Colbeck, taking a copy of *Bradshaw's Guide* from his desk drawer. 'I want to find out if N really does stand for Nathan Hawkshaw.'

The county town of Kent lay at the heart of what was popularly known as the Garden of England. Rich soil and a temperate climate combined to make it a haven for fruit-growers and the hops were reckoned to be the finest in the kingdom, spreading satisfaction and drunken stupor far and wide among the nation's beer drinkers. A parliamentary and municipal borough, Maidstone was an assize town with a long and varied history, its earlier ecclesiastical dominance reflected in the ancient, but expertly restored, Pilgrims' Chapel,

111

its ruined priory, its noble palace, formerly belonging to the Archbishop of Canterbury, and its imposing churches.

It was situated at a well-chosen point on the River Medway, a wide and sometimes turbulent waterway, the main artery of the town for centuries. From the wharves that lined the river, large quantities of local stone, corn, fruit, sand and other goods were shipped, and over fifty barges traded there regularly, giving employment to hundreds of people. The Medway was crossed by a stone bridge with five arches, and plundered assiduously by the local anglers. Occasional flooding was deemed to be an acceptable price to pay for the convenience of living beside such an important river.

Robert Colbeck reached the town by courtesy of the South Eastern Railway, the journey a continuous pleasure to someone who enjoyed travelling by train as much as he did. Since there was no direct line from London to Maidstone, he was obliged to change at Paddock Wood and eventually came into the station at the end of Hart Street on the western side of the town. It was market day and, though he did not get there until mid-afternoon, hundreds of customers still haggled beside the stalls, booths and carts that lined High Street, Week Street and King Street. Someone rang a hand bell, the last of the livestock complained noisily in their pens and the din was compounded by the incessant clucking of poultry in their baskets and by the competing cries of the vendors.

Even from the railway station, Colbeck could

hear the noise and he was grateful that he did not have to walk directly through the market, where his elegant attire would make him incongruous among the more homespun garments on show. As it was, he attracted a lot of curious glances. Maidstone Prison was a forbidding sight. Erected behind the Sessions House, it had four hundred night cells and was encircled by a high perimeter wall that acted as a stern warning to any would-be malefactors. The man on duty at the gate was so unaccustomed to the appearance of a Detective Inspector from Scotland Yard that he refused to admit Colbeck until word had been sent to the governor.

There was a long delay. Taken aback by news of his unexpected visitor, Henry Ferriday nevertheless agreed to see him, deciding that he would not have come all that way from London unless it were on a matter of some importance. Colbeck was admitted and escorted to the governor's office, a small, untidy, cheerless room that overlooked the exercise yard. Ferriday welcomed him with a warm handshake and an inquisitive frown. He waved the detective to a chair.

'Well,' he said, resuming his own seat behind the desk, 'to what do we owe the pleasure of this visit, Inspector?'

'I'm hoping that you can help me with an investigation.'

'We are always ready to do that.'

'It concerns the murder of Jacob Guttridge.'

'Yes,' said Ferriday, shaking his head, 'we saw mention of that in the newspapers. He was here only a matter of weeks ago, you know.'

113

'Was it the first time he'd carried out an execution at Maidstone?'

'No, no, Inspector. It would have been his third visit.'

Henry Ferriday was a lean man of middle years with hollow cheeks and large, mobile eyes. He had compensated for a dramatic loss of hair by trying to grow a beard but the experiment had been only a limited success. In his black frock coat, and with his sharp features, he looked like a giant crow. While he talked, he kept peering nervously over his shoulder as if fearing that someone would smash a way through the barred window behind him. From the way that the governor talked, Colbeck judged him to be a kind, humane man who had come into the prison service out of a sense of vocation and who still retained vestiges of an idealism that had largely melted away in the white hot furnace of daily experience.

'In the past,' he explained, 'we were happy with Mr Guttridge's services – insofar as any happiness can attend an execution, that is. Personally, I find them rather disgusting events and I hate being forced to witness them. My digestion is never the same for days afterwards.'

'Tell me about the most recent execution, if you will.'

'Nathan Hawkshaw?'

'Yes, Governor. Was he a local man?'

'He was a butcher in Ashford, twenty miles or so from here. And butchery was involved in his crime, alas,' he said, tossing another glance over his shoulder. 'Hawkshaw was hanged for the

114

murder of Joseph Dykes whom he hacked to death with a meat cleaver. It was a brutal assault. And the worst of it was that Hawkshaw refused so show the slightest remorse. He said that he was glad Dykes was dead though he insisted that he was innocent of the crime.'

'Was there any doubt about his guilt?'

'Not as far as the court was concerned, Inspector, and we are guided by the sentences that they hand down. Hawkshaw's was a capital offence so we sent for Mr Guttridge.'

'Do you happen to know the details of the case?' asked Colbeck. 'I'd be grateful for anything that you can tell me. This was the last execution carried out by Mr Guttridge and it may have some bearing on his death.'

'I fail to see how.'

'Humour me, if you please. I came in search of facts.'

'Then the person you should be talking to,' said Ferriday, getting up to cross to the door, 'is our chaplain, the Reverend Jones. He struggled hard with Nathan Hawkshaw but to no avail.' He opened the door. 'Narcissus will furnish you with all the details you need.'

'Narcissus?'

'That's his name, Inspector. Narcissus Jones.' He spoke briefly to someone in the corridor outside then closed the door. 'Our chaplain is Welsh. He's a man of strong opinions.'

'Not always the case with a man of the cloth.'

'Prison plays havoc with a man's spiritual values. Even the most pious Christian will question his faith when he has worked in this God-forsaken hell-hole for any length of time. Yet it has not affected the chaplain in that way,' said Ferriday, brushing an imaginary speck of dust from his lapel so that he had an excuse to look behind him. 'If anything, life within these walls has only reinforced his commitment.'

'That's comforting to hear.'

'Narcissus Jones is a species of saint.'

Colbeck was not at all sure that he wanted to discuss a murder investigation with a Welsh saint but he had no alternative. In any case, after the fulsome praise that the governor had heaped on the man, the detective was interested to meet him. Ferriday seemed to be slightly in awe of the chaplain, almost to the point of deference. Colbeck fished.

'You say that Nathan Hawkshaw protested his innocence?'

'Most prisoners do that, Inspector,' said the other, wearily. 'The worse their crimes, in my experience, the louder they deny their guilt. Hawkshaw was unusual in one respect, though, I have to concede that.'

'Oh?'

'A campaign was launched on his behalf.'

'What sort of campaign?' asked Colbeck. 'A plea for his release?'

'A full-throated demand for it,' replied Ferriday. 'Quite a sizeable number of people were involved. They had leaflets printed, claiming that Hawkshaw was innocent and they even brought banners and placards to the execution. It made the ordeal even more horrible.' There was a tap on the door. 'Ah, that will be the chaplain.' He

116

raised his voice. 'Come in!'

The door opened and the Reverend Narcissus Jones stepped into the room. He was even taller than Colbeck, a solid man in his forties with broad shoulders and huge hands. Dark hair of impressive luxuriance fell back from the high forehead and almost touched the edge of his clerical collar. His features were rugged, his nose bulbous, his eyes small and darting. Colbeck's first impression was that he bore less resemblance to a species of saint than to a species of farm animal. Ferriday was still on his feet. Introduced to the newcomer, Colbeck got up to exchange a handshake with him and to feel the power in his grip. Reverend Narcissus Jones liked to display his strength.

When all three of them were seated again, the governor explained the purpose of Colbeck's visit. The piggy eyes of the chaplain flashed.

'Oh, I remember Nathan Hawkshaw,' he said in a lilting voice that was deeper and more melodious than anything Colbeck had ever heard coming from a human mouth before. 'Distressing case. Very distressing. One of my rare failures as a chaplain. Is that not so, Governor?'

'You did your best.'

'I wrestled with him for days on end but I could find no way to awaken his conscience. Hawkshaw was adamant. Kept insisting that he was not responsible for the killing, thereby adding the crime of deceit to the charge of murder.'

'The chaplain even had to overpower the man,' recalled Ferriday.

'Yes,' said Jones, piqued by the memory. 'The

prisoner was so incensed with anger that he dared to strike at me and – what was far worse in my eyes – he had the audacity to take the Lord's name in vain as he did so. I felled him with a punch – God help me!'

'After that, we had to keep him under restraint.'

'From what the governor has been telling me,' said Colbeck to the muscular priest, 'this Nathan Hawkshaw was not the only person convinced of his innocence. He had a group of supporters, I believe.'

'A disorderly rabble from Ashford,' said Jones with a loud sniff. 'Thirty or more in number. They even tried to rescue Hawkshaw from the prison but the attempt was easily foiled. Instead, they chose to disrupt the execution.'

'Fortunately,' added Ferriday, 'we had advance warning that there might be trouble. Extra constables were on duty to keep the crowd under control and they were certainly needed.'

'That was largely Mr Guttridge's fault. He stirred them up to the very edge of mutiny. I've never seen such incompetence on a scaffold.'

'What happened?' asked Colbeck.

'The hangman made a few mistakes,' said Ferriday, mildly.

'A few?' boomed Jones. 'Let us be brutally frank, Governor. The fellow made nothing *but* mistakes. To begin with, he tried to take over my job and offer the prisoner spiritual sustenance. That was unforgivable.' He checked himself and spoke with more control. 'I know that one should not speak ill of the dead – especially if they die by violence – but I find it hard to think of Mr

118

Guttridge without feeling a surge of anger. Giving the prisoner a religious tract, indeed! Reading a ridiculous poem at him! And that was not the sum of his imperfections. As soon as he arrived here, we could smell the brandy on his breath.'

'Most executioners need a drink to steady their hand,' remarked Colbeck, tolerantly. 'Mr Cathcart is noted for his fondness for the bottle.'

'I had a drink myself beforehand,' confessed Ferriday.

'That may be, Governor,' said Jones, tossing his hair back, 'but you did not let it interfere with the discharge of your duties. That was not the case with Mr Guttridge. He tripped on the steps as he went up onto the platform.'

'Nervousness. The baying of that huge crowd upset him.'

'It did not upset me and many of them were abusing me by name.'

'You were an example to us all, Narcissus.'

'With the exception of the hangman.'

'What exactly did he do wrong?' inquired Colbeck.

'Everything, Inspector,' the Welshman told him. 'I thought that Hawkshaw was a benighted heathen but, to his credit, at the very last, he showed a glimmering of Christian feeling. When he saw there was no escape from his fate, he finally began to pray. And what does that fool of an executioner do, Inspector?'

'Tell me.'

'He pulled the bolt before the prayers were over.'

'It was most regrettable,' commented Ferriday.

119

'Mr Guttridge lost his nerve,' accused Jones, 'and fled from the scene without even checking that he had done his job properly.'

'I take it that he hadn't,' said Colbeck.

'No, Inspector. When the trap sprang open, Hawkshaw somehow contrived to get his heels on the edge so that he did not fall through it. You can imagine how that inflamed the crowd. The mood was riotous.'

'What did you do?'

'The only thing that we could do,' said Ferriday, flicking a glance behind him to check for eavesdroppers. 'I had Mr Guttridge brought out again and ordered him to dispatch the prisoner quickly. But, when he tried to push Hawkshaw's feet away from the trap, the man kicked out violently at him and – the sight will stay for me forever – his supporters urged him on with manic cries as they fought to get at us. Truly, I feared for my own life.'

'In the end,' said Jones, taking up the story, 'Mr Guttridge beat his legs away and he dropped through the trap, but the fall did not break his neck. He was jerking wildly around in the air. Everyone could see the rope twisting and turning. That really made passions rage.'

'I sent Guttridge below to pull on his legs,' said Ferriday, swallowing hard, 'but he could not even do that properly. One of the warders had to assist him. Nathan Hawkshaw was left hanging there, in agony, for well over five minutes. It was an abomination.'

'And Mr Guttridge was to blame?' said Colbeck.

'Regrettably, he was.'

'If all this took place in front of his loved ones, it must have fired some of them up to seek revenge against him.'

'Death threats were shouted from all sides.'

'I deplore those threats,' said Jones, 'but I sympathize with the impulse to make them. If I'm honest – and honesty is the essence of my character – *I* could have called for Mr Guttridge's head at that point in time. He was a disgrace to his calling. *Ieusi Mawr!*' he exclaimed with an angry fist in the air. 'Had there been another rope on the scaffold, I'd gladly have hanged that drunken buffoon alongside the prisoner, then swung on his legs to break that worthless neck of his.'

Henry Ferriday turned to Colbeck with a weak smile.

'I did warn you that the chaplain had strong opinions,' he said.

Chapter Six

Before he set out, Victor Leeming took the precaution of changing into a shabby old suit that he kept at the office for just such occasions. Although it was invariably crumpled, the clothing he wore to Scotland Yard every day was too close to that of a gentleman to allow him an easy passage through Bethnal Green, the most miserable and poverty-stricken district in the whole of the city. His aim was to be as non-descript as possible so that he could merge with his surroundings. For that reason, he traded his hat for a battered cap and his shoes for a pair of ancient boots. When he left the building, he looked more like a disreputable costermonger than a detective. Some of the cabs that he tried to hail refused to stop for him, fearing that he would be unable to pay his fare.

It was over a year since he had been in Bethnal Green but he remembered its notorious reek all too well. No sooner did he reach the area than it assaulted his nostrils once more. In a space enclosed between a hoarding on either side of the Eastern Counties Railway was a vast ditch that had been turned into an open sewer, filled with ever-increasing quantities of excrement, dead cats and dogs, rancid food and disgusting refuse of every imaginable kind. Passing within thirty yards of this stagnant lake, Leeming had to put a hand across his nose to block out the stench. Denizens of Bethnal Green had long been habituated to the stink of decomposition.

The Seven Stars lay on the edge of an infamous area known as the Nichol. Named after Nichol Street, one of its main thoroughfares, it was a stronghold for villains of every kind, fifteen acres of sin, crime and sheer deprivation that operated by rules entirely of its own making. Leeming was a brave man, raised in one of the roughest parts of London, but even he would not have tried to walk alone through the Nichol after dusk. Its filthy streets, shadowed lanes and dark passages were a breeding ground for thieves, pickpockets and prostitutes. Its squalid tenements, slum cottages and ramshackle pubs teemed with beggars, orphans, destitute families, ruthless criminals and fugitives from the law. Bethnal Green was a haven for the most desperate characters in the underworld.

Glad that he was visiting the place in broad daylight, Leeming noticed how many animals were roaming the streets. Snarling cats fought over territory with furious commitment while skinny dogs scavenged among the rubbish. The undernourished horses and donkeys that pulled passing carts looked as if they could barely stand. Loud squawks and even louder yells of encouragement disclosed that a cock-fight was being held nearby. Unwashed children played desultory games or lounged in gangs on corners. Cries of pain came from behind closed doors as violent men asserted their dominance over wives and mistresses.

Wherever he went, Leeming knew, dozens of pairs of eyes were upon him. He had never endured such hostile surveillance before. It was like a weight pressing down on him. When he entered the Seven Stars, however, the burden was immediately lifted. He collected a few casual looks from the ragged patrons scattered around the bar but they were too busy enjoying their drinks or their gossip to bother overmuch about the newcomer. Leeming sauntered across to the counter and ordered some beer. Filled with chairs and tables, the room was large, low and in a state of obvious neglect but its atmosphere was welcoming enough. The landlord served his customer with a toothless grin.

'There you are, sir,' he said as he put a foaming

tankard on the counter. 'Best beer in Bethnal Green.'

'So I heard.' Leeming paid for the drink then sipped it, managing a smile even though it was far too bitter for his taste. 'And he was right. You serve a good brew.'

'Ben, sir. Everyone calls me Ben. I own the place.'

'You run a good house, Ben.'

'Thank you.'

'My first visit won't be my last.'

The landlord appraised him. 'Where are you from, sir?'

'Clerkenwell.'

'Ah, I see.' A burst of cheering and applause came from the back of the establishment and Leeming turned his head questioningly. 'The lads are staging a bout or two. Fond of milling, sir?'

'That's why I came.'

'Then you're in the right place.'

Ben Millgate beamed proudly. He was a short, stubby man in his fifties with a bald pate that was tattooed with scars, and a craggy face. No stranger to a brawl himself, he had other scars on his bare forearms and both ears had been thickened by repeated punishment.

'Did you see the fight at Twyford?' asked Millgate.

'No – worse luck! I'd have given a week's wages to be there.'

'The Bargeman was robbed and so were we.'

'That's what I was told,' said Leeming, nodding seriously. 'They reckon that Mad Isaac fought dirty.'

124

'That lousy Jew was full of tricks,' said Millgate, wiping his nose with the back of his hand. 'So were his friends. I was there and saw it with my own eyes. When the Bargemen staggered back against the ropes, one of Mad Isaac's men punched him in the kidneys. Another time, he was hit with a cudgel. And, three times in a row, that sneaky Jew kicked him when he was on the ground.'

'He should have been disqualified.'

'The referee and the umpires had been bribed.'

'They must've been,' agreed Leeming. 'Rotten, I call it. I had money on the Bargeman to win. He's a true champion.'

'And fought like one as well. Gave no quarter.'

'So I gather. My friend was there to support him. More or less worships the Bargeman. In fact, it was Jake who told me about your beer. Comes in here a lot to watch the young boxers learning their craft.'

'Jake, you say?'

'Jake Bransby.'

'Oh, yes,' said Millgate, cheerily, 'I know him.'

'He's a bit on the quiet side.'

'That's him, sir, and no question. A shy fellow but he understands milling. He comes in regular, does Jake. Friend of yours, is he?'

'A good friend.'

'When I drew up a list to see how many of us would be going to the fight, Jake was one of the first to call out his name.'

'You went there as a group?'

'The Seven Stars sent over a hundred people to Twyford,' bragged Millgate. 'Well, you'd expect it. The Bargeman trains here.'

'How is he now, Ben? He must've taken a real beating.'

'Took one and gave one to Mad Isaac. But he's as strong as an ox. Back on his feet within a day or two. As a matter of fact,' he went on, head turning towards the back room as more applause rang out, 'he's watching the novices showing off what they've learned.'

'Then I'll take the opportunity to shake his hand,' said Leeming with genuine interest. 'I've followed his career from the start. I knew he had the makings of a champion when I saw him fight Amos Greer in a field near Newport Pagnall.'

'I was there as well. The Bargeman fair killed him.'

'He did at that. Greer was out cold.' He glanced around the bar. 'So all your regular customers went on that excursion train, did they?'

'Every last one of them.'

'What about newcomers?'

'Newcomers?'

'Strangers. People who drifted in for the first time.'

'We don't get many of those at the Seven Stars.'

'In that case, they would have stuck out.'

Millgate smirked. 'Like a pig in a pair of silk drawers.'

'Can you recall anyone who popped in here recently?' asked Leeming, pretending only casual interest. 'When you were drawing up that list for the excursion train, I mean?'

Ben Millgate's face went blank and he scratched the scars on the top of his head. A memory eventually seemed to come to the surface.

'Now that you mention it, sir,' he said, 'there *was* someone and he was certainly no Bethnal Green man. I could tell that just to look at the bugger. Odd thing is, he was asking about your friend, Jake Bransby.'

'Really? Could you describe this man?'

'Annie was the one who spoke to him, sir – she's my wife. You'd best ask her about it. Annie'll be in the back room with the others,' said Millgate, moving away. 'I'll take you through so that you can meet her. Bring your drink and you'll see the Bargeman in there as well.'

'Wonderful!' said Leeming.

Millgate lifted a hinged flap in the counter and opened the little door to step through into the bar. He led the visitor to the room at the rear then stepped back so that Leeming could enter it first. His arrival coincided with the loudest cheers yet as one of the young boxers knocked his opponent to the floor with a well-timed uppercut. The Sergeant was instantly enthralled. Crowded around the ring were dozens of people, veteran fighters, local men who followed the sport, eager youths hoping to take it up and a few women in gaudy dresses. Leeming also noticed a couple of well-dressed gentlemen, standing near the edge of the ring, members of the Fancy in search of new talent to sponsor, potential champions on whom they could wager extravagant amounts.

The fallen boxer got to his feet and was quickly revived by his bottleman. Scolded, advised and ordered to fight harder, he came out for the next round with greater determination. Both men

127

pounded away at each other. Ordinarily, Leeming would have watched with fascination had his attention not been diverted to the far corner where a legendary prizefighter was standing. It was the first time he had seen his hero so close and he marvelled at the size and bearing of the man. In the course of their fight, Isaac Rosen had left his signature all over Bill Hignett's face. One eye was still closed, both cheeks were badly puffed and there were ugly gashes above his eyebrows. The Bargeman's hands were heavily bandaged and some more bandaging could be seen under the brim of his hat but the various wounds only increased the man's stature in Leeming's eyes. He felt an almost childlike thrill.

Millgate, meanwhile, had been talking to his wife and to a couple of men standing beside her. They looked across at Leeming. Annie Millgate, a stringy woman with a vivacity that took years off her, tripped over to the visitor and took him companionably by the arm.

'I can tell you about that man, sir,' she said, pulling him away, 'but not in here. It's like Bedlam when a fight starts. Come into the yard where we can talk proper.'

'Thank you.'

'My husband says that you know Jake Bransby.'

'Very well,' replied Leeming, still admiring the Bargeman. 'He's told me about the Seven Stars so many times.'

'This way, sir.'

Annie Millgate opened a door and ushered him through it. Leeming found himself in a yard that was filled with empty crates and barrels. A mangy dog yelped. The detective turned to smile at the landlord's wife.

'You must be Annie,' he said.

But there was no time for proper introductions. Before he knew what was happening, Leeming was grabbed from behind by strong hands and spun round. Held by one man in a grip of iron, he was hit hard by someone who had been taught how and where to punch. The tankard fell from Leeming's fingers, hitting the ground and spilling its contents over his boots. His nose was soon gushing with blood and his body felt as if it were being trampled by a herd of stampeding horses. A fearsome blow to the chin sent him to the ground where he was kicked hard. The mangy dog sniffed him then licked his face.

Ben Millgate came out to get in a gratuitous kick of his own.

'Jake Bransby?' he said with a sneer. 'Think we can't read, do you? It was in all the newspapers. That two-faced bastard was a public hangman and he got what he deserved on that train.'

'What shall we do with him, Ben?' asked his wife.

'Like us to finish 'im off?' volunteered one of the men.

'We'd enjoy that,' said the other, baring his jagged teeth.

'No,' decreed Millgate, spitting on the ground. 'Annie will search him for money first then you can toss this nosey devil into a cesspit so that he'll stink of Bethnal Green for weeks to come. That'll teach him to come lying to me about Jake Bransby!'

'My father taught me how to make a Dog's Nose,' he said, stirring the concoction with a spoon. 'You got to get the proportions right, you see, Inspector. Warm porter, gin, sugar and nutmeg. Delicious!'

'I'm sure,' said Colbeck.

'Will you join me?'

'No, thank you, Sergeant. It's too strong for me.'

'My favourite tipple at the end of the day.'

The two men were in the snug little cottage that belonged to Sergeant Obadiah Lugg, a seasoned member of Maidstone's police force. Having learned that it was Lugg who had arrested Nathan Hawkshaw on a charge of murder, Colbeck tracked him down in his home on the edge of the town. A portly individual in his forties with a big, round, rubicund face, Lugg had an amiable manner and a habit of chuckling at the end of each sentence. He settled into the chair opposite his visitor and sipped his drink with patent relish.

'Perfect!' he cried.

'You deserve it, Sergeant. You do a valuable job in the town.'

'There's only fifteen of us in all, you know – two sergeants and a body of twelve men with Tom Fawcett as our inspector. Fifteen of us to police a town with over 20,000 people in it.'

'It must be hard work,' said Colbeck.

'Hard but rewarding, Inspector. When the force was founded in 1836, I joined it right away. I was a railway policeman before that. We made a difference from the start. The streets of Maidstone used to swarm with bad characters and loose women but not any more,' he said with a chuckle. 'Everyone will tell you how we cleaned the place up. Of course, Tom must take most of the credit.'

'Tom? Is that the Tom Fawcett you mentioned?'

'That's him. A drum-major in the army before he took over here and he made us all stand to attention.' Colbeck gave a half-smile as he thought of Superintendent Tallis. 'Trouble is that Tom is near seventy so he can't go on forever. Do you know what he told me?'

'I'd love to hear it, Sergeant,' said Colbeck, steering him away from his reminiscences, 'but I have a train to catch soon. What I'd really like you to tell me about is the arrest of Nathan Hawkshaw.'

'He resisted. I had to use my truncheon.'

'What were the circumstances of the crime?'

'There'd been bad blood between him and Joe Dykes for some time,' recalled Lugg, taking another sip of his drink. 'Hawkshaw had been heard threatening to kill him. Then this fair was held at Lenham and that's when it happened. The two of them had this quarrel. Next thing you know, Dykes is found dead behind some bushes. And I do mean dead,' he added with a chuckle. 'The body had been hacked to pieces like it was a side of beef.'

'Were there any witnesses?'

'Several people saw the argument between them.'

'Were any blows exchanged?'

'No, Inspector, nothing beyond a few prods and pushes. Everyone reckons that Dykes just laughed and went into the pub. An hour later, he'd been slaughtered.'

'So there were no witnesses to the actual killing?'

'None, sir. But it had to be Nathan Hawkshaw.'

'Why?'

'Because he hated Dykes so much. Think of them threats he'd made. And,' declared Lugg, as if producing incontrovertible proof, 'the murder weapon was one of Hawkshaw's meat cleavers. He admitted it.'

'Yet he protested his innocence.'

'I've never met a villain who didn't do that.'

'Nor me,' said Colbeck with a pained smile. 'You can catch them red-handed and they always have a plausible explanation. Tell me about Hawkshaw. Had he been in trouble with the police before?'

'They've only two constables in Ashford so it's hardly a police force. I interviewed both men and they spoke well of Nathan Hawkshaw. Said he was a good butcher and a decent family man. He kept himself out of mischief.'

'What about Dykes?'

'Ah,' replied Lugg, 'he was much more of a problem. Drunk and disorderly, assaulting a constable, petty theft – Joe Dykes had seen the inside of prison more than once. Nasty piece of work, he was. Even the chaplain found him a handful when he was put in Maidstone prison.' He grinned broadly. 'What did you think of Narcissus?'

Colbeck was tactful. 'The Reverend Jones

seemed to be dedicated to his work,' he said, quietly. 'It must be a thankless task.'

'I feel sorry sometimes for those shut away in there. Nobody quite like a Welshman for loving the sound of his own voice, is there? Narcissus can talk the hind leg off a donkey. Imagine being locked in a cell with him preaching at you through the bars.' He let out a cackle and slapped his thigh. 'No wonder Hawkshaw tried to hit the chaplain.'

'You heard about that incident?'

'Narcissus Jones told everyone about it, Inspector. That's the kind of man he is – unlike the Governor. Henry Ferriday would never tell tales about what happens behind those high walls. He's more secretive.'

'If Hawkshaw struck out at the chaplain,' noted Colbeck, 'he must be inclined to violence. Yet you say he'd no record of unruly behaviour.'

'None at all, Inspector.'

'What caused the animosity between him and Dykes?'

'All sorts of things.'

'Such as?'

'Emily, for start.'

'Emily?'

'Nathan Hawkshaw's daughter. Dykes tried to rape her.'

When he first came to his senses, Victor Leeming was lying in a cesspit surrounded by jeering children. There was blood down the front of his jacket and every part of his body was aching violently. Through his swollen lips, he could not

133

even muster the strength to shout at those who were enjoying his misfortune. In trying to move, he set off some fresh spasms of pain down his arms and legs. His body seemed to be on fire. It was the foul smell and the humiliation that finally got him out of there. Braving the agony, he hauled himself upright, relieved to find that he could actually stand on his own feet. While he gathered his wits, the children subjected him to another barrage of abuse. Leeming had to swing a bruised arm to get rid of them.

A frail old woman took pity on him and explained that there was a pump in a nearby street. Dragging himself there, he doused himself with water in order to bring himself fully awake and to get rid of the worst of the malodorous scum in which he was coated. When he slunk away from the pump, Leeming was sodden. Since no cab would dare to stop for him, he had to trudge all the way back to Whitehall in squelching boots, afraid that he might be accosted in the street by a uniformed constable on suspicion of vagrancy. Because of the smell, everyone he passed gave him a wide berth but he eventually got back to Scotland Yard.

Brushing past a couple of amused colleagues, he dived into the washroom, stripped to his underclothing and washed himself again from head to foot. He could not bear to look in a mirror. When he saw the bruises on his body, his first thought was how his wife would react to the hideous blotching. His sole consolation was that nothing appeared to be broken although his pride was in dire need of repair. The discarded suit was

134

still giving off an appalling stink so he bundled it up, gathered the other items of clothing and peeped out of the door. Seeing that the coast was clear, he tried to make a dash for his office but his weary legs would only move at a slow amble. Before the injured detective could reach safety, a bristling Edward Tallis suddenly turned into the corridor and held his nose in horror.

'Damnation!' he exploded. 'Is that *you*, Leeming?'

'Yes, Superintendent.'

'What on earth is that repulsive stench?'

Leeming sniffed the air. 'I can't smell anything, sir.'

'Well, everyone within a mile can smell *you*. What have you been doing, man – crawling through the sewers?' He saw the bruises on the Sergeant. 'And how did you get those marks on your body?'

'I was assaulted,' said Leeming.

'By whom?'

'Two men in Bethnal Green. They knocked me unconscious.'

'Dear me!' said Tallis, mellowing instantly. 'You poor fellow.'

Showing a compassion that took Leeming by surprise, he moved forward to hold him by the arm and help him into the office that the Sergeant shared with Inspector Colbeck. The Superintendent lowered the stricken detective into a chair then took the suit from him so that he could dump it in the wastepaper basket. After opening the window to let in fresh air, he returned to take a closer look at Leeming.

135

'No serious injuries?' he inquired.

'I don't think so, sir.'

'Let me send for a doctor.'

'No, no,' said Leeming, embarrassed to be sitting there in his underclothing. 'I'll be fine, sir. I was lucky. All I have are aches and pains. They'll go away in time. I just need to put on some clean things.'

'These, meanwhile, can go out,' decided Tallis, grabbing the wastepaper basket and tipping its contents unceremoniously through the open window. 'I'm sorry but I found that stink so offensive.' He replaced the basket beside the desk. 'Why don't I give you a few minutes to get dressed and spruce yourself up?'

'Thank you, Superintendent.'

'Comb your hair before you come to my office.'

'I will, sir. I didn't mean to turn up in this state.'

'Was it an unprovoked assault?'

'Yes and no,' said Leeming, ruefully. 'I think I upset someone when I asked a wrong question.'

'Well, I shall want to ask a few right ones in due course,' growled Tallis, resuming his normal role as the established martinet of the Detective Department. 'The first thing I'll demand to know is what the blazes you were *doing* in Bethnal Green?'

'Making inquiries, sir.'

'About what? No, no,' he said, quickly, stopping him with a raised palm before he could speak, 'I can wait. Make yourself presentable first. And dab some cold water on those lips of yours.'

'Yes, Superintendent.'

'I'll expect you in ten minutes. Bring the Inspector with you. I've no doubt that he'll be as interested as I am to hear how you got yourself in that condition.'

'Inspector Colbeck is not here at the moment.'

'Then where the devil is he?'

'In Maidstone.'

'Maidstone!' echoed the other. 'He's supposed to be solving a crime that took place in an excursion train at Twyford. Whatever has taken him to Maidstone?' He shuddered visibly. 'You don't need to tell me that. Inspector Colbeck has developed another theory, hasn't he?'

'Based on sound reasoning, sir.'

'And what about your visit to Bethnal Green?' asked Tallis with undisguised sarcasm. 'Was that based on sound reasoning as well?'

'Yes, sir.'

'You and I have something in common, Sergeant.'

'Do we, Superintendent?'

'Yes, we do. We're both martyrs to the Inspector's predilection for wild and often lunatic theories. So,' he said, pulling out his cigar case from an inside pocket, 'he decided to go to Maidstone, did he? I suppose that I should be grateful it was not the Isle of Wight.'

The return journey gave Robert Colbeck valuable thinking time. As the train rattled along, he reflected on what he had learned from his visit to Kent. Henry Ferriday and the Reverend Narcissus Jones had explained with dramatic clarity how the hangman's performance on the scaffold had embedded a fierce hatred in the family and friends of the condemned man. On his two previous visits to the town, Guttridge must have acquitted himself fairly well in order to be invited back a third time. It was to prove his downfall. Colbeck had no doubt whatsoever that the murder in the excursion train had been committed by someone who was in the crowd outside Maidstone prison on the fateful day.

Obadiah Lugg had also been a useful source of information. He was not only keen to describe how he had arrested Nathan Hawkshaw and taken him into custody, he was able to show his visitor copies of the local newspapers that contained details of the case and lurid accounts of the execution. Like the hangman, Lugg was a man who hoarded souvenirs of his work but, in the case of the chuckling Sergeant, they were far less disturbing. Along with the other members of the Maidstone police force, and supported by dozens of special constables, Lugg had been on duty during the execution of Hawkshaw and gave his own testimony to the ineptitude of the hangman and the effect that it had on an already restive crowd.

What interested Colbeck were the contradictory assessments of Hawkshaw's character and he struggled to reconcile them. As a butcher, the man had been liked and respected, leading an apparently blameless existence and causing no problems for the two constables representing law and order in Ashford. During his arrest, however, he had to be overpowered by Obadiah Lugg and the two men whom the Sergeant had wisely taken with him in support. At the prison, too, Hawkshaw had resorted to violence at one point though – having met Narcissus Jones – Colbeck could well understand how the chaplain's robust Christianity might prove irksome. Yet the same man who had struck out in frustration at an ordained priest had elected to pray on the scaffold before he was hanged. Was he an innocent man, searching for divine intervention in his hour of need, or had he finally admitted guilt before God and begged forgiveness for his crime?

It was clear that those who knew Hawkshaw best had a genuine belief in his innocence, an important factor in Colbeck's judgement of the man. Yet the evidence against him had been strong enough to support a death sentence and, according to all the reports of the trial that the detective had read in Lugg's collection of newspapers, Hawkshaw had been unable to account for his whereabouts at the time of the murder. It was a point that the prosecution team had exploited to the full and it had cost the prisoner his life.

Robert Colbeck was a former barrister, a man who had abandoned the histrionics of the courtroom to grapple with what he considered to be the more important tasks of preventing crime wherever possible and hunting down those who committed it. He could see from the newspaper accounts that Hawkshaw had not been well-defended by his barrister and that all the publicity had gone to the flamboyant man who led the prosecution. Wanting to know much more about the conduct of the trial, Colbeck made a note of his name and resolved to contact him.

Tonbridge flew past the window of his first class carriage but the Railway Detective was too lost in thought to notice it. He spared only a glance as they steamed through Redhill, his mind still engrossed by the murder of Joseph Dykes at Lenham and its relationship to a calculated killing on an excursion train. One thing was undeniable. Nathan Hawkshaw had motive, means and opportunity to kill a man he loathed. Since his daughter had been the victim of a sexual assault by Dykes, it was only natural that the butcher would confront him. Whether that confrontation led to a murderous attack, however, was an open question.

When he reached London, Colbeck had still not decided whether an innocent or a guilty man had gone to the gallows in Maidstone. The prison governor had insisted that the case was firmly closed now that Hawkshaw had been executed. The Inspector disagreed. It was time to resurrect the hanged man. One way or another – however long it might take – Colbeck was determined to find out the truth.

'How are you getting on, Maddy?' asked Caleb Andrews, standing behind her to look at the painting. 'Oh, yes,' he said, patting her on the back in appreciation, 'that's good, that's very good.'

'I'll have to stop soon. It's getting dark.'

'Sit beside the oil lamp.'

'I prefer natural light. I can see the colours properly in that.'

140

'You have a real gift, you know.'

'That's what Robert said.'

Madeleine stood back to admire her work, glad of her father's approval because he would not judge her work on artistic merit. As an engine driver, his concern was with accuracy and he could find no fault with her picture of a famous locomotive. After adding a touch more blue to the sky against which the *Lord of the Isles* was framed, she dipped her brush in a cup of water to clean it.

'You'll be painting in oils next,' said Andrews.

'No,' she replied. 'I prefer watercolours. Oils are for real artists.'

'You *are* a real artist, Maddy. I think so and I know that Inspector Colbeck does as well. He's an educated man. He knows about these things. I'm proud of you.'

'Thank you, Father.'

'That's the *Lord of the Isles* and no mistake,' he went on, slipping an arm around her shoulders. 'You've painted everything but the noise and the smell of the smoke. Well done!'

'It's not finished yet,' she said, moving away to take her paints and brush into the kitchen. She came back into the living room. 'I just hope that Robert likes it.'

'He'll love it, Maddy – or I'll know the reason why!'

Andrews laughed then watched her take the painting off the easel before standing both against the wall. He had always got on well with his daughter and enjoyed her affectionate bullying, but he knew that a time would come when she

141

would inevitably move out.

'Has the Inspector said anything to you?' he wondered, idly.

'About what?'

'Well...' He gave a meaningful shrug.

'About *what?*' she repeated, looking him in the eye.

'Something that a handsome man and a pretty young woman usually get round to talking about.'

'Father!'

'Well – has he?'

'Robert and I are just friends.'

'That's all that your mother and me were until she let me kiss her under the mistletoe one Christmas,' he remembered with a fond smile. 'The trouble was that her parents came in and caught us. Her father gave me such a talking to that my ears burned for a week. People were very strict in those days and I believe it was a good thing.' He shot her a quizzical glance. 'Do you think I'm strict enough with you, Maddy?'

'*You're* the person who needs a firmer hand,' she said, giving him a peck on the cheek, 'not me. And I've no complaints about the way you brought me up. How many other daughters have been allowed to sneak on to the footplate of a locomotive as I once was?'

'I could've lost my job over that.'

'You took the risk because you knew how much it meant to me.'

'And to me, Maddy. It was something we could *share.*' He sat down on the sofa. 'But you didn't answer my question. Have you and the Inspector got any kind of understanding?'

'Yes,' she replied with a touch of exasperation, 'we understand that we like each other as friends and that's that. Robert is too involved with his work to spare much time for me and I'm too busy running this house and looking after you.'

'At the moment.'

'Please!'

'Things could change.'

'Father, will you stop going on about it?'

'Well, I'm bound to wonder. He'd make a fine catch, Maddy.'

'Listen to you!' she cried. 'When I first met Robert, you kept telling me not to waste my time on someone who was out of my reach. He was above me, that's what you said. Too good for a girl from Camden.'

'That was before I got to know him proper. He may look fine and dandy but his father was only a cabinetmaker, a man who worked with his hands. I can respect that.'

'Try respecting me for a change.'

'I always do.'

'No, you don't, Father,' she said, vehemently. 'Left to you, I'd have been married off to Gideon Little, a fireman on the railway, somebody who suited you, regardless of what I felt about him. Now you're trying to push me at another man you like. Don't you think that I have the right to choose my own husband?'

'Calm down, calm down,' he said, getting to his feet.

'Then stop badgering me like this.'

'I was curious, that's all.'

'Robert and I are good friends. Nothing more.'

'It always starts out that way.'

'Nothing more,' she insisted. 'You must believe that.'

'Oh, I do, Maddy, but I can't ignore the signs.'

'What signs?'

'Him taking you out in that cab, for a start.'

'It was only for a ride,' she said, careful to say nothing about the visit to Hoxton. 'What was wrong with that?'

'Only that it's strange that a detective in the middle of a murder investigation can find time to take anyone for a ride in a Hansom cab. Some of the neighbours saw him pick you up from here. They told me how attentive he was.'

'Robert is a gentleman. He's always attentive.'

'Then there's the other signs,' he pointed out, marshalling his case. 'The ones you can't hide, no matter how much you try.'

'What are you talking about?'

'The way your voice changes when you mention him. The way your face lights up when he calls here. And look at that painting you've been working on,' he added, indicating it. 'When someone spends that amount of time and effort on a present for a man, he begins to look like more than a friend.'

'Robert loves trains, that's all.'

'There – you have a bond between you.'

'Father–'

'I've got eyes, Maddy. I can see.'

'Well, will you please stop *looking!*' she shouted.

Caught on a raw spot, Madeleine was torn between anger and embarrassment. It was no use asking her father to accept the situation because she did not fully comprehend it herself. When her emotions were in a tangle, however, the last thing she needed was to be questioned about her friendship with Robert Colbeck. Unable to contain her fury, she snatched up the painting and fled upstairs. Andrews heard her bedroom door slam shut. Annoyed with himself for upsetting her, he nevertheless felt able to sit down with a wry smile.

'I must remember to get some mistletoe for Christmas,' he said.

Even in the uncertain light from the gas lamp, Colbeck could see the damage inflicted on his face and, when Leeming got up to greet him, the Sergeant let out a grunt of pain. It was late evening when the Inspector got back to his office in Scotland Yard and he was distressed to find his colleague in such blatant discomfort. There was also a faint but very unpleasant whiff coming from him.

'What happened, Victor?' he asked.

'I saw seven stars at the Seven Stars,' said Leeming, laughing at his own feeble joke. 'I was fool enough to mention the name of Jake Bransby and took a beating for it.'

'How badly were you hurt?'

'I'll live, Inspector – just about. The Superintendent was so worried that he wanted to call in a doctor to examine me. Mr Tallis also made me wash three times but I still can't get rid of that stink.'

'How did you acquire it in the first place?'

'The worst possible way.'

145

Leeming had been waiting for a chance to tell his story to a more sympathetic audience and he left no detail out. What he could not tell Colbeck was who actually assaulted him and how he got from the yard at the rear of the public house to a cesspit some streets away. As he described the attack itself, his injuries started to throb violently and his swollen lips felt as if they had been stung by wasps. Reaching the end of his narrative, he took a long sip from the glass of water on the desk.

'I blame myself for this,' said Colbeck, apologetically.

'Why, sir?'

'I should never have sent you there.'

'I was getting on well until I tried to be too inquisitive.'

'I was hoping that they had not yet made the connection between Jacob Bransby and the public hangman but it was too much to ask. You have to admire his courage.'

'Yes,' agreed Leeming. 'Going in there among the ruffians of Bethnal Green when he must surely have stretched the necks of a few villains from that part of London. Just as well they never knew who he was or they'd have done more than sling him in a cesspit.'

'Your visit was not entirely wasted, Victor.'

'I hoped you'd say that.'

'You found out that almost everyone at the Seven Stars went off to support The Bargeman in that fight. They even drew up a list.'

'With a certain person from Hoxton near the top.'

'When the killer learned that,' said Colbeck, 'he didn't need to follow his victim in search of the right moment to strike. He knew that Guttridge would be on that excursion train – so he waited.'

'With that woman.'

'With or without that woman, Victor. That's another little mystery for us to solve. Was she involved or was she just another passenger?'

'I've no idea.'

'Perhaps we'll find out when we go to Ashford tomorrow.'

Leeming gaped. 'Ashford?'

'If you feel strong enough to accompany me.'

'Yes, yes. Of course.'

'Are you certain about that?'

'Yes, I am,' said the other, straightening his shoulders. 'It'll take more than a few punches to keep me put of action, sir – though my wife may not see it that way. I'm dreading the moment when I walk through that door tonight. You know how Estelle can carry on.'

'Would you like me to speak to her?'

'Oh, no.'

'But I can tell her what sterling work you were doing for us in Bethnal Green when you were set upon. Praise can be soothing.'

'Estelle will need more than a few kind words from you to calm her down, sir. Leave my wife to me. I know how to handle her. Meanwhile,' he went on, nodding in the direction of the door, 'make sure you have a good story ready for the Superintendent. He'll come storming in here any moment to ask why you went to Maidstone.'

'How did he react when you struggled back

here earlier?'

'He seemed very sorry for me at first – even helped me in here. And being the Superintendent, of course, he wanted retribution. Assaulting a police officer is a serious offence.'

'Except that they didn't know what your occupation was.'

'Thank God! I'd not be alive now, if they had.'

'Nobody involved in law enforcement is very welcome in Bethnal Green,' said Colbeck, 'and we both know why. It's the children I feel sorry for. They have no choice. If they're born there, crime is the only means by which they can survive.'

'Too true, sir.'

'So what did Mr Tallis want to do?'

'Send a bevy of constables to arrest the landlord and his wife,' said Leeming with a grimace, 'but I managed to talk him out of that. It was those two bruisers who set about me and I'd never recognise them again. Even if I did, it would be my word against that of everybody else in the Seven Stars and they'd swear blind that I was lying. I've got no witnesses to speak up for me.'

'That doesn't mean that we let these bullies get away with it, Victor,' said Colbeck, sharply, 'but I'm glad that you dissuaded the Superintendent from any precipitate action. It needs a more subtle approach. When time serves, we'll pay another visit to the Seven Stars.'

Leeming was vengeful. 'I'll look forward to that, sir.'

'Look forward to what?' demanded Tallis, bursting in through the door in time to hear the

148

words. 'Ah!' he said, seeing Colbeck, 'you've deigned to return from your unauthorised visit to Maidstone, have you?'

'It was a very productive trip, sir,' replied Colbeck.

'That's beside the point.'

'You must allow me some latitude in a murder inquiry.'

'I asked to be kept abreast of any developments. That means you inform me of your movements *before* the event rather than after it.'

'When I made the decision to go to Maidstone, you were in a meeting with the Commissioners and I could not interrupt that.'

'Then you should have waited until the meeting was over.'

'I'll not make any progress in this investigation by sitting on my hands in here, Superintendent,' said Colbeck, evenly. 'You demanded a speedy result so I moved with urgency.'

'So did I,' Leeming put in.

'Be quiet, Sergeant,' barked Tallis.

'Yes, sir.'

'And have a good bath before you come here tomorrow. You still smell like something that crawled out of a blocked drain.'

'Victor will not be in the office tomorrow,' said Colbeck. 'He and I will be going to Ashford in Kent.'

'How kind of you to tell me, Inspector!' returned the other with mock sweetness. 'It's always comforting to know where my detectives actually are.' His voice hardened. 'I trust that you have an extremely good reason for wanting to hare off to

149

Kent again.'

'Yes, sir. That's where the killer of Jacob Guttridge lives.'

'And what makes you think that?'

'The Inspector has this theory, sir,' interjected Leeming, earning himself such a glare of naked hostility from Tallis that he wished he had not spoken. 'I'd better leave it to him to explain.'

'Thank you, Victor,' said Colbeck.

Legs wide apart, Tallis folded his arms. 'I'm waiting, Inspector,' he said, coldly. 'I want to hear about this productive trip to Kent.'

'So do I,' said Leeming, eager to learn what progress had been made. 'You obviously fared a lot better than I did today. Did you get to Maidstone prison, Inspector?' He caught Tallis's eye again and took a hasty step backwards. 'Sorry, sir. I didn't mean to hold him up.'

Colbeck had made copious notes during his visit but he had no need to refer to them. His training as a barrister had sharpened his memory and given him an ability to assemble facts in the most cogent way. His account was long, measured and admirably lucid, making it easy for both men to understand why he had spent so much time in Maidstone. Victor Leeming was intrigued to hear about such colourful characters as Reverend Narcissus Jones and Obadiah Lugg but it was the accumulation of pertinent facts that weighed much more with the Superintendent. It was not long before the folded arms dropped to his side and the stern expression faded from his countenance.

When the recitation finally ended, Tallis came

150

close to a smile.

'You've done well, Inspector,' he admitted.

'Thank you, sir.'

'It looks as if you may at last have stumbled on a theory that has a grain of truth in it. Notwithstanding that, we are still a long way from making an arrest and that is what the Great Western Railway wants.'

'It's what we all want.'

'Then when do you expect it to take place?'

'In the fullness of time,' said Colbeck, smoothly.

'I need something more specific to tell the railway company,' said Tallis, 'and to appease the pack of reporters who keep knocking on my door.' He glanced at Leeming. 'I thank heaven that none of them were here when the Sergeant returned from Bethnal Green in all his glory. I tremble to think what the newspapers would have made of that.'

'I'd have been a laughing stock,' wailed Leeming.

'It's the bad publicity that concerns me. This Department has more than its share of critics. Whatever we do, we must not give them ammunition they can use against us.' He turned to Colbeck. 'So what do we tell them?'

'The same thing that we tell the railway company,' said Colbeck with a confident smile. 'That we have made significant progress but are unable to disclose details because the killer would be forewarned and might be put to flight. More to the point,' he continued, 'the Sergeant and I want to be able to shift our interest to Kent without having any reporters barking at our heels.'

151

'How long will we be in Ashford, sir?' asked Leeming, worriedly.

'A couple of days at least, Victor. Maybe more.'

'Then we'd have to stay the night there?'

'Your wife will have to forego the pleasures of matrimony for a short while, I fear,' said Colbeck, 'but she will be reassured by the fact that you're engaged in such an important investigation.'

'Only when you've taken that bath, Sergeant,' stipulated Tallis.

'Yes, sir,' said Leeming.

'I expect my men to be smart and well-groomed.' He turned a censorious eye on the elegant Inspector. 'Though there is no need to take my instructions in that regard to extremes.'

'We'll take an early train to Ashford,' said Colbeck, ignoring the barbed comment from his superior. 'I suggest that you bring enough clothing for five days, Victor.'

'Five days!' gulped Leeming. 'What about my wife?'

'She is not included in this excursion,' said Tallis, sourly.

'Estelle will miss me.'

'The sooner we bring this investigation to a conclusion,' observed Colbeck, 'the sooner you'll be back with your family. But we must not expect instant results here. The only way to solve the murder of Jacob Guttridge is to find out what really happened to Joseph Dykes.'

'But we know that,' asserted Tallis. 'He was killed by Hawkshaw.'

'That's open to question, Superintendent. Far

be it from me, as a barrister, to question the working of the judicial system, but I have a strange feeling – and it is only a feeling, not a theory – that there was a gross miscarriage of justice on the scaffold at Maidstone.'

Chapter Seven

Nothing revealed the essential difference between the two men as clearly as the train journey to Ashford that morning. Inspector Robert Colbeck was in his element, enjoying his preferred mode of travel and reading his way through the London newspapers as if sitting in a favourite chair at home. Sergeant Victor Leeming, on the other hand, was in severe discomfort. His dislike of going anywhere by train was intensified by the fact that his body was a mass of aching muscles and tender bruises. As their carriage lurched and bumped its clamorous way over the rails, he felt as if he were being pummelled all over again. Leeming tried to close his eyes against the pain but that only made him feel queasy.

'How can you do it, sir?' he asked, enviously.

'Do what, Victor?'

'Read like that when the train is shaking us about so much.'

'One gets used to it,' said Colbeck, looking over the top of his copy of *The Times*. 'I find the constant movement very stimulating.

'Well, I don't – it's agony for me.'

153

'A stagecoach would bounce you about just as much.'

'Yes,' conceded Leeming, 'but we wouldn't have this terrible noise and all this smoke. I feel safe with horses, Inspector. I hate trains.'

'Then you won't take to Ashford, I'm afraid.'

'Why not?'

'It's a railway town.'

Lying at the intersection of a number of main roads, Ashford had been a centre of communication for generations and the arrival of its railway station in 1842 had confirmed its status. But it was when the railway works was opened seven years later that its geographical significance was fully ratified. Its population increased markedly and a sleepy agricultural community took on a more urban appearance and edge. The High Street was wide enough to accommodate animal pens on market day and farmers still came in from a wide area with their produce but the wives of railwaymen, fitters, engineers and gas workers now rubbed shoulders with the more traditional customers.

The first thing that the detectives saw as they alighted at the station was the church tower of St Mary's, a medieval foundation, rising high above the buildings around it with perpendicular authority, and casting a long spiritual shadow across the town. A pervading stink was the next thing that impressed itself upon them and Leeming immediately feared that his bath the previous night had failed to wash away the noxious smell of the cesspit. To his relief, the stench was coming from the River Stour into which all the

154

town's effluent was drained without treatment, a problem exacerbated by the fact that there were now over six thousand inhabitants in the vicinity.

Carrying their bags, they strolled in the bright sunshine to the Saracen's Head to get a first feel of Ashford. Situated in the High Street near the corner with North Street, the inn had been the premier hostelry in the town for centuries and it was able to offer them separate rooms – albeit with low beams and undulating floors – at a reasonable price. Colbeck was acutely aware of the effort that it had cost the Sergeant to get up so early when he was still in a battered condition. He advised him to rest while he ventured out to make initial contact with the Hawkshaw family. Within minutes, Leeming was asleep on his bed.

Colbeck, meanwhile, stepped out from under the inn's portico and walked across the road to the nearby Middle Row, a narrow, twisting passage, where Nathan Hawkshaw and Son owned only one of a half-a-dozen butchers' stalls or shambles. The aroma of fresh meat mingled with the reek from the river to produce an even more distinctive smell. It did not seem to worry the people buying their beef, lamb and pork there that morning. Poultry and rabbits dangled from hooks outside the shop where Nathan Hawkshaw had worked and Colbeck had to remove his top hat and duck beneath them to go inside.

A brawny young man in a bloodstained apron was serving a female customer with some sausages. Colbeck noted his muscular forearms and the dark scowl that gave his ugly face an almost sinister look to it. When the woman left,

155

he introduced himself to Adam Hawkshaw, son of the condemned man, a hulking figure who seemed at home among the carcasses of dead animals. Hawkshaw was resentful.

'What do you want?' he asked, bluntly.

'To establish certain facts about your father's case.'

'We got no time for police. They helped to hang him.'

'I've spoken to Sergeant Lugg in Maidstone,' said Colbeck, 'and he's given me some of the details. What I need to do now is to get the other side of the story – from you and your mother.'

Hawkshaw was aggressive. *'Why?'*

'Because I wish to review the case.'

'My father's dead. Go back to London.'

'I understand the way that you must feel, Mr Hawkshaw, and I've not come to harass you. It may be that I can help.'

'You going to dig him up and bring him back to life?'

'There's no need for sarcasm.'

'Then leave us alone, Inspector,' warned Hawkshaw.

'Inspector?' said a woman, coming into the shop from a door at the rear. 'Who is this gentleman, Adam?'

Colbeck introduced himself to her and discovered that he was talking to Winifred Hawkshaw, a short, compact, handsome woman in her thirties with a black dress that rustled as she moved. She looked too young and too delicate to be the mother of the uncouth butcher. When she heard the Inspector's request, she invited him

156

into the room at the back of the property that served as both kitchen and parlour, leaving Adam Hawkshaw to cope with the two customers who had just come in. Colbeck was offered a seat but Winifred remained standing.

'I must apologise for Adam,' she said, hands gripped tightly together. 'He's taken it hard.'

'I can understand that, Mrs Hawkshaw.'

'After what happened, he's got no faith in the law.'

'And what about you?'

'I feel let down as well, Inspector. We were betrayed.'

'You still believe in your husband's innocence then?'

'Of course,' she said, tartly. 'Nathan had his faults but he was no killer. Yet they made him look like one in court. By the time they finished with him, my husband had been turned into a monster.'

'It must have affected your trade.'

'It has. Loyal customers have stayed with us, so have our friends who knew that Nathan could never have done such a thing. But a lot of people just buy meat elsewhere. This is a murderer's shop, they say, and won't have anything to do with us.'

There was resignation rather than bitterness in her voice. Winifred Hawkshaw did not blame local people for the way that they reacted. Colbeck was reminded of Louise Guttridge, another woman with an inner strength that enabled her to cope with the violent death of a husband. While the hangman's widow was sustained by religion,

157

however, what gave Winifred her self-possession was her belief in her husband and her determination to clear his name.

'Are you aware of what happened to Jacob Guttridge?' he asked.

'Yes, Inspector.'

'How did the news of his murder make you feel?'

'It left me cold.'

'No sense of quiet satisfaction?'

'None,' she said. 'It won't bring Nathan back, will it?'

'What about your son?' he wondered. 'I should imagine that he took some pleasure from the fact that the man who hanged his father was himself executed.'

'Adam is not my son, Inspector. He was a child of Nathan's first marriage. But, yes – and I'm not ashamed to admit this – Adam was thrilled to hear the news. He came running round here to tell me.'

'Doesn't he live here with you?'

'Not any more.'

'Why is that, Mrs Hawkshaw?'

'Never you mind.' She eyed him shrewdly. 'Why did you come here, Inspector?'

'Because the case interested me,' he replied. 'Before I joined the Metropolitan Police, I was a lawyer and was called to the bar. Almost every day of my life was spent in a courtroom involved in legal tussles. There wasn't much of a tussle in your husband's case. From the reports that I've seen, the trial was remarkably swift and one-sided.'

'Nathan had no chance to defend himself.'

'His barrister should have done that.'

'He let us down as well.'

'The prosecution case seemed to hinge on the fact that your husband was unable to account for his whereabouts at the time when Joseph Dykes was killed.'

'That's not true,' she said with spirit. 'Nathan began to walk home from Lenham but, when he'd gone a few miles, he decided to go back and tackle Joe Dykes again. By the time he got there, it was all over.'

'Mr Hawkshaw was seen close to the murder scene.'

'He didn't *know* that the body was lying there.'

'Were there witnesses who saw him walking away from Lenham?'

'None that would come forward in court.'

'Where was your stepson during all this time?'

'He was at the fair with his friends.'

'And you?'

'I was visiting my mother in Willesborough. She's very sick.'

'I'm sorry to hear that, Mrs Hawkshaw.'

'It's the least of my worries at the moment. If things go on as they are, we may have to sell the shop – unless we can prove that Nathan was innocent.'

'To do that, you'll need to unmask the real killer.'

'Gregory and I will do it one day,' she vowed.

'Gregory?'

'A friend of the family, Inspector.' A half-smile of gratitude flitted across her face. 'I don't know what we'd have done without Gregory Newman.

When others were turning away, he stood by us. It was Gregory who said we should start a campaign to free Nathan.'

'Did that involve trying to rescue him from Maidstone prison?'

'I know nothing of that,' she said, crisply.

'An attempt was made – according to the chaplain.'

Her facial muscles tightened. 'Don't mention that man.'

'Why not?'

'Because he only added to Nathan's suffering. Reverend Jones is evil. He kept on bullying my husband.'

'Is that what he told you?'

'Nathan wasn't allowed to tell me anything like that. They only let me see him in prison once. We had a warder standing over us to listen to what was said. Nathan was in chains,' she said, hurt by a painful memory, 'as if he was a wild animal.'

'So this information about the chaplain must have come from a message that was smuggled out. Am I right?' She nodded in assent. 'Do you still have it, by any chance?'

'No,' she replied.

Colbeck knew that she was lying. A woman who had made such efforts to prove her husband's innocence would cherish everything that reminded her of him, even if it was a note scribbled in a condemned cell. But there was no point in challenging her and asking to see the missive, especially as he already knew that there was an element of truth in its contents. The Reverend Narcissus Jones had made the prisoner's last few hours on earth far more uncomfortable than they need have been.

'Does this Mr Newman live in Ashford?'

'Oh, yes. Gregory used to be a blacksmith. He had a forge in St John's Lane but he sold it.'

'Has he retired?'

'No, Inspector,' she said, 'he's too young for that. Gregory took a job in the railway works. That's where you'll find him.'

'Then that's where I'll go in due course,' decided Colbeck, getting to his feet. 'Thank you, Mrs Hawkshaw. I'm sorry to intrude on you this way but I really do want the full details of this case.'

She challenged him. 'You think it's us, don't you?'

'I beg your pardon?'

'You're not really interested in Nathan, are you?' she said with a note of accusation. 'You came to find out if *we* killed that dreadful hangman. Well, I can tell you now, Inspector, that we're not murderers. Not any of us – and that includes my husband.'

'I'm sorry if I gave you the wrong impression,' he told her, raising both hands in a gesture of appeasement. 'Very few cases are reviewed in this way, I can assure you. I would have thought it would be in your interest for someone to examine the facts anew with a fresh pair of eyes.'

'That's not all that brought you here.'

'Perhaps not, Mrs Hawkshaw. But it's one of the main reasons.'

'What are the others?'

He gave a disarming smile. 'I've taken up

enough of your time. Thank you for being so helpful.' He was about to leave when he heard footsteps descending the stairs and a door opened to reveal a fair-haired girl in mourning dress. 'Oh, good morning,' he said, politely.

The girl was short, slender, pale-faced and exceptionally pretty. She looked as if she had been crying and there was a vulnerability about her that made her somehow more appealing. The sight of a stranger caused her to draw back at once.

'This is my daughter, Emily,' said Winifred, indicating her. 'Emily, this is Inspector Colbeck from London. He's a policeman.'

It was all that the girl needed to hear. Mumbling an excuse, she closed the door and went hurriedly back upstairs. Winifred felt impelled to offer an explanation.

'You'll have to forgive her,' she said. 'Emily still can't believe that it all happened. It's changed her completely. She hasn't been out of here since the day of the execution.'

Victor Leeming was dreaming about his wedding day when he heard a distant knock. The door of the church swung open but, instead of his bride, it was a plump young woman with a wooden tray who came down the aisle towards him.

'Excuse me, sir,' she said, boldly.

'What?'

Leeming came awake and realised that he was lying fully-clothed on the bed in his room at the Saracen's Head. The plump young woman was standing inside the doorway, holding a tray and staring at his bruised face with utter fascination.

'Did you hurt yourself, sir?' she asked.

'I had an accident,' he replied, leaping off the bed to stand up.

'What sort of accident?'

'It doesn't matter.'

'It would to me if I had injuries like that.'

'Who are you and what do you want?'

'My name is Mary, sir,' she said with a friendly smile, 'and I work here at the Saracen's Head. The other gentleman told me to wake you with a cup of tea at eleven o'clock and give you this letter.' She put the tray on the bedside table. 'There you are, sir.'

As she brushed his arm, he stepped back guiltily as if he had just been caught in an act of infidelity. It was a paradox. As a policeman in earlier days, Leeming had been used to patrolling areas of London that were infested with street prostitutes yet he was embarrassed to be alone in a room with a female servant. Mary continued to stare at him.

'Thank you,' he said. 'You can go now.'

'I don't believe it was an accident.'

'Goodbye, Mary.'

'Did it hurt, sir?'

'Goodbye.'

Ushering her out, he closed the door and slipped the bolt into place. Then he stirred some sugar into the tea and took a welcome sip. A clock was chiming nearby and his pocket watch confirmed that it was exactly eleven o'clock, meaning that he had slept for over two hours. Grateful to Colbeck for permitting him a rest, he opened the envelope on the tray and read his instructions, written in the neat hand that he knew so well. Leeming was not pleased by his orders but he seized on one benefit.

'At least, I don't have to go there by train!' he said.

Ashford was the home of the South Eastern Railway Company's main works, a fact that gave the town more kudos while inflicting a perpetual clamour upon it during working hours. The construction of a locomotive was not something that could be done quietly and the clang of industry had now become as familiar, if not as euphonious, as the tolling of a church bell. Robert Colbeck was delighted with an excuse to visit the works and he spent some time talking to the superintendent about the locomotives and rolling stock that were built there. To find the man he was after, Colbeck had to go to the boiler shop, the noisiest part of the factory a place of unremitting tumult as chains were used to manoeuvre heavy pieces of iron, hammers pounded relentlessly and sparks flew.

Gregory Newman was helping to lift a section of a boiler into position. He was a big man in his forties with a mop of dark hair and a full beard that was flecked with dirt. He used a sinewy forearm to wipe the sweat from his brow. Colbeck waited until he had finished the job in hand before he introduced himself, detached Newman from the others and took him outside. The boilerman was astonished by the arrival of a detective from Scotland Yard, especially one as refined and

164

well-dressed as Colbeck. He took a moment to weigh up the newcomer.

'How can you work in that din?' asked Colbeck.

'I was born and brought up in a forge,' said Newman, 'so I've lived with noise all my life. Not like some of the others. Three of the men in the boiler shop have gone stone deaf.'

'I'm not surprised.'

'They should have stuffed something in their ears.'

Newman had a ready grin and an affable manner, the fruit of a lifetime of chatting to customers while they waited for their horses to be shod or for him to perform some other task in his forge. Colbeck warmed to the man at once.

'Why did you stop being a blacksmith?' he said.

'This job pays me better,' replied the other, 'and locomotives don't kick as hard as horses. But that's not the real reason, Inspector. I used to hate trains at first but they've grown on me.'

'They're the face of the future, Mr Newman.'

'That's what I feel.'

'Though there'll always be a call for a good blacksmith.'

'Well, *I* won't hear it – not with all that hulla-baloo in the boiler shop. It's a world of its own in there.' His grin slowly faded. 'But you didn't come all the way here from London to hear me tell you that. This is about Nathan, isn't it?'

'Yes, Mr Newman. I've just spoken with his wife.'

'How is Win?'

'Holding up much better than I dared to expect,' said Colbeck. 'Mrs Hawkshaw was very

165

helpful. The same, alas, could not be said of her stepson. He doesn't have much respect for the law.'

'How could he after what happened?'

'Was he always so truculent?'

'Adam is a restless lad,' explained Newman, 'and he likes his own way. When he lived at home, he and Nathan used to argue all the time so I found him a room near the Corn Exchange. There's no real harm in Adam but he won't let anyone push him around.'

'How does he get on with his stepmother?'

'Not too well, Win is a good woman. She's done all she could for him but he was just too much of a handful for her. Then, of course, there was the problem with Emily.'

'Oh?'

'Adam was always teasing her. I'm sure it was only meant in fun,' said Newman, defensively, 'but I think it went too far sometimes. Emily's scared of him. It wasn't good for them to be sleeping under the same roof. They've nothing in common.'

'They share the same father, don't they?'

'No, Inspector. Emily is not Nathan's daughter.'

'I assumed that she was.'

'Win's first husband was killed in a fire,' said Newman, sadly, 'and she was left to bring up a tiny baby on her own. She and Nathan didn't get married until a year later. His wife had died of smallpox so he had a child on his hands as well – Adam.'

'I'm told that you were close to the Hawk-shaws.'

'We've been friends for years.'

'Was it a happy marriage?'

'Very happy,' returned the other, as if offended by the query. 'You can see that from the way that Win fought for his release. She was devoted to her husband.'

'But you ran the campaign on his behalf.'

'It was the least I could do, Inspector. Nathan and I grew up together in Ashford. We went to school, fished in the Stour, had our first pipe of tobacco together.' He smiled nostalgically. 'We were only twelve at the time and as sick as dogs.'

'Was Mr Hawkshaw a powerful man?'

'Stronger than me.'

'Strong enough to hack a man to death, then?' asked Colbeck, springing the question on him to gauge his reaction.

'Nathan didn't kill Joe Dykes,' asserted the other.

'Then who did?'

'Go into any pub in the town and you'll find a dozen suspects in each one. Joe Dykes was a menace. Nobody had a good word for him. If he wasn't getting drunk and picking a fight, he was stealing something or pestering a woman.'

'From what I heard, he did more than pester Emily Hawkshaw.'

'Yes,' said Newman, grimly. 'That was what really upset Nathan. The girl is barely sixteen.'

'I met her briefly earlier on.'

'Then you'll have seen how meek and defence-less she is. Emily is still a child in some ways. She was running an errand for her mother when Joe Dykes cornered her in a lane. The sight of a pretty face was all he needed to rouse him. He grabbed Emily, pinned her against a wall and tore her skirt as he tried to lift it.'

'Didn't she scream for help?' asked Colbeck.

'Emily was too scared to move,' said Newman, 'let alone call out. If someone hadn't come into the lane at that moment, heaven knows what he'd have done to her.'

'Was the incident reported to the police?'

'Nathan wanted to sort it out himself so he went looking for Joe. But, of course, he'd run away by then. We didn't see hide nor hair of Joe Dykes for weeks. Then he turned up at the fair in Lenham.'

'Were you there yourself?'

'Yes, Inspector.'

'Did you go with Nathan Hawkshaw?'

'No,' said Newman, 'I rode over there first thing on my own. I've a cousin who's a blacksmith in Lenham. A fair brings in plenty of trade so I helped him in the forge that morning. It made a nice change from the boiler shop.'

'So you didn't witness the argument that was supposed to have taken place between Hawkshaw and Dykes?'

'I came in at the end. There was such a commotion in the square that I went to see what it was. Nathan and Joe were yelling at each other and the crowd was hoping to see a fight. That's when I stepped in.'

'You?'

'Somebody had to, Inspector,' Newman continued, 'or things could have turned nasty. I didn't want Nathan arrested for disturbing the peace. So, when Joe goes off to the Red Lion, I stopped Nathan from following him and tried to talk some sense into him. If he wanted to settle a score, the square in Lenham was not the place to do it. He should have waited until Joe came out of the pub at the end of the evening when there was hardly anyone about.'

'So there would have been a fight of some sort?'

'A fight is different from cold-blooded murder.'

'But your friend was clearly in a mood for revenge.'

'That's why I had to calm him down,' said Newman, scratching his beard. 'I told him to go away until his temper had cooled. And that's what Nathan did. He set out for Ashford, thought over what I'd said then headed back to Lenham in a much better frame of mind.'

'Did he have a meat cleaver with him?'

'Of course not,' retorted the other.

'One was found beside the body. It had Hawkshaw's initials on it.'

'It was not left there by Nathan.'

'How do you know?'

'To begin with,' said Newman, hotly, 'he wouldn't have been so stupid as to leave a murder weapon behind that could be traced to him.'

'I disagree,' argued Colbeck. 'All the reports suggest that it must have been a frenzied attack. If someone is so consumed with rage that he's ready to kill, he wouldn't stop to think about hiding the murder weapon. Having committed the crime, Hawkshaw could have simply stumbled off.'

'Then where was the blood?'

'Blood?'

'I spoke to the farm lad who discovered the body, Inspector. He said there was blood everywhere. Whoever sliced up Joe Dykes must have been spattered with it – yet there wasn't a speck on Nathan.'

'He was a butcher. He knew how to use a cleaver.'

'That's what they said in court,' recalled Newman, bitterly. 'If he'd been a draper or a grocer, he'd still be alive now. Nathan was condemned because of his occupation.'

'Circumstantial evidence weighed against him.'

'Is that enough to take away a man's life and leave his family in misery? I don't give a damn for what was said about him at the trial. He was innocent of the crime and I want his name cleared.'

Gregory Newman spoke with the earnestness of a true friend. Colbeck decided that, since he had supervised the campaign to secure the prisoner's release, he was almost certainly involved in the doomed attempt to rescue him from Maidstone prison and in the upheaval during the execution. For the sake of a friend, he was ready to defy the law. Colbeck admired his stance even though he disapproved of it.

'You heard what happened to Jake Guttridge, I presume?'

'Yes, Inspector.'

'What did you think when you learned of the hangman's death?'

'He was no hangman,' said Newman, quietly. 'He was a torturer. He put Nathan through agony. When she saw the way that her husband

170

was twitching at the end of the rope, Win passed out. We had to take her to a doctor.'

'So you didn't shed a tear when you heard that Guttridge had met his own death by violent means?'

'I neither cried nor cheered, Inspector. I'm sorry for any man who's murdered and for those he leaves behind. Guttridge is of no interest to me now. All I want to do is to help Win through this nightmare,' he said, 'and the best way to do that is to prove that Nathan was not guilty.'

'Supposing – just *supposing* – that he was?'

Newman looked at him as if he had just suggested something totally obscene. There was a long silence. Pulling himself to his full height, he looked the detective in the eye.

'Then he was not the person I've known for over forty years.'

Colbeck was impressed with the man's conviction but he was still not entirely persuaded of Hawkshaw's innocence. He did, however, feel that the conversation had put him in possession of vital information. If the butcher had been wrongly hanged, and if Colbeck worked to establish that fact, then Gregory Newman would be a useful ally. Though the boiler maker had little trust in policemen, he had talked openly about the case with the Inspector and made his own position clear. There was much more to learn from him but this was not the time.

'Thank you, Mr Newman,' said Colbeck.

'Thank you for taking me away from work for a while.'

'I may need to speak with you again.'

'As you wish, Inspector. Do you want my address?'

'No, I think that I'd rather call on you here at the works.'

Newman grinned. 'Are you that fond of loco-motives, Inspector?'

'Yes,' said Colbeck, smiling. 'As a matter of fact, I am.'

Unable to hire a trap, they settled for a cart that had been used that morning to bring a load of fish to Ashford and that still bore strong aromatic traces of its cargo. When it set off towards Lenham and hit every pothole in the road, Victor Leeming could see that he was in for another painful ride. His companion was George Butter-kiss, one of the constables in the town, a scrawny individual in his thirties with the face of a startled ferret. Thankful to be driven, Leeming soon began to regret his decision to ask Butterkiss to take him. The fellow was over-eager to help, even in a uniform that was much too big for his spare frame, and he was desperately in awe of the Metropolitan Police. He spoke in an irritating nasal whine.

'What are our orders, Sergeant?' he asked, whipping the horse into a trot. 'This is wonderful for me, sir. I've never worked for Scotland Yard before.'

'Or ever again,' said Leeming under his breath.

'What are we supposed to do?'

'*My* instructions,' said Leeming, keen to stress that they had not been directed at Butterkiss, 'are to visit the scene of the crime, examine it

172

carefully then speak to the landlord of the Red Lion.'

'I know the exact spot where Joe Dykes was done in.'

'Good.'

'Sergeant Lugg showed it to me. He and his men came over from Maidstone to arrest Nathan Hawkshaw. There was no point, really. They should have left it to us.'

'Did you know Hawkshaw?'

'My wife bought all her meat from him.'

'What sort of man was he?'

'Decent enough,' said Butterkiss, 'though he wasn't a man to get on the wrong side of, I know that to my cost. Of course, I wasn't a policeman in those days. I was a tailor.'

'Really?' said Leeming, wishing that the man had stayed in his former occupation. 'What made you turn to law enforcement?'

'My shop was burgled and nobody did anything about it.'

'So you thought that you could solve the crime?'

'Oh, no, Sergeant. There was no chance of that. I just realised how horrible you feel when your property has been stolen. It was like being invaded. I wanted to save other people from going through that.'

'A laudable instinct.'

'Then there was the other thing, of course.'

'What other thing?'

'The excitement,' said Butterkiss, nudging him. 'The thrill of the chase. There's none of that when you're measuring someone for a new frock coat.

Well, I don't need to tell you, do I? You're another man who loves to hear the sound of a hue and cry.' He gave an ingratiating smirk. 'Would someone like me be able to work at Scotland Yard?'

'Let's talk about the case,' insisted Leeming, wincing as the wheel explored another pothole with jarring resonance. 'Do you think that Hawkshaw was guilty?'

'That's why they hanged him.'

'He wouldn't have been the first innocent man on the gallows.'

'There was no doubt about his guilt in my mind,' attested the driver. 'He and Joe Dykes were sworn enemies. It was only a matter of time before one of them did the other in. Joe broke into the butcher's shop once, you know.'

'Then why didn't you arrest him?'

'We couldn't prove it. Joe used to taunt Nathan about it. Boasted that he could walk in and out of any house in Ashford and nobody could touch him.'

'*I'd* touch him,' said Leeming, 'good and hard.'

'We gave him warning after warning. He ignored us.'

'What was this business about Hawkshaw's daughter?'

'It was his stepdaughter, Emily. Pretty girl.'

'Is it true that Dykes assaulted her?'

'Yes,' said Butterkiss. 'Someone disturbed them just in time.'

'Was the girl hurt?'

'Emily was very upset – who wouldn't be if they were pounced on by someone like Joe Dykes? It was a big mistake for her to go down that lane. It was one of his places, you see.'

'Places?'

'He used to take women there at night,' said the other, confidingly. 'You can guess the kind of women I mean. Even in a place like Ashford, we have our share of those. Joe would take his pleasure up against a wall and then, as like as not, refuse to pay for it.'

'And that's where this girl was attacked?'

'She thought she'd be safe in daylight.'

'It must have been a terrifying experience.'

'That's what fired Nathan up. He was very protective towards Emily. He went charging around the town in search of Joe but he'd had the sense to make himself scarce. If Nathan had caught him there and then,' said Butterkiss, flicking the reins to get a faster pace out of the horse, 'he'd have torn him apart. I've never seen him so angry.'

'Was he carrying a weapon of any kind?'

'A meat cleaver.'

Travelling with George Butterkiss had its definite compensations. Annoying as his manner might be, he was a fount of information about Ashford and its inhabitants and, since the murder case had been the only major crime in the area during his time as a policeman, he had immersed himself in its details. Victor Leeming overcame his dislike of the man and let him talk at will. Long before they reached Lenham, he had acquired a much clearer understanding of what had brought him and Colbeck to Kent.

'Is this it, Mr Butterkiss?' he asked.

'Yes, Sergeant. The very spot.'

175

'Where exactly was the body lying when discovered?'

'Here,' said the policeman, dropping obligingly to the ground and adopting what he believed to be the appropriate position. 'This is where the torso was, anyway,' he added. 'Some of the limbs were scattered about. They never found the other bit.'

'What other bit?'

Butterkiss got to his feet. 'Joe Dykes was castrated.'

It was the first time that Leeming had heard that particular detail and it shook him. They were in a clearing in the woods near Lenham, a quiet, private, shaded place that would have beckoned lovers rather than a killer and his victim. Birds were singing, insects were buzzing, trees and bushes were in full leaf. To commit a murder in such a tranquil place was like an act of desecration.

'Who found the body?'

'A lad from a nearby farm, taking a short-cut home from the fair.'

'I'll need to speak to him.'

'He was the one who spotted Nathan close to here.'

'Let's talk to the landlord of that pub first,' said Leeming. 'That was where Dykes was drinking before he came out to meet his death.'

'Will this go into your report, Sergeant?'

'What?'

'The way I was able to demonstrate where the corpse lay,' said Butterkiss with a willing smile. 'I'd appreciate a mention, sir. It will help me to

176

get on as a policeman. A lot of people in Ashford still treat me as if I was still a tailor. But I'm not – I'm one of *you* now.'

Leeming choked back a comment.

Since there were so few customers that afternoon, Adam Hawkshaw elected to close the butcher's shop early. After bringing in everything that had been on display on the table outside, he took off his apron and hung it up. Then he opened the door at the rear of the shop and went into the room. Winifred Hawkshaw was seated beside Emily with a comforting arm around the girl. Both of them looked up. After a glance from her mother, Emily went off upstairs. Winifred stood up to confront her stepson.

'I told you to knock before you came in.'

'Why?' he asked, insolently. 'It's my house as well.'

'You moved out, Adam.'

'I still own a share of this place now that my father's dead. He always said that he'd leave it to me.'

'He changed his mind.'

'You *made* him change it, you mean.'

'I don't want another row with you,' she said, wearily. 'Not now, please. You'll be able to see the will in due course.' She noticed that he had no apron on. 'Have you shut up shop already?'

Adam was surly. 'No point in staying open,' he said. 'The only customer I had this afternoon was a woman who didn't buy anything. Came to complain about the beef we sold her. And you know why.'

177

'Yes.' Winifred bit her lip. 'We can't get the best meat any more. Mr Hockaday refused to supply us when your father got arrested.'

'So did Bybrook Farm. We have to pay a higher price now for meat that's only half as good. It's killing our trade.' He heard footsteps over his head and looked up. 'How is she now?'

'Much the same.'

'Has she started to talk again yet?'

'No, Adam,' she replied, sorrowfully. 'Emily has hardly spoken more than a few words to me since this all began. She spends most of her time up there in her room, frightened to come out.'

'She never was one for saying much.'

'Emily needs time to recover – just like the rest of us. We could all do with a period of peace and quiet.'

'How can we get that when some Inspector from London turns up to cause trouble?' he snarled. 'You were wrong to talk to him like that.'

'Why?'

'Policemen are all the same, even fancy ones like that. You never know what they really want.'

'I know what Inspector Colbeck is after.'

'What?'

'He wants to find out who killed the public hangman.'

'So do I,' said Adam, eyes glinting, 'because I'd like to shake his hand. Guttridge being murdered was the one good thing to come out of all this. I hope he died in torment.'

'That's a vile thing to say!' she chided.

'He killed my father.'

'I lost a husband that day, Adam,' she told him,

178

'but I don't want vengeance against those involved. I just want the stain to be wiped away from our name so that we can hold up our heads in this town again.'

'We may not be staying long enough for that,'

'We *have* to, Adam. We can't crawl away in disgrace.'

'The shop is the only thing that keeps us here,' he said, jerking a thumb over his shoulder, 'and most people walk straight past it. I'm not a butcher any more. I'm Nathan Hawkshaw's son – a killer's whelp.'

It was remarkable how much information they had garnered between them in the course of one day. When the two detectives met over a meal at the Saracen's Head that evening, Robert Colbeck and Victor Leeming compared notes and disussed what their next move ought to be. Though no firm conclusions could yet be reached, the Inspector felt that the visit to Ashford had already proved worthwhile.

'He's here, Victor,' he announced. 'I feel it.'

'Who is?'

'The killer.'

'Which one, sir?'

'I beg your pardon?'

'The man who murdered Joseph Dykes or the one who finished off Jacob Guttridge in that excursion train?'

'The second of the two. That's what brought us here, after all. Until we've solved that particular crime, Mr Tallis will hound us from morn till night – and he's quite right to do so.'

'That's the only advantage of being here,' said Leeming, rubbing a buttock as he felt another twinge. 'We're out of the Superintendent's earshot. We can breathe freely.'

'Not with that smell from the river.'

'Going back to Nathan Hawkshaw for a minute...'

'Yes?'

'Before we came here, you had a few doubts about his guilt.'

'More than a few, Victor.'

'And now?'

'Those doubts remain,' said Colbeck, spearing a piece of sausage with his fork. 'I spent the afternoon talking to people in the town who knew the butcher well – his friends, his doctor, even the priest at St Mary's Church. They all agreed that it was so out of character for Hawkshaw to commit murder that they couldn't believe he was culpable.'

'I've come round to the opposite view, sir.'

'Why?'

'According to the George Butterkiss, there was another side to the butcher. He liked an argument for its own sake. When he used to be a tailor – Butterkiss, that is, not Hawkshaw – he made a suit for him and got a mouthful of abuse for his pains. It was as if Hawkshaw was finding fault on purpose so that he could have a good quarrel with the tailor.'

'Did he buy the suit in the end?'

'Only when Butterkiss had made a few slight changes.'

'Maybe there *were* some things wrong with it.'

180

'I don't think so,' said Leeming, munching his food. 'Butterkiss reckons that he only started the argument so that he could get something off the price. The tailor was browbeaten into taking less for his work. That's criminal.'

'It's business, Victor.'

'Well, it sums up Hawkshaw for me. He was no saint.'

'Nobody claims that he was,' said Colbeck, 'and I know that he could be argumentative. Gregory Newman told me that Hawkshaw and his son were always gnawing at some bone of contention. It's the reason that Adam Hawkshaw moved out of the house. Nothing you've said so far inclines me to believe that Hawkshaw was a killer.'

'You're forgetting the daughter, sir.'

'Emily?'

'When she told her stepfather she'd been assaulted by Dykes, he grabbed a meat cleaver and went out looking for him. That doesn't sound like an innocent man to me.'

'What it sounds like is someone who acted purely on impulse. He may have brandished a weapon but that doesn't mean he would have used it – especially in a public place where there'd be witnesses. In those circumstances,' said Colbeck, 'most fathers would respond with blind rage. You have a daughter of your own, Victor. What would you do if some drunken oaf molested Alice?'

'I'd be after him with a pair of shears!' said Leeming.

'I rest my case.'

'Only because you didn't meet the lad who saw Hawkshaw near the place where the murder occurred. I did, Inspector. He gave evidence in court that, when he walked home through the woods, Hawkshaw was trying to hide behind some bushes. He was furtive,' insisted Leeming, 'like he'd done something wrong.'

'Did the youth speak to him?'

'He tried to but Hawkshaw scurried off into the undergrowth. Why did he do that if he had nothing to hide?'

'I don't know,' admitted Colbeck.

'It was because he'd just hacked Joseph Dykes to death.'

'Maybe, maybe not.'

'I'll stick with maybe, sir. The victim was castrated, remember. Only a father who wanted revenge for an attempted rape of his daughter would do that. It has to be Hawkshaw.'

'Did you talk to the landlord of the Red Lion?'

'Yes,' said Leeming. 'He gave evidence in court as well. He told me that Dykes went in there that day, drank a lot of beer and made a lot of noise, then rolled out as if he didn't have a care in the world.'

'What was he doing in that wood?'

'I can't work that out, sir. You'd only go that way if you wanted to get to the farm beyond. It was where that lad worked, you see. My theory is that Dykes may have made himself a den in there.'

'Take care, Victor!' said Colbeck with a laugh. 'We can't have you succumbing to theories as well. In any case, this one doesn't hold water. If there had been a den there, it would have been found when the police made a thorough search of the area.'

'Dykes slept rough from time to time. We know that for certain.'

'But even he wouldn't bed down in the middle of the afternoon when there was a fair to enjoy and several hours more drinking to get through. What took him there at that specific time?'

'Hawkshaw must have lured him there somehow.'

'I think that highly unlikely.'

'How else could it have happened?'

'I intend to find out, Victor,' said Colbeck. 'But only after we've caught the man who stalked Jake Guttridge on that excursion train.'

'We know so little about him, sir.'

'On the contrary, we know a great deal.'

'Do we?' asked Leeming, drinking his beer to wash down his food. 'The only thing we can be sure of is that he's almost illiterate.'

'Why do you say that?'

'Because of that warning note you found at Guttridge's house.'

'Go on.'

'It was nothing but a scrawl. Half the words weren't even spelled properly. The person we want is obviously uneducated.'

'I wonder,' said Colbeck. 'People who can't write usually get someone to do it for them. The man who sent that message to the hangman may have *wanted* to appear unlettered by way of disguise. But there's another factor to weigh in the balance here.'

'Is there, sir?'

'The man who killed Jake Guttridge may not be the one who sent him that note. He could well be someone else altogether.'

'That makes him even more difficult to track down,' said Leeming, popping a potato into his mouth. 'We're looking for a needle in a very large haystack, Inspector.'

'A small haystack, perhaps,' said Colbeck, sipping his wine, 'but that should not deter us. We know that we're looking for a local man with some connection to Nathan Hawkshaw. Someone so outraged at what happened to his friend that he'd go in search of the hangman to wreak his revenge. The killer was strong, determined and cunning.'

'Have you met anyone who fits that description, sir?'

'Two people at least.'

'Who are they?'

'The son is the first,' Colbeck told him. 'From the little I saw of him, I'd say he had the strength and determination. Whether he'd have the cunning is another matter.'

'Who's the other suspect?'

'Gregory Newman. He was Hawkshaw's best friend and he led the campaign on his behalf. My guess is that he even tried to rescue him from Maidstone prison and he'd have to be really committed to attempt something as impossible as that.'

'If he was a blacksmith, then he'd certainly be strong enough.'

'Yes,' said Colbeck, 'but he didn't strike me as

184

a potential killer. Newman is something of a gentle giant. Since the execution, all his efforts have been directed at consoling the widow. He's a kind man and a loyal friend. The priest at St Mary's spoke very highly of him. Gregory Newman, it transpires, has a bed-ridden wife whom he looks after lovingly, even to the point of carrying her to church every Sunday.'

'That *is* devotion,' agreed Leeming.

'A devoted husband is unlikely to be a brutal murderer.'

'So we come back to Adam Hawkshaw.'

'He'd certainly conform to your notion that an uneducated man sent that note,' explained Colbeck, using a napkin to wipe his lips. 'When I left the shop yesterday, he was lowering the prices on the board outside. He'd chalked up the different items on offer. Considering that he must have sold pheasant many times, he'd made a very poor shot at spelling it correctly.'

Leeming grinned. 'He's lucky he didn't have to spell asphyxiation.'

'He's certainly capable of inflicting it on someone.'

'It's that warning note that worries me, sir.'

'Why?'

'Guttridge had one and he ended up dead.'

'So?'

'According to George Butterkiss,' said Leeming, pushing his empty plate aside, 'someone else had a death threat as well. Sergeant Lugg, that policeman from Maidstone, told him about it. The note that was sent sounds very much like the one that went to the hangman. The difference is that the man who received it just laughed and tore it up.'

'Who was he, Victor?'

'The prison chaplain, sir – the Reverend Narcissus Jones.'

Though his job at Maidstone prison was onerous and wide-ranging, Narcissus Jones nevertheless found time for activities outside its high stone walls. He gave regular lectures at various churches and large audiences usually flocked to hear how he had conceived it as his mission to work among prisoners. He always emphasized that he had converted some of the most hardened criminals to Christianity and sent them out into society as reformed characters. With his Welsh ancestry, he had a real passion for choral singing and he talked lovingly about the prison choir that he conducted. Jones was a good speaker, fluent, dramatic and so steeped in Biblical knowledge that he could quote from Old and New Testaments at will.

He had been on good form at Paddock Wood that night, rousing the congregation to such a pitch that they had burst into spontaneous applause at the end of his talk. Everyone wanted to congratulate him afterwards and what touched him was that one of those most effusive in his praise was a former inmate at the prison who said that, in bringing him to God, the chaplain had saved his life. When he headed for the railway station, Jones was still beaming with satisfaction.

He did not have long to wait for the train that would take him back to Maidstone. Selecting an empty carriage, he sat down and tried to read his

Bible in the fading light. A young woman then got into the carriage and sat opposite him, gaining a nod of welcome from the chaplain. He decided that she had chosen to join him because the sight of his clerical collar was a guarantee of her safety. She was short, attractive and dark-haired but she was holding a handkerchief to her face as if to dab away tears. At a signal from the stationmaster, the train began to move but, at the very last moment, a man jumped into the carriage and slammed the door behind him.

'Just made it!' he said, sitting down at the opposite end from the others. 'I hope that I didn't disturb you.'

'Not at all,' replied Jones, 'though I'd never care to do anything as dangerous as that. Are you going as far as Maidstone?'

'Yes.'

'And what about you, my dear?' asked the chaplain, turning to the woman. 'Where's your destination?'

But she did not even hear him. Unable to contain her sorrow, she began to sob loudly and press the handkerchief to her eyes. Jones put his Bible aside and rose to his feet so that he could bend solicitously over her. It was a fatal error. As soon as the chaplain's back was turned to him, the other man got up, produced a length of wire from his pocket and slipped it around the neck of Narcissus Jones, pulling it tight with such vicious force that the victim barely had time to pray for deliverance. When the train stopped at the next station, the only occupant of the carriage was a dead prison chaplain.

Chapter Eight

Robert Colbeck had always been a light sleeper. Hearing the footsteps coming up the oak staircase with some urgency, he opened his eyes and sat up quickly in bed. There was a loud knock on his door.

'Inspector Colbeck?' said a voice. 'This is Constable Butterkiss.'

'One moment.'

'I have a message for you, sir.'

Colbeck got out of bed, slipped on his dressing gown and unbolted the door. He opened it to admit George Butterkiss who had come to the Saracen's Head at such speed that he had not even paused to button up his uniform properly.

'What's the problem, Constable?'

'I'm sorry for the delay,' gabbled Butterkiss, almost out of breath, 'but they didn't realise that you were in Kent. They sent a telegraph message to London and it was passed on to Scotland Yard. When they found out you were in Ashford, they asked us to get in touch with you straight away.'

'Calm down,' said Colbeck, putting a hand on his shoulder. 'Just tell me what this is all about.'

'There's been another murder, sir.'

'Where?'

'In a train on its way to Maidstone.'

'Do you know who the victim was?'

'The prison chaplain – Narcissus Jones.'

Colbeck felt a pang of regret. 'Where's the body?'

'Where it was found, sir,' said Butterkiss, deferentially. 'They thought you'd want to see it before it was moved.'

'Someone deserves congratulations for that. I hope that the same person had the sense to preserve the scene of the crime so that no clues have been lost. Sergeant Leeming needs to hear all this,' he went on, stepping into the passage to bang on the adjoining door. 'Wake up. Victor! We have to leave at once.'

Leeming took time to come out of his slumber and to adjust to the fact that someone was pounding on the door. He eventually appeared, bleary-eyed and wearing a flannel nightshirt. Colbeck invited him into his own room then asked Butterkiss to give a succinct account of what he knew. It was a tall order for the former tailor. Overwhelmed at being in the presence of two Scotland Yard detectives, albeit it in night attire, he started to jabber wildly, embroidering the few facts that he knew into a long, confused, meandering narrative.

'That's enough,' said Colbeck, cutting him off before he had finished. 'We'll find out the rest when we get there.'

Butterkiss was eager. 'Will you be needing my assistance, sir?'

'You've already given that.'

'There must be something that I can do, Inspector.'

'There is,' said Colbeck, glad to get rid of him. 'Arrange some transport to get us to the station as fast as possible.'

'Very good, sir.'

'Only not that cart that stinks of fish,' warned Leeming.

'I'll find something,' said Butterkiss and he rushed out.

'Get dressed, Victor. We must be on our way.'

The Sergeant was hungry. 'What about breakfast?'

'We'll think about that when we reach Maidstone. Now hurry up, will you? They're all waiting for us.'

'What's the rush, Inspector? The chaplain isn't going anywhere.' Leeming put an apologetic hand to his mouth. 'Oh dear! I shouldn't have said that, should I?'

The baker's shop in North Street was among the earliest to open and Winifred Hawkshaw was its first customer that morning. Clutching a loaf of bread still warm from the oven, she was about to cross the High Street when she saw two familiar figures coming towards her on a little cart. Gregory Newman gave her a cheery wave and brought the horse to a halt. Seated beside him and swathed in a rug, in spite of the warm weather, was his wife, Meg, a thin, wasted creature in her forties with a vacant stare and an open mouth.

'Good morning,' said Winifred. 'How is Meg today?'

'Oh, she's very well,' replied Newman, slipping a fond arm around his wife, 'aren't you, Meg?' She looked blankly at him. 'It's Win. You

190

remember Win Hawkshaw, don't you?' His wife nodded and gave Win a crooked smile of acknowledgement. 'She's not at her best this time of the morning,' explained her husband, 'but the doctor said that she must get plenty of fresh air so I take her for a ride whenever I can.' He looked up as a few dark clouds began to form. 'We went before work today because it may rain later.'

'You're wonderful with her, Gregory.'

'You were there when I made my marriage vows before the altar. In sickness and in health means exactly what it says, Win. It's not Meg's fault that she's plagued by illness.'

'No, of course not.'

'But how are you? I've been meaning to call in.'

'I'm fine,' said Winifred. 'Well, as fine as I'll ever be, I suppose.'

'What about Emily?'

'She's still the same, I'm afraid. Emily seems to be lost in a bad dreams most of the time. I just can't reach her, Gregory.'

'Things will improve soon.'

'Will they?' she asked with a hint of despair. 'There's been no sign of it so far. Emily can go a whole day without even speaking.'

Newman glanced at his wife to show that he had experienced the same problem many times. Win marvelled at the patience he always showed. She had never known him complain about the fact that he had to care for a woman whose mind was crumbling as fast as her body. His example gave Win the courage to face her own domestic difficulties.

191

'Did an Inspector Colbeck come to see you, Gregory?'

'Yes,' he said with a grin. 'We had a nice, long chat that kept me out of that madhouse of a boiler room for a while. I took him for a shrewd man though he was far too smartly dressed for a town like Ashford.'

'I talked to him as well. Adam refused.'

'That was silly of him.'

'He hates policemen.'

'I don't admire them either,' confessed Newman, 'but I'm ready to accept their help when it's offered. We know that Nathan didn't commit that murder but we still haven't managed to find out who did. I reckon that this Inspector Colbeck might do the job for us. I'll speak to Adam and tell him to talk to the Inspector.'

'I can't promise it will do any good.'

'How is he?'

'Still hurting like the rest of us,' said Winifred, 'but he wants to hurt someone back. It doesn't matter who it is to him. Adam just wants to strike out.'

'Are you still having trouble at the shop?'

'Our custom is slowly drying up. Mr Hockaday won't supply us with meat any more and Bybrook Farm turned us down as well.'

'Bybrook!' he said, angrily. 'That's unforgivable.'

'No, Gregory It's only natural.'

'Nathan was not guilty of that murder.'

'He was hanged for it – that's enough for them.'

'Let me go to Bybrook Farm and have a word.'

'There's no point.'

'There's every point, Win. You've been buying their meat and poultry for years. It's high time someone told them about loyalty.'

'It's good of you to offer,' she said, reaching up to squeeze his arm, 'but you can't fight all our battles for us. You've done more than enough as it is and we can never repay you.'

'I don't look for repayment. I simply want to see some justice in this world. Think of all the money that Nathan paid to Bybrook Farm over the years – and to Silas Hockaday. They ought to be *ashamed*.'

'You'd better go. I don't want to make you late for work.'

'We must talk more another time.'

'I'd like that, Gregory.'

'And so would I.' He turned to his wife. 'Wouldn't I, Meg?' She continued to stare unseeingly in front of her. 'One of her bad days, I'm afraid. Meg will be better next time we meet.'

'I'm sure.' She raised her voice. 'Goodbye, Meg.'

'Goodbye, Win,' he said, clicking his tongue to make the horse move off again. 'And I won't forget to speak to Adam. He listens to me.'

'Sometimes.'

'He's the man of the house now. He's got responsibilities.'

'Yes,' she murmured, 'that's the trouble.'

After watching the cart rattle on up the High Street, she went back to Middle Row in time to find her stepson trying to chalk up some information on the board outside the shop. He wrote in large, laborious capitals.

'Good morning, Adam,' she said. 'You're up early.'

He smirked. 'I didn't sleep at all last night.'

'When was the body actually discovered?' asked Inspector Colbeck.

'First thing this morning,' replied Lugg.

'Why was there such a delay?'

'It was the last train from Paddock Wood and it stayed here all night. When it was due to leave this morning, someone tried to get into this carriage and found the chaplain.'

'Didn't anyone check that the carriages were empty last night?'

'The guard swears that he walked the length of the train and looked through all the windows but, of course, he couldn't see anyone lying on the floor now, could he?'

Colbeck was pleased to encounter Sergeant Obadiah Lugg again but he wished that it could have been in more propitious circumstances. After taking a train from Ashford, the two detectives had changed at Paddock Wood so that they could travel on the Maidstone line. News of the crime had spread quickly through the town and a crowd had gathered at the station to watch developments. Colbeck was relieved to see that Lugg had deployed his men to keep the inquisitive and the purely ghoulish at bay while the Inspector went about his work.

The scene that confronted him was very similar to the one he had found at Twyford, except that the wider gauge of the Great Western Railway had allowed for a carriage with more generous proportions. The prison chaplain was lying on his back, his mouth agape, his eyes wide open as if straining to leave their sockets. Rigor mortis had set in, turning the face into a marble carving of pain. Above his clerical collar was a dark red circle of dried blood. When he knelt to examine the wound, Colbeck saw that something very sharp and unyielding had cut deep into the neck of Reverend Narcissus Jones.

There were signs of a struggle – the victim's clothing was in disarray, his hair was unkempt, the padding on one seat had been badly torn – but it was one that the chaplain had clearly lost. Underneath his head was his Bible, acting as a spiritual pillow. On the floor near his hand was a small button that did not belong to the victim. Colbeck picked it up and saw the strands of cotton hanging from it.

'He managed to tear this from his attacker by getting a hand behind him,' said Colbeck. He indicated the gash in the padding. 'That could well have been caused by the heel of his shoe when he was threshing about.'

'The chaplain wouldn't give up without a fight, Inspector.'

'Unfortunately, he was caught off guard.'

'How?' said Lugg. 'If there are only two of you in a carriage, it's hard for one man to surprise the other.'

'Not if a third person distracts the victim.'

'A third person?'

'A woman, for instance,' explained Colbeck. 'When I spoke to the stationmaster at Paddock Wood, he remembers a woman on the platform

195

though he didn't see her board the train.'

'Very few women travel alone at that time of the evening.'

'Exactly. That's why this one interests me.'

'I've talked to our own stationmaster,' said Lugg, keen to show that he had not been idle, 'and he recalls that the train was two-thirds empty when it reached Maidstone. Albert knew most of them by name because he's been here for years. No stranger got off that train, he swears to that. Only regular travellers on the line.'

'The killer and his accomplice – if there was one, that is – would never have stayed on the train until it reached here. My guess is that the murder took place shortly after they left Paddock Wood because the killer could not take the risk that someone might get into the same carriage when they stopped at Yalding.'

'In that case,' concluded Lugg, 'he must have strangled the chaplain to death then made his escape at the station.'

'No, Sergeant.'

'Why not?'

'Because someone might have seen him getting off the train,' said Colbeck. 'And if, as I believe, there was a woman with him, they would surely have been noticed by the railway staff.'

Lugg was baffled. 'Then where and how did they get off, sir?'

'I can't give you a precise location but it's somewhere the other side of Yalding. The train slows down well short of the station and there's a grassy bank that runs along the side of the line.'

'You think that the killer jumped off?'

'That's what I'd have done in his place, wouldn't you?'

'Well, yes,' said Lugg, wrinkling his brow in concentration. 'I suppose that I would, sir. Except that I'm a bit old for anything as daring as leaping out of a moving train.'

'Approaching the station, it only goes at a snail's pace but it would still take some agility to get off. That tells us something about the killer.'

'What about this woman you mentioned?'

'She, too, must be quite athletic.'

'Younger people, then?'

'We'll see, Sergeant, we'll see.'

'Two people, leaping from the train,' said Lugg, rubbing his chin as he meditated. 'Surely, some of the other passengers would have spotted them doing that.'

'Only if they happened to be looking out of the window at the time. This, as you can see, is near the end of the train. There are only two carriages and a guard's van behind it. Naturally,' he went on, 'we'll speak to all the passengers who were on that train last night but, since there were so few of them, I doubt that we'll find a witness.'

'No, Inspector. If someone had seen people hopping off the train, they'd have reported it by now. The killer obviously chose the point to jump off very carefully.'

'Someone who knows this line well.'

Colbeck continued with his meticulous examination of the body and the carriage while Lugg looked on with fascination. After searching the dead man's pockets, Colbeck lifted the head so that he could slip the Bible out from under it.

197

He opened it at the page with the marker in it and read the text.

'Amazing how his head came to rest on that, isn't it?' said Lugg with his characteristic chuckle. 'Almost as if God's hand was at work.'

'It was the killer's hand, Sergeant,' announced Colbeck. 'He put the Bible there deliberately so that he could leave us this message.'

'Message?'

'St. Paul's Epistle to the Romans – chapter 12. He's crossed out verse 19 in order to make his point.'

'And what's that?'

'Something that every Christian knows – Vengeance is mine; I will repay, saith the Lord.' He closed the Bible and put it aside. 'It seems as if someone is determined to do the Lord's work for Him.'

Victor Leeming had been efficient. Having taken statements from the guard and the stationmaster, he had located a handful of passengers who had travelled on the train the previous evening and spoken to them as well. When he saw Colbeck coming down the platform towards him with Sergeant Lugg, he went swiftly forward to meet the Inspector.

'One of the managers of the South Eastern Railway is here, sir,' he said. 'He wants to know when the service can be resumed – so do all the people you see queueing outside the ticket office.'

'As soon as the body is removed,' said Colbeck, 'the train is all theirs, but I'd recommend that they detach that particular carriage. Nobody will want to travel in it now, anyway. Can you pass that on, Sergeant Lugg?'

'Yes, Inspector,' replied Lugg, 'and I've got men standing by with a stretcher – and with a blanket. The chaplain deserves to be covered when we carry him past that mob. I'm not having them goggling at Mr Jones. It's indecent.'

'Well, Victor,' said Colbeck as the policeman waddled off, 'have you discovered anything of value?'

'Not really, sir.'

'I thought not.'

'It was getting dark by the time that the train reached Maidstone last night so the guard couldn't see much when he glanced in through the windows. To be honest,' he added, 'I doubt if he even looked. He was too anxious to get home to his supper.'

'What about the stationmaster? Albert some-one, I gather.'

'Albert Scranton, crusty old soul. He recog-nised all the people who got off that train and said that everything looked perfectly normal. He wonders if the murder could have happened during the night.'

'While the train was out of commission?'

'Yes, Inspector – after he'd closed the station.'

'And how did the chaplain come to be in the railway carriage of a train that wasn't going any-where?'

'That's what I asked him,' said Leeming. 'Mr Scranton reckoned that he could have been tricked into meeting someone here.'

'Impossible,' said Colbeck, dismissing the

199

notion at once. 'There was a ticket in the dead man's pocket showing that he was travelling from Paddock Wood to Maidstone. Since he didn't get off here, he must have been killed during the journey.'

'So where did the murderer get off?'

'Somewhere on the other side of Yalding station.'

Leeming blinked. 'While the train was still *moving?*'

'Yes, Victor. It's only three miles or so between Paddock Wood and Yalding. The chaplain must have been dispatched shortly after the train left so that the pair of them had time to make their escape.'

'The pair of them?'

'I'm fairly certain that he had an accomplice.'

'You mean that woman?'

'Let's be off,' said Colbeck, using a hand to ease him into a walk. 'I'll give you all the details on the way there.'

'Where are we going, sir?'

'To prison, Victor.'

Henry Ferriday was more apprehensive than ever. Unable to sit still, he paced nervously up and down his office in the vain hope that movement would ease the tension that he felt. A rap on the door startled him and he called for the visitor to identify himself before he allowed him in. It was one of the men on duty at the prison gate, bringing news that two detectives from Scotland Yard were waiting to see him. Minutes later, Robert Colbeck and Victor Leeming were escorted to the

200

governor's office. When the Sergeant was introduced to Ferriday, he was given a clammy handshake. All three men sat down.

'This is an appalling business,' said Ferriday,
still reeling from the shock. 'Quite appalling.'

'You have my deepest sympathy,' said Colbeck,
softly. 'I know how much you relied on the
chaplain.'

'Narcissus was vital to the running of this
prison, Inspector. He exerted such influence over
the inmates. I don't know how we'll manage
without him. He's irreplaceable.'

'Is it true that he had a death threat some weeks
ago?'

Ferriday was taken aback. 'How on earth do
you know that?'

'That's immaterial. It was in connection with
the execution of Nathan Hawkshaw, wasn't it?'

'Yes, it was.'

'Did you happen to see the note?'

'Of course. Narcissus and I had no secrets
between us.'

'Can you recall what it said?'

'Very little, Inspector. Something to the effect
of 'We'll kill you for this, you Welsh bastard' –
only the spelling was dreadful. It was clearly
written by an ignorant man.'

'Ignorant men can still nurture a passion for
revenge.'

'Did you take the threat seriously?' asked
Leeming.

'Yes, Sergeant.'

'And what about the chaplain?'

'Narcissus shrugged it off,' said Ferriday, 'and

threw the note away. He refused to be frightened by anything. That was his downfall.'

'Did he take no precautions outside the prison?' said Colbeck.

'He didn't need to, Inspector. Well, you've met him. He was a big man, strong enough to look after himself. And having worked with villains for so long, he had a second sense where danger was concerned.'

'Not in this case,' observed Leeming.

'Do we have any idea what actually happened?' said Ferriday, looking from one to the other. 'All I know is that his body was discovered in a railway carriage this morning. How was he murdered?'

Colbeck gave him a brief account of his examination of the murder scene and told him that the body had now been removed from the train. The governor flinched when he heard about the Bible being placed under the head of the dead man and the verse that had been picked out.

'What kind of vile heathen are we dealing with here?' he shouted.

'A very clever one,' admitted Colbeck. 'This is the second murder that he's committed on a train and he's escaped on both occasions.'

'He must be caught, Inspector!'

'He will be.'

'This is one execution in which I'll take some pleasure,' said the governor, bunching his fists. 'He deserves to hang until every last breath is squeezed out of his miserable body.' He collected himself. 'Narcissus Jones was a great man. The whole prison will mourn him. It's not given to many chaplains to possess such extraordinary gifts.'

'He was a striking individual,' agreed Colbeck.

The governor looked over his shoulder. 'This prison is a sewer,' he said, contemptuously. 'We have the scum of the earth in here.'

'There's no need to tell us that,' said Leeming with a dry laugh. 'Our job is to catch the devils and send them on to places like this.'

'Most of them sneer at authority and go straight back to a life of crime as soon as we let them out. At least,' Ferriday went on, 'that's what used to happen until Narcissus Jones was appointed here. He gave the men a sense of hope and self-respect. He *improved* them as human beings. That's what made him so popular among the men.'

Colbeck had doubts on that score. 'I take it that the chaplain had a room at the prison?' he said.

'Yes, Inspector. He more or less lives within these walls.'

'But he did venture out?'

'From time to time.'

'What we need to establish is how the killer knew that he would be travelling on that train from Paddock Wood.'

'I can tell you that,' said Ferriday. 'The chaplain was much in demand as a speaker at churches and Christian gatherings. Most of the invitations he received had, of necessity, to be turned down because of his commitments here but he did like to give a talk or take a service somewhere once or twice a month.'

'Events that would have been advertised in a parish magazine.'

'And in the local newspapers, Inspector Colbeck. Our chaplain was a man of some renown. If you go to the church in Paddock Wood where he spoke yesterday, I daresay you'll find that they had a board outside for weeks in advance with details of his talk. It was St Peter's, by the way,' he added. 'They'll be horrified to hear the news.'

'So will everyone else,' said Leeming. 'Killing a man of the cloth is about as low as you can sink. I mean, it's sacrosanct.'

'Sacrilege,' corrected Colbeck, gently.

'I call it diabolical,' said Ferriday.

While they were talking a distant noise had begun inside the prison, slowly building until it became audible enough for them to become aware of it. All three of them looked at the window. The sound got progressively louder, spreading swiftly from wing to wing of the establishment with gathering force. Raised voices could be heard but the dominating note had a metallic quality to it as if a large number of inmates were using implements to beat on the bars of their cells in celebration. In its menacing rhythm, a concerted message was being sent to the governor by the only means at the prisoners' disposal. As the noise rose to a climax, Leeming looked across at the governor.

'What's that?' he asked.

'I'll have it stopped immediately,' declared Ferriday, getting up angrily from his seat and going to the door. 'That's intolerable.'

'Someone has heard the news of his death already,' noted Colbeck as the governor flung open the door to leave. 'Perhaps the chaplain was

204

not as universally popular as you believed.'

The loss of Emily Hawkshaw's appetite was almost as worrying to her mother as the long silence into which the girl had lapsed. She refused more meals than she ate and, of those that were actually consumed, the major portion was always left on the plate. Emily was in no mood to eat anything at all that morning.

'Come on, dear,' coaxed Winifred. 'Try some of this bread.'

'No, thank you.'

'It's lovely and fresh. Eat it with a piece of cheese.'

'I'm not hungry.'

'Some jam, then.'

'No.'

'You must eat *something*, Emily.'

'Leave me be, Mother.'

'Please – for my sake.' The girl shook her head. 'If you go on like this, you'll make yourself ill. I can't remember the last time you had a decent meal. In the past, you always had such a good appetite.'

They were in the room at the rear of the shop, facing each other across the kitchen table. Emily looked paler than ever, her shoulders hunched, her whole body drawn in. She had never been the most lively and outgoing girl but she had seemed very contented in the past. Now she was like a stranger. Winifred no longer knew her daughter. As a last resort, she tried to interest her in local news.

'Mr Lewis, the draper, is going to buy the shop

next door to his premises,' she told her. 'He wants to expand his business. Mr Lewis is very ambitious. I don't think it will be long before he's looking for another place to take over as well.' She gave a sigh. 'It's nice to know that someone in Ashford is doing well because we're not. Things seem to get worse each day. Adam says that hardly anybody came into the shop this morning.' Her voice brightened. 'Oh, I saw Gregory earlier on, did I tell you? He was taking his wife for a drive before he went off to the railway works. I know that *we* have our sorrows,' she continued, 'but we should spare a thought for Gregory. His wife has been like that for years and she'll never get any better. Meg can't walk and she can't speak. She has to be fed and seen to in every way by someone else. Think what a burden that must place on Gregory yet somehow he always stays cheerful.' She bent over the table. 'Can you hear what I'm saying?' she asked. 'We have to go on, Emily. No matter how much we may grieve, we have to go on. I know that you loved your father and miss him dreadfully but so do we all.' Emily's lower lip began to tremble. 'What do you think he'd say if he were here now? He wouldn't want to see you like this, would he? You have to make an *effort.*'

'I'll go to my room,' said Emily, trying to get up.

'No,' said Winifred, extending a hand to take her by the arm.

'Stay here and talk to me. Tell me what you *feel.* I'm your mother – I want to help you through this but I need some help in return. Don't you understand that?'

Emily nodded sadly. Winifred detached her arm. There was a long, bruised silence then it seemed as if the girl was finally about to say something but she changed her mind at the last moment. After a glance at the food on the table, she turned towards the door. Temper fraying slightly, Winifred adopted a sterner tone.

'If you won't eat your meals,' she warned, 'then there's only one thing I can do. I'll have to call the doctor.'

'No!' cried Emily, suddenly afraid. 'No, no, don't do that!'

And she fled the room in a flood of tears.

It was early evening before the two detectives finally got back to Ashford, having made extensive inquiries both in Maidstone and in Paddock Wood. Both of their notebooks were filled with details relating to the latest crime. On reaching the station, they were greeted by the three defining elements of the town – the grandeur of its church, the smell of its river and the cacophony of its railway works. A steady drizzle was falling and they had no umbrella. Colbeck was still grappling with the problems thrown up by the new investigation but Victor Leeming's mind was occupied by a more immediate concern. It was the prospect of dinner at the Saracen's Head that exercised his brain and stimulated his senses. The only refreshment they had been offered all day was at the prison and the environment was hardly conducive to any enjoyment of food. When they turned into the High Street, he began to lick his lips.

As they approached the inn, they saw that George Butterkiss was standing outside, his uniform now buttoned up properly and his face aglow with the desire to impress. He stood to attention and touched his helmet with a forefinger. Thoroughly damp, he looked as if he had been there some time.

'Did you find any clues, Inspector?' he asked, agog for news.

'Enough for us to act upon,' replied Colbeck.

'You will call upon us in due course, won't you?'

'If necessary, Constable.'

'How was the chaplain killed?'

'Quickly.'

'We can't discuss the details,' said Leeming, irritated by someone who stood between him and his dinner. 'Inspector Colbeck was very careful what information he released to the press.'

'Yes, yes,' said Butterkiss. 'I understand.'

'We know where to find you, Constable,' said Colbeck, walking past him. 'Thank you for your help this morning.'

'We appreciated it,' added Leeming.

'Thank you!' said Butterkiss, beaming like a waiter who has received a huge tip. 'Thank you very much.'

'By the way,' advised Leeming, unable to resist a joke at his expense. 'That uniform is too big for you, Constable. You should see a good tailor.'

He followed Colbeck into the Saracen's Head and made for the stairs. Before they could climb them, however, they were intercepted. Mary, the plump servant, hurried out of the bar. She subjected Leeming's face to close scrutiny.

'Those bruises are still there, Sergeant.'

'Thank you for telling me,' he said.

'Is there nothing you can put on them?'

'We were caught in the rain,' explained Colbeck, 'and we need to get out of these wet clothes. You'll have to excuse us.'

'But I haven't told you my message yet, Inspector.'

'Oh?'

'The gentleman said that I was to catch you as soon as you came back from wherever it is you've been. He was very insistent.'

'What gentleman, Mary?'

'The one who's taken a room for the night.'

'Did he give you a name?'

'Oh, yes,' she said, helpfully.

Leeming was impatient. 'Well,' he said, as his stomach began to rumble, 'what was it, girl?'

'Superintendent Tallis.'

'What!'

'He's going to dine with you here this evening.'

Suddenly, Victor Leeming no longer looked forward to the meal with quite the same relish.

Gregory Newman finished his shift at the railway works and washed his hands in the sink before leaving. Many of the boilermen went straight to the nearest pub to slake their thirst but Newman went home to see to his wife. During working hours, Meg Newman was looked after by a kindly old neighbour, who popped in at intervals to check on her. Since the invalid spent most of her time asleep, she could be left for long periods.

When he got back to the house, Newman found that the neighbour, a white-haired woman in her sixties, was just about to leave.

'How is she, Mrs Sheen?' he asked.

'She's been asleep since lunch,' replied the other, 'so I didn't disturb her.'

'Did she eat much?'

'The usual, Mr Newman. And she used the commode.'

'That's good. Thank you, Mrs Sheen.'

'I'll see you tomorrow morning.'

'I'll take Meg for another ride before I go to work.'

He went into the house and opened the door of the front room where his wife lay in bed. She stirred. Newman gave her a token kiss on the forehead to let her know that he was back then he went off to change out of his working clothes. When he returned, his wife woke up long enough to eat some bread and drink some tea but she soon dozed off again. Newman left her alone. As he ate his own meal in the kitchen, he remembered his promise to Winifred Hawkshaw. After washing the plates and cutlery, he looked in on his wife again, saw that she was deeply asleep and slipped out of the house. The drizzle had stopped.

He knew exactly where he would find Adam Hawkshaw at that time of the evening. A brisk walk soon got him to the High Street and he turned into the Fountain Inn, one of the most popular hostelries in the town. The place was quite full but nobody was talking to Hawkshaw, seated alone at a table and staring into his tankard with a quiet smile on his face. Walking jauntily into the bar, Newman clapped Hawkshaw on the shoulder by way of greeting. He then bought some beer for both of them and took the two glasses across to the table.

'I was hoping to catch you, Adam,' he said, sitting down.

'Just in time. I'll have to leave soon.'

'Where are you going?'

'That would be telling.'

Adam Hawkshaw grinned wolfishly then finished the dregs of his own drink before picking up the other tankard. He seemed in good spirits. Raising the tankard to Newman in gratitude, he took a long sip.

'How's business?' asked Newman.

'Bad,' said the other, 'though it did pick up this afternoon. Best day we've had all week. What about you, Gregory?'

'Boiler-making is a good trade. I was never apprenticed to it but those years in the forge stood me in good stead. The foreman is amazed how quickly I've picked things up.'

'Do you miss the forge?'

'I miss chatting to the customers,' said Newman, 'and I loved working with horses but the forge had to go. It was unfair on Meg to make so much noise underneath her bedroom. The new house is much quieter and she can sleep downstairs.'

'How is she?'

'As well as can be expected.' Newman lent over the table. 'But I haven't told you the news yet,' he said with a glint. 'One advantage of working by the railway station is that word travels fast. Our foreman heard it from the guard on a train to Margate. He's dead, Adam.'

'Who is?'

'The prison chaplain.'

'Never!'

'Murdered on a train last night,' said Newman, 'and I'm not going to pretend I wasn't pleased to hear it. Narcissus Jones made your father suffer in that prison.'

'Yes.'

'And someone called him to account.'

Adam Hawkshaw seemed unsure how to react to the tidings. His face was impassive but his eyes were gleaming. He took a long drink of beer from his tankard then wiped his mouth with a sleeve.

'That's great news, Gregory,' he said. 'Thank you.'

'I thought you'd be delighted.'

'Well, I don't feel sorry for that Welsh bastard, I know that.'

'Win ought to be told. It might cheer her up.' Newman sat back. 'I spoke to her early this morning. She said that you wouldn't talk to Inspector Colbeck.'

'Nor to any other policeman,' said Hawkshaw, sourly.

'But he might help us.' The other snorted. 'He might, Adam. We've all tried to find the man who *did* kill Joe Dykes but we've got nowhere so far. And we have jobs to do, people to support. This detective has the time to conduct a proper search.'

'Keep him away from me.'

'If we can convince him that your father was

innocent, we'll get him on our side – don't you see?'

'He thinks we killed that hangman.'

'That doesn't mean we don't *use* him, Adam.'

'Forget it.'

'Win agrees,' said Newman. 'If we co-operate with this Inspector, he may do us all a favour and help to clear your father's name. You want the man who really killed Joe Dykes to be caught, don't you?'

Hawkshaw gave him a strange look then took another long sip from his tankard. Wiping his mouth again, he got to his feet.

'Thanks for the beer, Gregory.'

'Where are you going?'

'I've got to see somebody.'

Without even a farewell, Adam Hawkshaw walked out of the bar.

Robert Colbeck was sporting a red silk waistcoat when he joined his superior for dinner and Edward Tallis glared at it with unconcealed distaste. Victor Leeming's apparel was far more conservative but he was criticised by the Superintendent for being too untidy. It did not make for a pleasant meal. Tallis waited until they had ordered from the menu before he pitched into the two detectives.

'What the deuce is going on?' he demanded. 'I send you off to solve one railway murder and a second one is committed.'

'We can hardly be blamed for that, sir,' said Colbeck.

'But it happened right under your noses.'

'Paddock Wood is some distance from here and

213

the chaplain was killed somewhere beyond it. We have a rough idea of the location.'

'How?'

'Because we walked beside the line,' said Leeming, able to get a word in at last. 'The Inspector's theory was right.'

'It wasn't a theory, Victor,' said Colbeck, quickly, 'because we know that the Superintendent frowns upon such things. It was more of an educated supposition.'

'Don't try to bamboozle me,' warned Tallis.

'It would never cross my mind, sir.'

Leeming took over. 'Inspector Colbeck believed that the killer committed his crime soon after the train left Paddock Wood, then jumped off it before it reached the first station at Yalding.'

'A preposterous notion!' said Tallis.

'We proved it.'

'Yes,' said Colbeck. 'A shallow embankment runs alongside the line outside Yalding. We found a place where there were distinct footprints, as if someone had landed heavily and skidded down the grass. My supposition was correct.'

'I dispute that,' said Tallis. 'Those marks could have been caused by someone else – children, playing near the line, for instance.'

'A child would not leave a murder weapon behind, sir.'

'What?'

'We found it in some bushes close to the footprints.'

'A piece of wire,' said Leeming, 'covered in blood.'

'Then why didn't you bring it back with you?'

asked Tallis. 'That's the kind of evidence we desperately need.'

'It's upstairs in my room, Superintendent,' Colbeck reassured him. 'The stationmaster at Yalding was kind enough to give me a bag in which to carry it. So at least we know where and precisely how the prison chaplain met his death.'

'What we really need is a suspect.'

'Two of them, sir.'

Tallis was sceptical. 'Not this phantom woman again, surely?'

'She was no phantom, sir,' said Leeming. 'There were two clear sets of footprints beside the railway line. The Inspector guessed it the moment we heard the news. The woman was there to distract the victim.'

'Both of them will hang when they're caught.'

'Yes,' said Colbeck, 'for the two murders.'

'You're certain we're dealing with the same killer here?'

'Without a shadow of doubt, sir.'

'Convince me,' said Tallis, thrusting out his chin.

Colbeck had rehearsed his report in advance. It was clear and concise, containing a description of what the Inspector had found at the scene of the crime and the supporting evidence that had been gathered. Leeming felt impelled to add his own coda.

'We even called at St Peter's church in Paddock Wood,' he said. 'They still had the board that advertised the talk by the Reverend Jones. A large congregation turned up with lots of strangers among them.'

'Including, I should imagine, the killer,' said Tallis.

'He and this woman must have followed the chaplain to the station and seized their opportunity.'

'Yes,' said Colbeck. 'They realised that there wouldn't be many people on that train so there was a good chance that their victim would get into an empty carriage. The rest we know.'

'It means that I now have *two* railway companies demanding action from me,' complained Tallis. 'If anything, the management of the South Eastern Railway is even more strident. They say that disasters come in threes. Which is the next railway company to harry me?'

The waiter arrived with the first course and the discussion was suspended for a little while. Colbeck nibbled his bread roll and Leeming overcame his discomfort in the presence of the Superintendent to tuck into his soup. Only when Tallis had tasted his own first mouthful of soup was he ready to resume.

'This all began with an illegal prizefight,' he noted.

'With respect, sir,' said Colbeck, 'it goes back before that. It really started with the murder of Joseph Dykes.'

'That case is closed.'

'Not to the people who believe Hawkshaw was wrongly hanged.'

'Courts of law do not make errors on that scale.'

'It's conceivable that they did so in this instance,' said Colbeck. 'But, in one sense, it doesn't really matter. It's a question of perception, sir. The people who supported Nathan Hawkshaw saw what they honestly believed was an innocent man going to the gallows. They went to exhaustive lengths on his behalf.'

'So?'

'One of those people is the man we're after, Superintendent, and there are dozens to choose from. What happened at Twyford, and on that train last night to Maidstone, is rooted here in Ashford. The killer is probably less than a couple of hundred yards from where we sit.'

'Then find him, Inspector.'

'We will. Meanwhile, precautions have to be taken.'

'Of what kind?'

'We have to ensure that Jacob Guttridge and Narcissus Jones are not joined by a third victim,' said Colbeck. 'We're dealing with a ruthless man here. He may not be content with killing the hangman and the prison chaplain. Other people may be in danger as well.'

'What other people?'

'For a start,' said Leeming, chewing a bread roll, 'the policeman who came here to arrest Hawkshaw. His name is Sergeant Lugg.'

'Empty your mouth before you speak,' snapped Tallis.

'Sorry, sir.'

'Sergeant Lugg has been warned,' said Colbeck, 'but the person we need to contact is the barrister who led the prosecution team. He tore the case for the defence apart and made the guilty verdict inevitable.'

'What's his name?'

'Patrick Perivale, sir. I'm wondering if he received one of those death threats as well.'

'Where are his chambers?'

'In Canterbury. I'm sending Victor over there tomorrow.'

Leeming was uneasy. 'Not by train, I hope.'

'By any means you choose. Mr Perivale must be alerted.'

'Very sensible,' said Tallis. 'We don't want another murder on our hands. You, I presume, will be remaining here, Inspector?'

'Yes, sir,' replied Colbeck, 'but I require your assistance. The petition for the release of Nathan Hawkshaw was sent to the Home Secretary, who refused to grant a reprieve. I'd be grateful if you could get a copy of the names on that petition from the Home Office.'

'Can't you ask for the names from that fellow who organised the campaign? What did you call him – Gregory Newland?'

'Newman, and the answer is no. He knows why we're in the town and he's not going to betray one of his friends by volunteering his name. We'll have to dig it out for ourselves. The only place we can get the full list is from The Home Office.'

'Use your influence, Superintendent,' said Leeming.

'We'd be eternally grateful, sir.'

Tallis was unconvinced. 'Will that really help to solve the murder of the prison chaplain?'

'And that of Jacob Guttridge,' said Colbeck, firmly. 'Somewhere in that list of names is the man that we want and – in all probability – his female accomplice.'

Winifred Hawkshaw was pleased to see her visitor. After a fruitless attempt to get her daughter to eat anything more than a slice of apple, she gave up and slumped in a chair. Emily retired to her room once more. Winifred could do nothing but brood on a malign Fate. A once happy home was now a place of unrelieved misery. The arrival of Gregory Newman lifted her out of her gloom.

'Hello,' she said, accepting a kiss on the cheek. 'Come in.'

'I won't stay long,' he told her, removing his hat and going into the parlour ahead of her. 'I have to get back to Meg soon.'

'Of course. Sit down for a moment, anyway.'

'I will.'

'Can I get you some tea?'

'No, thank you.' Newman took a seat and Winifred sat opposite him. They exchanged a warm smile. 'I had a few words with Adam earlier on. He was in a peculiar mood.'

'He's been strange all day, Gregory. But at least he was civil to us and we must be thankful for that. Since the execution, Adam's been like a bear with a sore head.'

'I had some glad tidings for him.'

'Oh?'

'The prison chaplain was murdered on a train last night.'

'Mr Jones?' She gave a cry of delight but was instantly penitent. 'God forgive me for rejoicing in the death of another!'

'You're entitled to rejoice, Win.'

219

'No, it's wrong. He was a man of the cloth.'

'Are you forgetting what Nathan said about him?'

'It makes no difference. This is awful news. How did he die?'

'I don't know the details,' said Newman, disappointed by her response. 'Our foreman passed it on to me. All that he picked up was that the chaplain was found dead in a railway carriage at Maidstone.'

'Did you tell this to Adam?'

'Yes, and I thought that he'd be glad as well.'

'Wasn't he?'

'It was difficult to say, Win. There was hardly any reaction at all and that was surprising when you think of the way that he damned the chaplain at the execution. It's odd,' Newman went on, scratching his beard, 'but it was almost as if Adam already knew.'

'How could he?'

'I don't know and he didn't stay long enough for me to find out. He rushed off. Adam said that he had somewhere to go and, judging by the way he left, it must have been somewhere important.'

'He told me that he didn't sleep at all last night.'

Newman was puzzled. 'Then what is the lad up to?' He dismissed the subject and turned his attention to her. 'Let's put him aside for the moment, shall we? The person I'm really worried about is you, Win.'

'Why?'

'You looked so drawn and harassed when I saw you this morning. So desperately tired. To be honest, I thought you were sickening for something.'

'Don't fret about me, Gregory.'

'But I do.'

'I'm worn down, that's all,' she explained. 'This whole business has dragged on for so long. Nathan's arrest was such a shock to me and the trial was unbearable. As for the execution...'

'You shouldn't have been there. I did try to stop you.'

'He was my husband. I *had* to be there.'

'It was too much to ask of any wife, Win. It was foolish to put yourself through all that suffering outside Maidstone prison.'

'Nathan wanted me, Gregory. I gave him my word.'

She looked down at her hands as unpleasant memories surged back to make her temples pound. He could see her struggling to compose herself. Newman gave her time to recover. When she eventually glanced up, she manufactured a smile.

'I'm sorry. I try not to think about it or the pain floods back.'

'I know.'

'At least Emily was spared the sight. It would have been cruel to make her go with us. She adored Nathan – he could *talk* to her somehow. Emily always turned to him for help, not me.'

'He was a good father to her.'

'She trusted him.'

He looked upwards. 'She spends all her time in her room?'

'Yes, it's so worrying. She won't eat and she

221

won't speak to me.'

'Would you like *me* to talk to her?'

'You?'

'Yes,' said Newman, persuasively. 'Emily and I always got on very well. She adored horses so she'd spend hours watching me at work in the forge. She talked all the time then. If a horse was well-behaved, I'd let her hold the bridle sometimes. Emily liked that.'

'Nathan always talked about buying her a pony of her own.'

'Let me see if *I* can draw her out.'

Win was hesitant. 'I'm not sure that it would do any good.'

'It will certainly do no harm. Bring her down.'

'Well...'

'And leave us alone for five minutes,' he suggested.

Winifred considered the request for some time before she agreed to it. At length she went upstairs and Newman could hear a muted discussion with her daughter. Emily's voice then rose in protest but it was instantly silenced by her mother's rebuke. After another minute, tentative footsteps came down the stairs and the girl entered the room.

Newman stood up and gave her a welcoming smile.

'Hello, Emily,' he said.

'Hello.'

'I haven't seen you for a while. Come and sit down so that I can have a proper look at you.' She glanced nervously around the room then perched on the edge of an upright chair near the door.

222

'That's better,' he said, resuming his own seat. 'I was just talking to your mother about they way that you used to hold the horses for me at the forge.'

'Yes.'

'You enjoyed that, didn't you?' Emily nodded. 'I don't work as a blacksmith any more but I've still got my own horse and cart. If ever you want to come for a ride, you only have to ask. You can take the reins.'

'Thank you.'

'It's important to get out. You mustn't lock yourself away in your room like a hermit. We all miss Nathan terribly,' he went on, lowering his voice to a soothing whisper. 'When I take my wife to church on Sundays, the first prayer I say is for your father. Do you pray for him as well?'

'All the time.'

'But we haven't seen you in church for weeks. You mustn't be afraid of what other people may say,' he told her. 'You've just as much right as anyone to go to St Mary's. There are one or two narrow-minded busybodies who may turn up their noses when they see anyone from this family but you've nothing at all to be embarrassed about, Emily. Your father was innocent.'

'I know,' she said, 'that's what makes it so hard to bear.'

'You loved him dearly, didn't you?' said Newman. 'Nathan was so proud of you. He was always talking about his lovely daughter. That's how he thought of you, Emily – as his own child. And you looked on him as your real father, didn't you?'

'I tried.'

'You were a proper family, all four of you.'

She shifted on her seat. 'Can I go now, Mr Newman?'

'Am I upsetting you in some way?'

'No, no.'

'Because we both want the same thing, Emily, you know that, don't you? I'll strain every bone in my body to prove that your father did not commit that crime. That's why I got that petition together,' he said, 'and you saw how many people signed that.'

'You did so much for us, Mr Newman.'

'Then let me do a little more,' he offered, spreading his arms. 'Let me help you through this period of mourning. *Share* your grief, Emily. Talk to your mother about it. Come to church with us and show the town that you can bear this loss because you know in your heart that your father was not a killer. Stand up and be *seen*.'

'I can't, Mr Newman,' she said, shaking her head.

'Why not?'

'Don't ask me that.'

'But we're entitled to know. Your father was the best friend I ever had, Emily,' he said, soulfully, 'and I stood by him until the end. I'll not give up on him now. Nathan may be dead but he still needs us to speak up for him, to show everyone how hard we'll fight to protect his good name. You care, don't you?'

'Yes,' she said, tearfully. 'I care more than anyone.'

'Then why can't you open your heart to us?'

She stood up. 'Let me go,' she bleated, taking out a handkerchief.

'Wait,' he said, getting up to cross over to her. 'Just tell me one thing, Emily. Why are you pushing away the people who love you? Mourn for your father with the rest of us.'

'No, Mr Newman!'

'It's the right and proper way.'

'I'm sorry but I can't do it.'

'Why ever not?'

'You wouldn't understand.'

'Why not?' he pressed.

She looked him in the eyes. 'Because I feel too *ashamed*.'

Chapter Nine

After a hearty breakfast and a discussion as to how the investigation would proceed, Superintendent Edward Tallis was driven in a trap to Ashford station to catch a train back to London. Both detectives were pleased to see him go but it was Victor Leeming who really savoured his departure. Slapping his thigh, he let out a controlled whoop of delight.

'He's gone at last!' he cried.

'He was only here for about twelve hours,' Colbeck pointed out.

'It seemed much longer somehow. If I have to spend a night away from my wife, I'd rather not do it under the same roof as Mr Tallis. It unsettled me, knowing that His Lordship was only a few doors away. I took ages to get off and I expect that you did as well.'

'No, I slept extremely well.'

'Well, I didn't. It's not the same without Estelle,' said Leeming. 'I missed her, Inspector.'

'And I'm sure that she missed you just as much, Victor. The sooner we solve these crimes, the sooner you can get back to her.'

Having bidden farewell to their superior, they were still under the portico outside the Saracen's Head. It was relatively early but the town was already busy. People were bustling around the streets, shops were getting ready to open and the pandemonium from the railway works showed that the first shift of the day had begun. Across the road from them, an ironmonger was going slowly through his morning routine of displaying his wares outside his shop. He heaved out a long tin bath.

'That's what I could do with,' said Leeming, covetously. 'A bath.'

'Take one back to your wife as a present.'

'I meant that I'd like to soak in warm water for half an hour.'

'I was only teasing you,' said Colbeck, smiling. 'There's no time for either of us to relax, I fear. You need to be on your way to Canterbury.'

'How will I find this Mr Perivale?'

'His chambers are in Watling Street. Get his address from there.'

'What if he doesn't live in the city?'

'Then go out to where he does live,' instructed Colbeck. 'The man could be unaware of the danger that he's in. But that's not the only reason you must speak to him, Victor. He was a key figure in the trial of Nathan Hawkshaw. I've several questions I'd like you to put to him,' he said, extracting a folded sheet of paper from his pocket and handing it over. 'I've written them down for you. Peruse them carefully.'

'Wouldn't it be better if you put them to him in person?'

'Ideally, yes.'

'You were a barrister. You talk the same language as this man.'

'Unfortunately, I can't be in two places at once.'

'Where will you be, sir?'

'Here in Ashford, for the most part,' replied Colbeck. 'I want to make some inquiries at the station then I need to have a longer talk with Winifred Hawkshaw and with Gregory Newman. To mount the sort of campaign that they did was a formidable challenge to anyone yet they brought if off somehow.'

'It failed all the same.'

'That's irrelevant. When I paid my first visit to Maidstone, I saw some of the leaflets calling for Hawkshaw's release, and Sergeant Lugg showed me the advertisements placed in the local newspapers. They were all well-written and must have cost money to produce. Who penned that literature and how could they afford to have it printed?'

'Are they likely to tell you?'

'It depends how I ask.'

'I'd better go and find Constable Butterkiss,'

said Leeming. 'He's promised to drive me to Canterbury in a trap. If he keeps on at me about the Metropolitan Police, it's going to be a very long journey. Oh, I do hope that I can get back home soon!' he went on, earnestly. 'I miss everything about London. And so do you, I daresay, sir.'

'My place is here in Kent at the moment.'

'Even you must have regrets.'

'Regrets?'

'Yes,' said Leeming, broaching a topic he had never touched on before. 'You must be sorry to be apart from Miss Andrews. I know that you like to spend time with her occasionally.'

'I'll certainly look forward to seeing her again,' admitted Colbeck, smiling to himself at the unexpected mention of her name, 'but Madeleine understands that my work always takes precedence.'

'That won't stop the lady missing you, sir.'

Madeleine Andrews scanned the newspaper report with a combination of interest and horror. Her father was eating his breakfast at their house before going off to work. She indicated the paper.

'Have you seen this?' she asked.

'I read it on the way back from the shop, Maddy. When I saw that Inspector Colbeck was on the front page again, I knew you'd want to see it for yourself.'

'A prison chaplain has been murdered.'

'Yes.'

'What kind of monster could want to kill a priest?'

'Oh, I can think of one or two priests *I'd* like to have met in a dark alley,' said Andrews with a grim chuckle.

'Father!' she said, reproachfully.

'I'm only being honest, Maddy. When I was a boy, there was a Canon Howells at St Saviour's who could make a sermon last a whole afternoon, and he'd give you such a clout if you dozed off in the middle. I should know. I had a clip around my ear from him more than once.'

'This is not something to joke about.'

'It's no joke. I'm serious. Canon Howells was a holy terror and his deacon, Father Morris, was even worse.' He swallowed the last of his porridge. 'But I don't think you have to look very far to find the man who killed that Reverend Jones.'

'What do you mean?'

'It was obviously someone who'd been in Maidstone prison.'

'That's not what Robert thinks,' said Madeleine, pointing to the article on the front page. 'He's certain that the murderer was the same man who killed the public hangman in that excursion train.'

'Yes, a former prisoner with a grudge.'

'Robert is the detective. You keep to driving trains.'

'I'm entitled to my opinion, aren't I?' he asked, combatively.

'You'd give it in any case,' she said, fondly, 'whether you're entitled to or not. You've got an opinion on everything, Father. Nobody can silence Caleb Andrews – even when he's wrong.'

229

'I'm not wrong, Maddy.'

'You don't know all the facts of the case.'

'I know enough to make a comment.'

'I'd sooner trust Robert's judgement.'

'Well, he does have an eye for picking things out,' he said, wryly, 'I have to admit that. After all, he picked you out, didn't he?'

'Please don't start all that again,' she warned. 'You should be off.'

'Let me finish this cup of tea first.'

'Which train are you driving today?'

'London to Birmingham.'

'You must know that route by heart.'

'I could drive it with my eyes closed,' he boasted, draining his cup and getting up from the table. 'Thanks for the breakfast, Maddy.'

'You need a good meal inside you at the start of the day.'

'You sound like your mother.'

'What time will I expect you?'

'Not too late.'

'Will you be going for a drink first?'

'Probably,' he replied, taking his hat from the peg behind the front door. 'I'll call in for a beer or two and tell them all what I think about this latest murder. They listen to me.'

'Do you give them any choice?'

'I've got this instinct, Maddy. Whenever there's a serious crime, I always have this strange feeling about who committed it. Look at this case of the dead chaplain.'

'It's shocking.'

'The person who done him in just has to be someone who was locked up in that prison and

230

took against the Reverend Jones. It was the same with that hangman,' he went on, putting on his hat and opening the front door. 'All prisoners hate Jack Ketch because he could be coming for them with his noose one day.'

'Yes,' she said, immersed in the paper again.

'That's enough to make anyone want revenge.'

'Maybe.'

'I know that I would if I was put behind bars.'

'Of course.'

'Goodbye, Maddy. I'm off.'

'Goodbye.'

'Don't I get my kiss?' he whined.

But she did not even hear his complaint. Madeleine had just noticed a small item at the bottom of the page. Linked to the main story, it reminded her poignantly of the last time that she had seen Robert Colbeck. An idea suddenly flashed into her mind. Caleb Andrews had to manage without his farewell kiss for once.

As soon as the shop opened, Adam Hawkshaw brought some meat out and started to hack it expertly into pieces before setting them out on the table. Other butchers were also getting ready for customers in Middle Row but all they had in response to their greeting was a curt nod of acknowledgement. The first person to appear in the passage was Inspector Colbeck. He strolled up to Adam Hawkshaw.

'Good morning,' he said, politely.

'I've nothing to say to you.'

'Are you always so rude to your customers?'

'Customers?'

'Yes,' said Colbeck. 'I didn't come to buy meat but I am shopping for information and I'm not leaving until I get it. If you insist on refusing to speak to me, of course, I may have to arrest you.'

'Why?' rejoined the other, testily. 'I done nothing wrong.'

'Obstructing a police officer in the exercise of his duties is a crime, Mr Hawkshaw. In other words, a decision confronts you.'

'Eh?'

'We can either have this conversation here and now or we'll have it when you're in custody. It's your choice.'

'I got to work in this shop.'

'Then we'll sort this out right away, shall we?' said Colbeck, briskly. 'Where were you the night before last?'

'That's my business,' retorted Hawkshaw.

'It also happens to be my business.'

'Why?'

'I need to establish your whereabouts during that evening.'

'I was in my room,' said the other, evasively. 'Satisfied now?'

'Only if we have a witness who can verify that. Do we?' Hawkshaw shook his head. 'I thought not.'

'I was on my own.'

'Gregory Newman told me that you rented a room near the Corn Exchange. There must have been someone else in the house at the time. Your landlord, for instance?'

'I can't remember.'

'I'll ask him if *he* remembers.'

'He wouldn't know,' said Hawkshaw. 'I come and go as I please.'

'I've just been talking to the stationmaster at Ashford station. He recalls a young man of your build and colouring, who took a train to Paddock Wood on the evening in question.'

'It must have been someone else, Inspector.'

'Are you quite certain of that?'

Hawkshaw met his gaze. 'I was alone in my room all evening.'

'Studying the Bible, I daresay.'

'What?'

'No,' said Colbeck on reflection, glancing at the board beside him. 'I don't think you have much time for reading – or for writing either. That's evident. I doubt if you'd even know where to find St Paul's Epistle to the Romans, would you?' Hawkshaw looked mystified. 'There you are,' Colbeck went on, 'that wasn't too difficult was it? I'll have some more questions for you in time but I'll not hold you up any longer. I need to speak to your stepmother now.'

'She's not in,' claimed the butcher.

'Then I wonder whose face I saw in the bedroom window when I crossed the High Street just now. Is it possible that Mrs Hawkshaw has a twin sister living over the shop?' Hawkshaw glowered at him. 'Excuse me while I speak to someone who's a little more forthcoming.'

Meat cleaver in his hand, Hawkshaw moved across to block his way but the determination in Colbeck's eye made him change his mind. He stood aside and the detective went into the shop before tapping on the door at the rear. It was not

233

long before he and Winifred Hawkshaw were sitting down together in the parlour. He held his top hat in his lap. She was watchful.

'I finally had a conversation with your stepson,' he said.

'Oh?'

'He seems to be having a problem with his memory.'

'Does he, Inspector?'

'Yes, Mrs Hawkshaw. He tells me that he spent the night before last alone in his room yet a witness places him – or someone very much like him – at the railway station that evening. Have you any idea where he might have been going?'

'Adam was where he said he was.'

'How can you be so sure?'

'Because we brought him up to be honest,' said Winifred, stoutly. 'I know you think he might have had something to do with the murder of the prison chaplain but you're wrong. Adam is like his father – he's been falsely accused.'

'I haven't accused him of anything, Mrs Hawkshaw.'

'You suspect him. Why else are you here?'

'I wanted to eliminate him from my inquiries,' said Colbeck, levelly, 'and I did so by discovering if he had any acquaintance with the New Testament. Patently, he does not. The reason I wanted to see you is to ask a favour.'

She was suspicious. 'What sort of favour?'

'When your husband was arrested, several people rallied around you and supported your campaign.'

'Nathan had lots of friends.'

'Did you keep a record of their names?'

'Why should I do that?'

'Because you knew how to organise things properly.'

'That was Gregory's doing, Inspector.'

'I fancy that you were intimately involved in every aspect of the campaign, Mrs Hawkshaw. You had the biggest stake in it, after all. He was your husband. That's why you fought tooth and nail to save him.'

'Yes,' she said, proudly, 'and I'd do the same again.'

'I respect that.'

'Yet you still think Nathan was guilty.'

'Oddly enough, I don't,' he told her. 'In fact, having learned more details of the case, I'd question the safety of the conviction.'

'Do you?' Winifred Hawkshaw regarded him with frank distrust. 'Or are you just saying that to trick me?'

'Trick you into what?'

'I'm not sure yet.'

'All I want to know is who helped you in your campaign and how you funded the whole thing? There's no trickery in that, is there?'

'I can't remember all the names,' she said. 'There were far too many of them. Most people paid a little towards our expenses.'

'And what about the rescue attempt at Maidstone prison?'

'I told you before – I know nothing of that.'

'But you must have approved of it.'

'If I thought I could have got my husband out,' she said, 'I'd have climbed over the wall of the

235

prison myself.' She looked at him quizzically. 'Are you married, Inspector?'

'No, I'm not.'

'Then you'll never understand how I felt. Nathan was everything to me. He came along at a very bad time in my life when I had to fend alone for Emily and myself. Nathan saved us.'

'But he wasn't your first husband, was he?'

'No, he wasn't. Martin was killed in an accident years ago.'

'In a fire, I believe. What were the circumstances exactly?'

'Please!' she protested. 'It's painful enough to talk about one husband who was taken away from me before his time. Don't ask me about Martin as well. I've tried to bury those memories.'

'I'm sorry, Mrs Hawkshaw. It was wrong of me to bring it up.'

'Have you finished with me now?'

'One last question,' he said, choosing his words with care. 'Your second husband had good reason to loathe Joseph Dykes. What impelled him to go after the man was the assault on your daughter, Emily. Can you recall what she told you about that incident?'

'Why should you want to know that?'

'It could be important. What precisely did she say to you?'

'Nothing at all at the time,' answered Winifred, 'because I wasn't here. I was visiting my mother. It was Nathan who had to console her. As soon as he'd done that, he left Adam in charge of the shop and charged off to find Joe Dykes.'

'With a meat cleaver in his hand.'

'You sound just like that barrister at the trial.'

'I don't mean to, Mrs Hawkshaw,' he apologised. 'Your daughter had just been through a frightening experience. She must have told your husband enough about it to make him seek retribution. Though I daresay that she reserved the full details for you.'

'No,' she confessed. 'That's the strange thing. She didn't.'

'But you're her mother. Surely, she confided in you?'

'If only she had, Inspector. I tried to get the story out of her but Emily refused to talk about it. She said that she wanted to forget it but there's no way that she could do that. In fact,' she went on as if realising something for the first time, 'that's when it really started.'

'What did?'

'This odd behaviour of hers. Emily pulled away from me. We just couldn't talk to each other properly again. I don't know what Joe Dykes did to her in that lane but I was his victim as well. He took my daughter away from me.'

Victor Leeming was in luck. When he got to the venerable city of Canterbury, he discovered that Patrick Perivale was at his chambers, interviewing a client. The detective did not mind waiting in the gracious Georgian house that served as a base for the barrister. After a ride through the countryside with Constable George Butterkiss at his most aggravating, Leeming felt that he was due some good fortune. Taking out the piece of paper that Colbeck had given him, he memorised the questions by repeating them over and over again in his head. Eventually, he was shown into a large, well-proportioned, high-ceilinged room with serried ranks of legal tomes along one wall.

Standing in the middle of the room, Patrick Perivale did not even offer him a handshake. A smart, dark-haired, dapper man in his forties with curling side-whiskers, he wore an expression of disdain for lesser mortals and he clearly put his visitor in that category. The bruising on Leeming's face made him even less welcome to someone who resented unforeseen calls on his time.

'What's this all about, Sergeant?' he inquired, fussily.

'The trial of Nathan Hawkshaw.'

'That's history. There's no cause to reopen it.'

'I simply want to discuss it, sir.'

'Now?' said Perivale, producing a watch from his waistcoat pocket and looking at it. 'I have another appointment soon.'

'You'll have to hear me out first,' said Leeming, doggedly.

'Must I?'

'Inspector Colbeck was most insistent that I should warn you.'

'About what?' asked the other, putting his watch away. 'Oh, very well,' he went on, going to the chair behind his desk. 'I suppose that you'd better sit down – and please make this visit a short one, Sergeant.'

'Yes, sir.' Leeming lowered himself into a high-backed leather armchair that creaked slightly. 'Are you aware that the man who hanged Nathan Hawkshaw was murdered recently?'

238

'I do read the papers, you know.'

'Then you'll also have picked up the information that the Reverend Jones, the prison
chaplain from Maidstone, was killed the night
before last in a railway carriage.'

'Is this some kind of test for me on recent news
events?'

'Both murder victims received death threats
from someone.'

'Not for the first time, I warrant.'

'But it was for the last,' stressed Leeming. 'One
of them heeded the warning but was nevertheless
killed. The other – the chaplain – took no notice
of the threat and lost his life as a result.'

'I was truly sorry to hear that,' said Perivale. 'I
met the chaplain once and he struck me as a
fellow of sterling virtue – not always the case with
Welshmen. As a nation, they tend to veer towards
the other side of the law.'

'Did *you* receive a death threat, sir?'

'That's none of your damned business,
Sergeant!'

'I think that it is.'

'I refuse to divulge any information about what
I receive in relation to my cases. It's a question of
professional confidentiality.'

Leeming was blunt. 'I'd say it was a question of
staying alive.'

'That's a very offensive remark.'

'There's a pattern here, sir. Two people have
had–'

'Yes, yes,' said the barrister, interrupting him. 'I
can see that, man. When you deal with criminal
law, you inevitably make enemies but that does

not mean you let the imprecations of some worthless villain upset the even tenor of your life.'

'So you *did* get a death threat.'

'I didn't say that. What I am telling you – if only you had the grace to listen – is that I am very conscious of the dangers appertaining to my profession and I take all sensible precautions. To be more precise,' he continued, opening a drawer to pull out a gun, 'I always carry this when I go abroad in the streets. It's a Manton pocket pistol.'

'Jacob Guttridge was armed as well but it did him no good.'

'Thank you for telling me, Sergeant.' He put the pistol away then stood up. 'Now that you've delivered your message, you can go.'

'But I haven't asked the questions yet, sir.'

'What questions?'

'The ones given to me by Inspector Colbeck.'

'I don't have time to play guessing games.'

'The Inspector used to be a barrister,' said Leeming, irritated by the other man's pomposity. 'Of course, he worked in the London criminal courts where they get the important cases that provincial barristers like you would never be allowed to touch. If you don't help me,' he cautioned, 'then Inspector Colbeck will come looking for you to know the reason why. And he won't be scared off by that toy pistol of yours either.'

Patrick Perivale was checked momentarily by Leeming's forthrightness but he soon recovered his natural arrogance. One hand on a hip, he gave a supercilious smile.

'Why did your Inspector leave the bar?'

'Because he wanted to do something more worthwhile.'

'Nothing is more worthwhile than convicting criminals.'

'They have to be caught first, sir,' said Leeming. 'Besides, you don't always see justice being done in court, do you? I've sat through too many trials to know that. I've watched guilty men go free because they had a clever barrister and innocent men convicted because they didn't.'

'I hope that you don't have the effrontery to suggest that Nathan Hawkshaw was innocent.'

'I don't know the facts of the case well enough, sir, but Inspector Colbeck has studied it in detail and he's raised a few queries.'

'He's too late. Sentence has been passed.'

'It was passed on the hangman and the prison chaplain as well.'

'Are you being frivolous, Sergeant?'

'No, sir,' said Leeming, 'I was just pointing out that this case is by no means over for those who feel aggrieved on Hawkshaw's behalf. Two lives have been lost already. We'd like to catch the killer before anyone else joins the list. To do that, we need your help.'

'What can I possibly do?'

'Tell us something about the trial. Newspaper reports can only give us so much. You were *there*.'

'Yes,' said the other with self-importance, 'and I regard it as one of my most successful cases. The reason for that is that I refused to be intimidated. I had to walk through a baying crowd outside the court and defy the howling mob in the public gallery.'

'The judge had them cleared out, didn't he?'

'Not before they'd made their point and weaker vessels would have been influenced by that. I was simply spurred on to get the conviction that Hawkshaw so obviously deserved.'

'And how did you do that?'

'By making him crack under cross-examination.'

'He maintained his innocence until the end.'

'But he'd already given himself away by then,' said Perivale with a note of triumph in his voice. 'He could not give a convincing explanation of where he was at the time of the murder. That was his undoing, Sergeant. He had no alibi and I taunted him with that fact.'

'He claimed that he walked away from Lenham to think things over and then returned in a calmer frame of mind.'

'Calmer frame of mind – balderdash! The fellow was in a state of sustained fury. He had to be to inflict such butchery on his victim. It was an assault of almost demonic proportions.'

'I know. I visited the scene of the crime.'

'Then you'll have seen how secluded it was. Hawkshaw chose it with care so that he'd not be disturbed.'

'But how did he persuade Dykes to join him there?'

'That's beside the point.'

'I don't think so,' said Leeming, remembering one of Colbeck's notes. 'Dykes would hardly agree to meet him in a private place when he knew that the butcher was after him. He'd have stayed drinking in the Red Lion where he was safe. And what proof is there that Hawkshaw was in that part of the woods, anyway?'

'He was seen there by a witness.'

'After the event. Yet there was no blood on him.'

'You're dragging up the same feeble argument as the defence,' said the barrister. 'Because there was no blood on him, they argued, he could not have committed such a violent crime. Yet there was a stream nearby. Hawkshaw could easily have washed himself clean.'

'What about his clothing? He couldn't wash blood off that.'

'Quite right. That's why his coat mysteriously disappeared.'

'His coat?'

'Yes,' continued Perivale, almost crowing over him. 'That's one little detail that you and the Inspector missed. When he went to that fair in Lenham, Hawkshaw was wearing a coat. A number of witnesses testify to that, including his son. Later, however, when he was observed by the youth returning to the farm, he had no coat on and was thoroughly dishevelled, as if he'd been involved in vigorous exercise. In other words,' he said, coming to the end of his peroration, 'he discarded his coat because it was spattered with the blood of his victim.'

'Was the coat never found?'

'No – he must have buried it somewhere.'

'Then why wasn't it discovered? The police searched the area.'

'They were only looking for a certain part of Joseph Dykes's anatomy that had gone astray – a fact that tells you everything about the mentality of the killer. Taken together, the missing coat and the absence of an alibi put Hawkshaw's neck into the hangman's noose. Hundreds of people were at that fair with more arriving every minute. If Hawkshaw really had walked off towards Ashford, somebody *must* have seen him but no witnesses could be found.'

'So where do you think he was?'

'Searching the wood for a place to commit a murder.'

'In the hope that Dykes would happen to pass by later on?'

'He enticed him there somehow.'

'I wouldn't be enticed by an angry butcher with a meat cleaver.'

'You never met Nathan Hawkshaw,' countered the barrister. 'He was an evil man and capable of any ruse. You never saw the murder dancing in those black eyes of his. When I had him in the dock,' he said, raising a finger, 'I showed the jury what he was really like. I put him under such stern cross-examination that this decent, kind, popular, reasonable man that all his friends claimed him to be suddenly turned into a snarling animal. I've never seen such a vivid expression of guilt on the face of any prisoner.'

'You have no reservations about that trial then?'

'None whatsoever.'

'What's happened since has not alarmed you in any way?'

'I'm upset that two men have died unnecessarily and in such a brutal way, but I have no fears at all for my own safety. When I led the

244

prosecution in that trial, I was doing my bounden duty.'

'And you believe that you convicted the right man.'

'Without a scintilla of doubt,' said Perivale, lapsing into his courtroom manner. 'The evidence against Nathan Hawkshaw was quite overwhelming. Any other barrister in my place – including your Inspector Colbeck – would have done exactly the same thing as me and striven hard for a death sentence.'

'I hope that you won't make a habit of this, Inspector,' said Gregory Newman with a laugh. 'If you keep taking me away from my work, the foreman will start to dock my wages.'

'I won't keep you long.'

'We could hardly talk in the boiler shop.'

'That's a pity,' said Colbeck. 'I'd have been interested to see more of what goes on in there.'

'You really like locomotives, don't you?'

'They fascinate me.'

'They fascinate lots of people, Inspector, but only if they're running along railway lines. You're the first person I've ever met who wants to see how they're built.'

'Very noisily, by the sound of it.'

Newman grinned. The two men were standing outside the railway works in Ashford. A train was just leaving the station, adding to the industrial uproar and sending up clouds of smoke into an overcast sky. Colbeck waited until it had rolled past them.

'I like to know the way that things are put

245

together,' said Colbeck. 'I come from a family of cabinetmakers, you see. As a boy, I was always intrigued at the way that my father could take a pile of wood and turn it into the most exquisite desk or wardrobe.'

'There's nothing quite so fancy in making a boiler.'

'It takes skill and that impresses me.'

'You wouldn't say that if you worked here,' said Newman. His grin was inviting. 'What can I tell you this time, Inspector?'

'I'd like to hear how far you've got.'

'In what?'

'Your search for the man who *did* kill Joseph Dykes.'

'Not as far as we'd like,' conceded the other, 'but we won't give up. The trouble is that we have such limited time. That holds us back.'

'Us?'

'Me and the friends helping me.'

'How many of them are there?'

'A handful,' said Newman, 'and you can include Win Hawkshaw as well. Nobody is more eager to track down the culprit than Win.'

'Do you have any suspects?'

'Yes, Inspector. One, in particular.'

'Why didn't you mention him before?'

'Let's be frank about this. You didn't come to Ashford because you thought Nathan was innocent, did you? You only came to find out who killed Jake Guttridge and now you have the murder of the prison chaplain on your plate.'

'All three murders are closely linked.'

'But only two of them have any interest for

246

you,' said Newman.

'That's untrue. If you have any new information relating to the murder of Joseph Dykes, I
want to hear it.'

'Why?'

'I told you, Mr Newman. I like to know the way
that things are put together, whether they're
desks, wardrobes, steam locomotives or crimes. I
thrive on detail.'

The other man scratched his beard as he pon-
dered. Like Winifred Hawkshaw, he had a deep
distrust of policemen but he seemed to sense that
Colbeck might be different from the general run.

'His name is Angel,' he said.

'Your suspect?'

'Yes. We don't know his surname – he may not
even have one – but he's been through here a
number of times over the years. I once shoed a
horse for him, only to discover that he'd stolen it
from Bybrook Farm.'

'Did you report it to the police?'

'Of course, but Angel was long gone by then. I
didn't catch sight of him again for eighteen
months. He moves around, Inspector. He's half-
gypsy. That type never settle.'

'Why do you think that he was Dykes's killer?'

'He was at that fair in Lenham. I saw him going
into the Red Lion with my own eyes. According
to the landlord, he and Joe Dykes had a disagree-
ment over something or other. When Joe left,
Angel must have sneaked out after him.'

'Do you have any proof of that?'

'None at all. But we know how Angel can
harbour grudges.'

247

'Dykes was killed with a meat cleaver belonging to Nathan Hawkshaw. How could this man possibly have got hold of that?'

'By stealing it, Inspector. The day before the fair, it went missing from the shop along with a number of other items. Nathan told them that at the trial,' said Newman with a hint of anger, 'but they didn't believe him. That weasel of a prosecution barrister said that Nathan could have faked the burglary himself.'

'Was this other man – Angel – mentioned in court?'

'I raised his name but nobody would listen to me.'

'You have no firm evidence, then?'

'Not yet, maybe,' said Newman, 'but I'll beat it out of Angel when he shows that ugly face of his in Ashford again.'

'I should imagine he'll have the sense to keep well clear of here.'

'We'll find him somehow, Inspector.'

'And then?'

Newman grinned. 'He'll be passed on to the police.'

'I hope so,' warned Colbeck. 'We don't want anyone taking the law into their own hands. You said that a small number of you are looking out for this man.'

'That's right.'

'Perhaps you'd give me their names, Mr Newman. And while we're on the subject, I'd appreciate the names of everyone who supported the campaign to free Hawkshaw.'

'I'm afraid that I can't do that, Inspector.'

'Why not?'

'Because there are far too many of them to remember. In any case, some people simply gave some money to our fighting fund. They only did that if they could remain anonymous.'

'I see.'

'As for the handful I mentioned, you've already met one of them.'

'Adam Hawkshaw?'

'Yes. The others wouldn't want their names to be known.'

'Is that a polite way of saying that you won't divulge them?'

'I can see why you became a detective,' said Newman with amusement. He became brusque. 'If you want us on your side, you've got to help us in return. Angel is the man we want. Find him, Inspector.'

'There are other suspects at the top of my list first.'

'An innocent man was hanged. Doesn't that matter to you?'

'It matters a great deal, Mr Newman. Innocent or guilty, his death has already provoked two murders. What other crimes are there to come?' He changed his tack. 'How well do you know Emily Hawkshaw?'

'As well as anyone, I suppose,' said Newman, hunching his shoulders. 'My wife and I were not blessed with children – Meg was struck down when she was still a young woman. Nathan let us share his family. Both of the children used to come and watch me at the forge, especially Emily. She was there every day at one time.'

'Why has she drawn away from her mother?'

'What makes you ask that?'

'I spoke to Mrs Hawkshaw earlier,' explained Colbeck. 'She was upset at the way that she and her daughter seem to have lost touch. She traced it back to the assault made by Joseph Dykes.'

'That put the fear of death into Emily.'

'Then you'd expect her to turn to her mother. Yet she didn't.'

'I know.'

'Have you *any* idea why that might be?'

'No, Inspector,' said Newman, sadly. 'I don't. As a matter of fact, I had a word with the girl yesterday and asked her why she spurned her mother at a time when they needed to mourn together. At first, Emily wouldn't say anything at all. When I pushed her, she told me that she wanted to be left alone because she felt ashamed at Nathan's death.'

'Ashamed?'

'She feels responsible for it somehow.'

'That's absurd.'

'She's only a young girl, after all. In her eyes, none of this would have happened if she hadn't been attacked in that lane. She ran home in tears to Nathan and he swore that he'd make Joe Dykes pay. Can you see it from Emily's point of view, Inspector?'

'Yes – she gave her stepfather a motive.'

'It helped to put him on that scaffold.'

'Was Emily at the fair that day?'

'Yes, she went with Adam.'

'Did they stay together?'

Newman chuckled. 'I can see that you don't

250

know much about country fairs,' he said. 'It's a big event for us. We don't just go there to buy and sell. There are games, dances, races, competitions and they even put on a little play this year. Emily and Adam would have split up and enjoyed the fair in their own way.'

'Did either of them witness the argument with Dykes?'

'I can't honestly say.'

'You were the one who stopped Hawkshaw from going into the Red Lion after Dykes. You persuaded him to go home, didn't you?'

'That's right, Inspector.'

'Then why didn't either of the children go as well?'

'I've no idea. I was back in my cousin's forge by then.'

'I find it surprising that Emily, in particular, didn't go with him.'

'He was in no real state for company, Inspector. He stalked off.'

'But I'm told he was very protective towards his stepdaughter.'

'He was, believe me.' He caught sight of someone out of the corner of his eye. 'Ah,' said Newman, grimacing, 'the foreman has come out to see why I'm not earning my pay. I'll have to go, Inspector.'

'Of course. Thank you for your help.'

'If you want to talk to me again, come to my house in Tufton Street. Number 10. You'll find me sitting with my wife most evenings,' he said, walking away. 'I don't go far from Meg.'

'I'll bear that in mind,' said Colbeck.

There were several moments when Madeleine Andrews regretted the impulse that had taken her to Hoxton again, but she felt obscurely that her visit might be of some help to Robert Colbeck and that made her stay. Never having been in a Roman Catholic church before, she felt like an intruder and, since she was wearing black, the charge of impostor could be levelled at her as well. The morning newspaper had printed the bare details of Jacob Guttridge's funeral. Madeleine was one of a pitifully small congregation. The widow and the other mourners occupied the front row of seats while she remained at the rear of the church.

Even from that distance, she found the service profoundly moving, conducted by Father Cleary in a high-pitched voice that reached every corner of the building without effort. The burial was even more affecting and, though she only watched it from behind one of the statues in the graveyard, Madeleine felt as if she were actually part of the event. Louise Guttridge tossed a handful of earth on to the coffin then turned away. The rest of the mourners took their leave of Father Cleary and dispersed.

To Madeleine's horror, the widow walked slowly in her direction. The interloper had been seen. Madeleine feared the worst, expecting to be castigated for daring to trespass on private grief, for attending the funeral of a man she had never known and could not possibly admire. Pursing her lips, she braced herself for deserved censure. Louise Guttridge stopped a few yards from her and beckoned with a finger.

'Come on out, please,' she said.

'Yes, Mrs Guttridge,' agreed Madeleine, emerging from her refuge.

'I thought it was you, Miss Andrews.'

'I didn't mean to upset you in any way.'

'I'm sure that you didn't. You came out of the goodness of your heart, didn't you?' She looked around. 'That's more than I can say for my son. Michael and his wife could not even bother to turn up today. You, a complete stranger, have more sympathy in you than our only child.'

'It was perhaps as well that he did stay away, Mrs Guttridge.'

'Yes, you may be right.'

'At a time like this, you don't want old wounds to be opened.'

'That's true, Miss Andrews.'

'Your son has his own life now.'

'Rebecca is welcome to him!'

Louise Guttridge's face glowed with anger for a second then she went off into a reverie. It lasted for minutes. All that Madeleine could do was to stand there and wait. She felt highly embarrassed. When she saw that Father Cleary was heading their way, Madeleine squirmed and wished that she had never dared to go to Hoxton that morning. She began to move slowly away

'Perhaps I should go, Mrs Guttridge,' she said.

'No, no. Wait here.'

'I sense that I'm in the way.'

'Not at all,' said the other woman, taking her by the wrist.

'Stay here while I speak with Father Cleary. I

253

need to talk to you alone afterwards.' She gave a semblance of a smile. 'And don't worry about me, Miss Andrews. Jacob has been laid to rest now and I'm at peace with myself. God has provided.'

Edward Tallis was feared for the strong discipline he enforced but he was also respected for his effectiveness. As soon as he reached London, he drafted a letter to the Home Office in response to Colbeck's request. Sent by hand, it prompted an instant response and he was able to dispatch the document to Ashford. It arrived by courier that afternoon as Robert Colbeck and Victor Leeming sat down to a late luncheon at the Saracen's Head. The Inspector took the long sheet of paper out of the envelope with a flourish.

'Here it is, Victor,' he said, unfolding it. 'The petition I wanted.'

'Well done, Mr Tallis!'

'I knew that he wouldn't let us down.'

'I never believed that the Home Secretary would bother to keep this sort of thing,' said Leeming. 'I imagined that he'd tear it into strips and use them to light his cigars.'

'You're being unfair to Mr Walpole. His duty is to consider every appeal made on behalf of a condemned man. In this case, he did not see any grounds for a reprieve.'

'They wanted more than a reprieve, sir.'

'Yes,' said Colbeck as he read the preamble at the top of the petition. 'It's an uncompromising demand for Nathan Hawkshaw's freedom, neatly written and well-worded.'

'How many names in all?'

'Dozens. Fifty or sixty, at least.'

Leeming sighed. 'Will we have to speak to them all?'

'No, Victor. My guess is that the man we're after will be somewhere in the first column of names. Those are the ones they collected first, the ones they knew they could count on.'

'Who's at the top, sir – Hawkshaw's wife?'

'Yes,' replied Colbeck, 'followed by his son. At least, I take it to be Adam Hawkshaw's signature. It's very shaky. Then we have Gregory Newman, Timothy Lodge, Horace Fillimore, Peter Selling and so on. The one name we don't seem to have,' he said, running his eye down the parallel columns, 'is that of Emily Hawkshaw. Now, why wouldn't the girl sign a petition on behalf of her stepfather?'

'You'll have to ask her, Inspector.'

'I will, I promise you.'

'Are there any women on the list – apart from the wife, that is?'

'Quite a few, Victor. By the look of it, most of the names are beside those of their husbands but there are one or two on their own.'

'Perhaps she's one of them.'

'She?'

'The female accomplice you believe is implicated.'

'I think that there's a good chance of that. However,' said Colbeck, setting the petition aside, 'let's order our meal and exchange our news. I long to hear how you got on. Was your visit to Canterbury productive?'

'Far more productive than the journey there

and back, sir.'

'Constable Butterkiss?'

'He keeps on treating me as if I'm a recruiting sergeant for the Metropolitan Police,' grumbled Leeming. 'I had to listen to his life story and it was not the most gripping adventure I've heard. Thank heavens I never became a tailor. I'd hate to be so servile.'

'He'll learn, I'm sure. He's raw and inexperienced but I sense that he has the makings of a good policeman. Bear with him, Victor. Apart from anything else, he can help us to identify the people on this list.'

The waiter took their order and went off to the kitchen. Leeming was able to describe his jarring encounter with Patrick Perivale. He quoted some of the barrister's remarks verbatim.

'He was exactly the sort of man you said he'd be, Inspector.'

'The egotistical type that never admit they can make a mistake. I've met too many of those in the courtroom,' said Colbeck.

'Winning is everything to them. It doesn't matter if a human life is at stake. All that concerns them is their standing as an advocate.'

'I could see how Mr Perivale had built his reputation.'

'Why – did he hector you?'

'He tried to,' said Leeming, 'but I put him in his place by telling him that you'd been a barrister in London.'

'No word of thanks for warning him, then?'

'He was insulted that we'd even dared to do so.'

'Outwardly, perhaps,' decided Colbeck, 'but it

256

was all bravado. I can't believe that even he will ignore the fact that two murders have already been committed as a result of that trial.'

'I agree, sir. I reckon that he loaded that pistol of his as soon as I left. At one point,' said Leeming with a laugh, 'I thought he'd fire the thing at me. I got under his skin somehow.'

'You were right to do so, Victor, or you'd have learned nothing.'

'What worried me was that detail about the missing coat.'

'Yes, that disturbs me as well.'

'Hawkshaw was unable to explain its disappearance.'

'I can see why the prosecution drew blood on that point,' said Colbeck, thoughtfully. 'It further undermined Hawkshaw's defence. Nothing you've told me about him has been very flattering or, for that matter, endearing, but Mr Perivale must be an able man or he'd not have been retained in the first place. Unlike us, he saw all the evidence and made a judgement accordingly. I'm beginning to wonder if my own assumptions have been wrong.'

'You think that Hawkshaw was guilty?'

'It's a possibility that we have to entertain, Victor.'

'Then why are so many people certain of his innocence?' asked Leeming, touching the petition. 'They must have good cause.'

'Yes,' said Colbeck, 'they must. But thank you for making the journey to Canterbury. It's thrown up some valuable information.'

'What about you, sir?'

'Oh, I, too, have made a number of discoveries.'

Colbeck went on to describe what he had gleaned from the various people to whom he had talked that morning. In the middle of his account, the first course arrived and they were able to start their meal while the Inspector continued. Leeming seized on one detail.

'Adam Hawkshaw went to Paddock Wood that night?' he said.

'Someone resembling him did.'

'Can't you get the stationmaster to make a positive identification? All we have to do is to take Hawkshaw along to the station.'

'Even if it *was* him on that train from Ashford, it doesn't mean that he was implicated in the murder. Adam Hawkshaw can barely write. How could someone that illiterate be able to pick out a verse in the Bible to serve his purpose?'

'Was he travelling alone?'

'Yes, Victor, and that's another point in his favour. He had no female companion. Given his surly manner,' said Colbeck, 'I doubt if he ever will have one. I'm certain that he lied to me about being at home that evening but I don't think he's a suspect for the chaplain's murder.'

'Who else travelled from Ashford to Paddock Wood on that train?'

'Several people. Some of the men from the railway works live there and use the line regularly. The only reason that Adam Hawkshaw – or the person who looked like him – stayed in the stationmaster's mind was that he was so irascible.'

'I still think that Hawkshaw needs watching.'

'He'll stay under observation, Victor. Have no fear.'

'What about this other character?' asked Leeming, spooning the last of his soup into his mouth. 'This gypsy that they're looking for?'

'His name is Angel, apparently.'

'He could turn out to be an Angel of Death.'

'If he really exists.'

'Is there any doubt about that, Inspector?'

'I don't know,' said Colbeck, sprinkling more salt on his food. 'I'm not entirely sure how I feel about Gregory Newman. He's very plausible but he's obviously keeping certain things from me. This story about someone called Angel being the potential killer of Dykes might just be a way of misleading us.'

'Why would Newman want to do that?'

'We're policemen, Victor. We represent the law that sent his best friend to the gallows. He could be trying to confuse us out of spite.'

'I'm confused enough already,' admitted Leeming.

'We can soon find out if Newman was telling the truth. You simply have to ask your assistant if he's even heard of this man, Angel.'

'My assistant?'

'Constable Butterkiss,' said Colbeck, 'and while you're at it, show him this petition and ask him where we could find the first ten people on that list, excluding Newman and the Hawkshaw family.'

'Why must I always be landed with George Butterkiss?'

'The two of you clearly have an affinity, Victor.'

'Is that what it's called?' Leeming was disconsolate. 'I can think of a very different word for it, sir.'

He sat back while the waiter cleared the plates away. 'What will you be doing this afternoon?'

'Trying to speak to Emily Hawkshaw. There's something about her behaviour that troubles me. I want to find out what it is.'

Emily lay on her bed and stared up at the ceiling. She was so preoccupied that she did not hear the tap on the door. When her mother came into the room, the girl sat up guiltily.

'You startled me,' she said.

'I didn't mean to do that, Emily. I just came to warn you.'

'About what?'

'Inspector Colbeck just called again,' said Winifred Hawkshaw. 'He's very anxious to talk to you.'

Emily was alarmed. 'Me?'

'Yes.'

'Why?'

'It's nothing to be afraid of, dear,' said her mother, sitting on the bed beside her. 'He needs to ask you a few questions, that's all.'

'Is he still here?'

'No, I thought you'd need fair warning so I told him that you were asleep. The Inspector will be back later.'

'What do I say to him?'

'The truth, Emily He's trying to help us.'

'None of the other policemen did that.'

'Their minds were already made up. They'd decided that your father was guilty and that was that. Inspector Colbeck is different. You'll have to speak to him, dear. He won't go away.'

'What does he want to know?'

'You'll find out when he comes back.'

'Didn't he say?'

'He did wonder why you didn't sign that petition for your father's release,' said her mother, 'and I told him it was because you were too young, but he still felt your name should have been there. So do I, really.' She touched the girl's arm. 'Why wasn't it?'

'I don't know.'

'Gregory asked you to sign but you refused.'

'I had too many things on my mind,' whimpered the girl. 'I just couldn't bring myself to do it somehow. As soon as I saw that list of names, I lost heart. I *knew* that it would do no good.'

'It showed everyone what we felt, Emily.'

'I felt the same.'

'Then you should have been part of it.'

Emily stifled a cry then began to convulse wildly. Putting her arms around the girl, her mother tried to control the spasms but to no avail. Emily seemed to be in the grip of a seizure.

'What's wrong with you?' asked Winifred, tightening her hold on her daughter. 'Emily, what's wrong?'

Robert Colbeck had been in the town for over twenty-four hours without really exploring it properly. While he waited to speak to Emily Hawkshaw, therefore, he decided to stroll around Ashford and take the measure of the place. It also gave him an opportunity to reflect on what he had learned earlier and to sift through the evidence that Leeming had obtained from his visit to

261

Canterbury. The solution to the two murders aboard trains, he felt, still lay buried in the case of Nathan Hawkshaw. Until he could unearth the truth about the first killing, he was convinced that he would never catch those responsible for the other crimes. Deep in thought, he ambled gently along.

Industry was encroaching fast but Ashford was still largely a pleasant market town with a paved High Street at its heart and an ancient grammar school that, for well over two hundred years, had educated privileged pupils and turned them into useful citizens. Shops dominated the centre of the town. It was in the side-streets that houses, tenements and artisans' villas abounded. Having stopped to admire the soaring church tower of St Mary's, Colbeck read some of the inscriptions on the gravestones surrounding it, sobered by the thought that Nathan Hawkshaw had been deprived of his right to a last resting place there.

Continuing his walk, he went in a loop around the town so that he could see every aspect of it, his striking appearance causing much interest among the townspeople and more than a few comments. When he finally returned to the High Street, he elected to call once more on Emily Hawkshaw but, before he could turn into Middle Row, he saw what at first he took to be some kind of mirage. Walking towards him with purposeful strides was an attractive young woman in a dress that he had seen once before. Colbeck rubbed his eyes to make sure that they were not deceiving him. At that moment, the woman saw him and quickened her step at once. Colbeck was astonished and excited to see her.

It was Madeleine Andrews.

Chapter Ten

Robert Colbeck escorted her into the Saracen's Head and indicated some chairs. When they sat opposite each other near the window, he beamed at her, still unable to believe that she had come all the way from London to see him. For her part, Madeleine Andrews was delighted to have found him so quickly and to have been made so welcome. She was amused by the look of complete surprise on his face.

'What's the matter, Robert?'

'Did you really take the train by yourself?' he asked.

'My father's an engine driver,' she reminded him. 'I'm well used to the railway, you know.'

'Young ladies like you don't often travel alone. Except, of course,' he added, gallantly, 'that there's nobody quite like you, Madeleine.' She smiled at the compliment. 'You create your own rules.'

'Do you disapprove?'

'Not in the least. But how did you know where to find me?'

'Your name was on the front page of the newspaper. The report said that you were conducting an investigation in Ashford.'

'Ah, well,' he said with a sigh, 'I suppose it was

too much to ask to keep my whereabouts secret for long. We'll have a batch of reporters down here in due course, assailing me with questions I refuse to answer and generally getting in my way. I'd hoped to avoid that.' He feasted his eyes on her. 'I'm so pleased to see you, Madeleine.'

'Thank you.'

'Where were you going when I saw you in the High Street?'

'To the Saracen's Head.'

'You *knew* that I was staying here?'

'No,' she replied, 'but I guessed that you'd choose the best place in the town. When I asked at the station where that would be, they directed me here.'

He laughed. 'You're a detective in your own right.'

'That's what brought me to Ashford.'

Mary interrupted them to see if they required anything. Colbeck ordered a pot of tea and some cakes before sending the girl on her way. He switched his attention back to Madeleine again.

'I'm a detective by accident,' she explained. 'I don't know why but, when I saw that Jacob Guttridge's funeral was being held today, I took it into my head to go to it.'

He was stunned. 'You went to Hoxton *alone?*'

'I do most things on my own, Robert, and I felt perfectly safe inside a church. Unfortunately, there was hardly anyone there for the service. It was very sad.'

'What about Michael Guttridge?'

'No sign of him – or of his wife. That upset his mother.'

264

'You spoke to her?'

'Yes,' said Madeleine. 'I didn't mean to. I kept out of the way during the ceremony and didn't think that she even knew I was there. But Mrs Guttridge did notice me somehow. She said how grateful she was to see me then invited me back to the house.'

'What sort of state was she in?'

'Very calm, in view of the fact that she'd just buried her husband. Mrs Guttridge must have a lot of will power. After my mother's funeral, I was unable to speak, let alone hold a conversation like that.'

'I put it down to her religion.'

'She told me that her priest, Father Cleary, had been a rock.'

'Why did she invite you back to the house?'

'Because she wanted to talk to someone and she said that it was easier for her to speak to a stranger like me.'

'So you were a mother-confessor.'

'Mrs Guttridge seemed to trust me,' said Madeleine. 'She didn't admit this but I had the feeling that she was using me to get information back to you. She's not an educated woman, Robert, but she's quite shrewd in her own way. She knew that you only took me to the house because she was more likely to confide in a woman.'

'I'm glad that I did take you, Madeleine,' he said with an admiring glance. 'Extremely glad.'

'So am I.'

'Much as I like Victor, you're far more appealing to the eye.'

'Oh, I see,' she said with mock annoyance, 'I

265

was only there as decoration, was I?'

'Of course not,' he replied. 'I took you along for the pleasure of your company and because I thought that Mrs Guttridge would find you less threatening than a Detective Inspector from Scotland Yard.'

'She did, Robert.'

'What did you learn this time?'

'Quite a lot,' said Madeleine. 'After we left the house that day, she prayed for the courage to go into the room that her husband had always kept locked. It was a revelation to her.'

'I took away the most distressing items in his bizarre collection but I had to leave some of his souvenirs behind – and his bottles of brandy.'

'It was the alcohol that really upset her. She only agreed to marry Jacob Guttridge because he promised to stop drinking. She firmly believed that he had. But what disturbed her about that room,' she went on, 'was how dirty and untidy it was. She called it an animal's lair. You saw how house-proud she was. She was disgusted that her husband spent so much time, behind a locked door, in that squalor.'

'Gloating over his mementos and drinking brandy.'

'It helped Mrs Guttridge to accept his death more easily. She said that God had punished him for going astray. When she saw what was in that room, she realised that her husband's life away from her was much more important to him than their marriage. I tried to comfort her,' said Madeleine. 'I told her that very few men could meet the high moral standards that she set.'

'Jacob Guttridge went to the other extreme. He executed people on the gallows then gloried in their deaths.' Colbeck chose not to mention the hangman's passion for retaining the clothing of his female victims. 'It gave him a weird satisfaction of some sort. But I'm holding you up,' he said, penitently. 'Do please go on.'

'It was what she told me next that made me come here, Robert. On the day when he hanged Nathan Hawkshaw, his wife expected him home that night. But he never turned up.'

'He was probably too afraid to leave the prison in case the mob got their hands on him. What explanation did he give her?'

'That he was delayed on business.'

'Had that sort of thing happened before?'

'Once or twice,' she said. 'Mrs Guttridge was vexed that, as soon as he got home on the following day, he went straight out again to see some friends in Bethnal Green.'

'He must have been going to the Seven Stars.'

'What's that?'

'A public house where fighters train. As an avid follower of the sport, Guttridge knew it well – though he called himself Jake Bransby whenever he was there. Over a hundred people from the Seven Stars went to that championship contest on the excursion train.'

'How did you find that out?'

'Victor Leeming visited the place for me,' said Colbeck, 'though he was not exactly made welcome.' He flicked a hand. 'However, I'm spoiling your story. I'm sorry.'

'It was what happened afterwards that puzzled

Mrs Guttridge,' she said, 'though she thought nothing of it at the time.'

'Of what?'

'That evening – when he got back from Bethnal Green – her husband seemed to have been running and that was most unusual for him. He was out of breath and sweating. For the next few weeks, he never stirred out of the house after dark. He used to go off to these 'friends' regularly, it seems, but he suddenly stopped altogether.'

'Did she know why?'

'Not until a few days after her husband had been murdered. One of her neighbours – an old Irish woman – was leaving some flowers on her step when Mrs Guttridge opened the door and saw her there. They'd never talked properly before,' said Madeleine, 'but they'd waved to each other in the street. The old woman lived almost opposite.'

'And?'

'She remembered something.'

'Was it about Guttridge?'

'Yes, Robert. She remembered looking out of her bedroom window the night that he came hurrying back home. A man was following him. He stood outside the house for some time.'

'And Guttridge said nothing to his wife about this man?'

'Not a word. I thought it might be important so I made a point of calling on the old lady – Mrs O'Rourke, by name – when I left.'

'That was very enterprising.'

'She told me the same story.'

'Was she able to describe this man?'

'Not very well,' said Madeleine, 'because it was getting dark and her eyesight is not good. All she could tell me was he was short and fat. Oh, and he walked in this strange way.'

'With a limp?'

'No, he waddled from side to side.'

'Age?'

'Mrs O'Rourke couldn't be sure but the man wasn't young.' She smiled hopefully. 'Was I right to pass on this information to you?'

'Yes,' he said, 'and I'm very grateful. It could just be someone he fell out with at the Seven Stars but, then, a man spoiling for a fight wouldn't have gone all the way back to Hoxton to confront him. He would have tackled Guttridge outside the pub,' he went on, recalling what had happened to Leeming. 'It sounds to me as if this man was more interested in simply finding out where Guttridge lived.'

'Do you think that he might be the killer?'

'It's possible, Madeleine, but unlikely.'

'Why?'

'A short, fat man with a strange walk doesn't strike me as someone who could overpower Jacob Guttridge, not to mention Narcissus Jones. I shook hands with the prison chaplain. He was a powerful man.'

'Then who do you think this person was, Robert?'

'An intermediary,' he decided. 'Someone who found out where the hangman lived and who established that he'd be on that excursion train. He could be the link that I've been searching for,' said Colbeck, 'and you've been kind enough to

269

find him for me.'

'Ever since you took me to Hoxton, I feel involved in the case.'

'You are – very much so.'

Mary arrived with a tray and set out the tea things on the table. She stayed long enough to pour them a cup each then gave a little curtsey before going out again. Colbeck picked up the cake stand and offered it to Madeleine.

'Thank you,' she said, choosing a cake daintily, 'I'm hungry. I was so anxious to get here that I didn't have time for lunch.'

'Then you must let me buy you dinner in recompense.'

'Oh, I can't stay. I have to get back to cook for Father. He likes his meal on the table when he comes home of an evening.' She nibbled her cake and swallowed before speaking again. 'I made a note of the train times. One leaves for London on the hour.'

'I'll come to the station with you,' he promised, 'and I insist that you take the rest of those cakes. You've earned them, Madeleine.'

'I might have one more,' she said, eyeing the selection, 'but that's all. What a day! I attend a funeral, go back to Hoxton with the widow, talk to an Irishwoman, catch a train to Ashford and have tea with you at the Saracen's Head. I think that I could enjoy being a detective.'

'It's not all as simple as this, I'm afraid. You only have to ask Sergeant Leeming. When he went to the Seven Stars in Bethnal Green, he was beaten senseless because he was asking too many questions.'

'Gracious! Is he all right?'

'Victor has great powers of recovery,' Colbeck told her. 'And he's very tenacious. That's imperative in our line of work.'

'Is he here with you in Ashford?'

'Of course. At the moment, he's questioning one of the local constables and he'll stick at it until he's found out everything that he needs to know.'

'Let's start with the names at the top of the list,' said Victor Leeming, showing him the petition. 'Do you know who these people are?'

'Yes, Sergeant.'

'Begin with Timothy Lodge.' He wrote the name in his notebook. 'Does he live in Ashford?'

'He's the town barber. His shop is in Bank Street.'

'What manner of man is he?'

'Very knowledgeable,' said George Butterkiss. 'He can talk to you on any subject under the sun while he's cutting your hair or trimming your beard. What you must never do is to get him on to religion.'

'Why not?'

'Timothy is the organist at the Baptist church in St John's Lane. He's always trying to convert people to his faith.'

'We can forget him, I think,' said Leeming, crossing the name off in his notebook. 'Who's the next person on the list?'

'Horace Fillimore. A butcher.'

'That sounds more promising.'

'Not really, Sergeant,' contradicted Butterkiss.

271

'Horace must be nearly eighty now. Nathan Hawkshaw used to work for him. He took the shop over when Horace retired.'

Another name was eliminated from the notebook as soon as Leeming had finished writing it. The two men were in an upstairs room above the tailor's shop where Butterkiss had once toiled. Having sold the shop, he had kept the living accommodation. Even in his own home, the constable wore his uniform as if to distance himself from his former existence. Pleased to be involved in the murder investigation again, he described each of the people on the list whose signatures he could decipher. One name jumped up out him.

'Amos Lockyer!' he exclaimed.

'Who?'

'Right here, do you see?'

'All I can see is a squiggle,' said Leeming, glancing at the petition. 'How on earth can you tell who wrote that?'

'Because I used to work alongside Amos. I'd know that scrawl of his anywhere. He taught me all I know about policing. He left under a cloud but I still say that this town owed a lot to Amos Lockyer.'

'Why was that?'

'He was like a bloodhound. He knew how to sniff out villains.'

'Yet he's no longer a policeman?'

'No,' said Butterkiss with patent regret. 'It's a great shame. Amos was dismissed for being drunk on duty and being in possession of a loaded pistol. There were also rumours that he took bribes but I don't believe that for a second.'

272

'Why were you surprised to see his name on the list?'

'Because he doesn't live here any more. Amos moved away a couple of years ago. The last I heard of him, he was working on a farm the other side of Charing. But the main reason that I didn't expect to see his name here,' said Butterkiss in bewilderment, 'is that I'd expect him to side with the law. How could he call for Nathan Hawkshaw's release when the man's guilt was so obvious?'

'Obvious to you, Constable,' said Leeming, 'but not to this friend of yours, evidently. Or to everyone else on that list.'

'How many more names do you want to hear about?'

'I think I have enough for the time being. You've been very helpful, especially as you've been able to give me so many addresses as well.' He closed his notebook. 'Inspector Colbeck wanted to know if you'd ever heard of a man called Angel.'

'Angel?' Butterkiss gave a hollow laugh. 'Everyone in Kent has heard of that rogue.'

'There is such a person then?'

'Oh, yes. As arrant a villain as ever walked. Nothing was safe when Angel was around. He'd steal for the sake of it. He made Joe Dykes look like a plaster saint.'

'We were told that he may have been at the Lenham fair.'

'I'm sure that he was because that's where the richest pickings are. Angel loved crowds. He was a cunning pickpocket. At a fair in Headcorn, he once stole a pair of shire horses.'

273

'Someone had *those* in their pocket?'

'No, no,' said Butterkiss, unaware that he was being teased. 'They were between the shafts of a wagon. When the farmer got back to the wagon, the horses had vanished. Angel had gypsy blood and gypsies always have a way with animals.'

'Did you ever meet him?'

'I tried to arrest him once for spending the night in the Saracen's Head without paying. The nerve of the man!'

'What happened?'

'It was raining hard and he needed shelter. So he climbed in, as bold as brass, found an empty room and made himself at home. Before he left, he stole some food from the kitchen for breakfast.'

'The fellow needs locking up for good.'

'You have to catch him first and that was more than I managed to do. Angel is as slippery as an eel. The person who can really tell you about him is Amos Lockyer.'

'Why?'

'Because he had a lot of tussles with him,' said Butterkiss. 'Amos managed to find him once and put him behind bars. Next morning, when he went to the cell, the door was wide open and Angel had fled. The next we heard of him, he was running riot in the Sevenoaks area.'

'How would he have got on with Joseph Dykes?'

'Not very well. Joe was just a good-for-nothing, who stole to get money for his beer. Angel was a real criminal, a man who turned thieving into an art. He boasted about it.'

'Was he violent?'

'Not as a rule.'

'What if someone was to upset Angel?'

'Nobody would be stupid enough to do that or they'd regret it. He was a strong man – wiry and quick on his feet.'

'Capable of killing someone?' said Leeming.

'Angel is capable of *anything*, Sergeant.'

Winifred Hawkshaw was so concerned about her daughter that she went to call the doctor. Occupied with other patients, he promised to call later on to see the girl. The anxious mother went straight back to Middle Row and up to Emily's bedroom. To her dismay, it was empty. After searching the other rooms, she rushed downstairs where Adam Hawkshaw was starting to close up the shop for the day.

'Where's Emily?' she asked.

'I've no idea.'

'She's not in her room – or anywhere else.'

'I didn't see her go out.'

'Have you been here all the time?'

'Yes,' he said. 'Except when I went to buy some tobacco.'

'Emily's run away,' decided her mother.

'That's silly – where could she go?'

'I don't know, Adam, but she's not here, is she? Emily hasn't been out of the house for weeks but, as soon as my back is turned, she's off. Lock up quickly,' she ordered. 'We've got to go after her.'

'She'll come back in her own good time,' he argued.

'Not when she's in that state. I've never known

her have a fit like that. There's something very wrong with Emily. Now, hurry up,' she urged. 'We must find her!'

Surrounded by a graveyard in which leafy trees threw long shadows across the headstones, St Mary's church had stood for four centuries. It was at once imposing and accessible, a fine piece of architecture that never forgot its main function of serving the parish. Emily Hawkshaw attended the church every Sunday with her family and they had always sat in the same pew halfway down the nave. This time, she ignored her usual seat and walked down the aisle to the altar rail before kneeling in front of it. Hands clasped together, she closed her eyes tight and prayed for forgiveness, her mind in turmoil, her body shaking and perspiration breaking out on her brow. She was in a positive fever of contrition.

Madeleine Andrews had travelled from London to Ashford in a second class compartment but Colbeck was so happy to see her, and so grateful for the information she brought, that he insisted on buying her a first-class ticket for the return journey. He removed his hat to give her a kiss on the hand then waved her off, standing wistfully on the platform until the train had rounded a bend and disappeared from sight. Deeply moved by her visit, Colbeck felt that it had been more than a pleasant interlude. What she had learned in Hoxton might well serve to confirm his theory about how a man who courted anonymity had been traced to his home. Madeleine's attendance at a funeral had been opportune.

Deciding to call on Emily Hawkshaw again, Colbeck left the station and made for Church Street. He had already resolved to say nothing to his Sergeant about the unheralded visitor. Victor Leeming was too old-fashioned and conventional to believe that a woman could be directly involved in the investigative process. It was better to keep him – and, more importantly, Superintendent Tallis – ignorant of Madeleine's part in the case. The Metropolitan Police was an exclusively male preserve. Robert Colbeck was one of the very few men who even dallied with the notion of employing female assistants.

As he approached St Mary's church, his mind was still playing with fond memories of taking tea with Madeleine at the Saracen's Head. A loud scream jerked him out of his reverie. Ahead of him, pointing upwards with horror, was a middle-aged woman. The handful of people walking past the church immediately stopped and followed the direction of her finger. Colbeck saw the slim figure at once. Holding one of the pinnacles on top of the tower was a young woman in a black dress, trying to haul herself on to the parapet. It was Emily Hawkshaw.

Recognising her at once, Colbeck broke into a run and dashed into the church, shedding his hat and frock coat as he did so and diving through the door to the tower. He went up the steps as fast as he could, going up past the huge iron bells and feeling a first rush of air as he neared the open door at the top. When he emerged into daylight, he saw that Emily was poised between life and death, clinging to the pinnacle while standing precariously on the parapet. Intent on flinging herself off, the girl seemed to be having second thoughts.

Colbeck inched slowly towards her so that he would be in her field of vision. In order not to alarm her, he kept his voice calm and low.

'Stay there, Emily,' he said, 'I'll help you down.'

'No!' she cried. 'Stay back.'

'I know that you must hate yourself even to think of doing this but you must remember those who love you. Do you really want to *hurt* your family and your friends?'

'I don't deserve to be loved.'

'Come down from there and tell me why,' he suggested, moving closer. 'Killing yourself will solve nothing.'

'Keep away from me – or I'll jump.'

'No, Emily. If you really meant to do it, you'd have gone by now. But you knew that there would be consequences, didn't you? Others would suffer terribly, especially your mother. Don't you think she's been through enough already?'

'I've been through it as well,' sobbed the girl.

'Then share your suffering with her. *Help* each other, Emily.'

'I can't.'

'You must,' he said, gently. 'It's the only way.'

'God will never forgive me.'

'You won't find forgiveness by jumping off here. To take your own life is anathema. To do it on consecrated ground makes it even worse. This is a church, Emily. You understand what that means, don't you?'

She began to tremble. 'I just can't go on.'

'Yes, you can. It won't always be like this. Time heals even the deepest wounds. You have a long life ahead of you. Why destroy it in a moment of despair? You're loved, Emily,' he said, taking a small step towards her. 'You're loved and *needed.*'

The girl fell silent as she considered what he had said and Colbeck took it as a good sign. But she was still balanced perilously on the edge of the parapet. One false move on his part and she might jump. From down below, he could hear sounds of a crowd gathering to watch. Emily Hawkshaw had an audience.

'You know that this is wrong,' he told her, moving slightly closer. 'You were christened in this church and brought up in a God-fearing household. You know that it mustn't end this way. It will leave a stain on the whole family.'

'I don't care about that.'

'What *do* you care about? Tell me. I'm here to listen.'

'You wouldn't understand,' she said, trembling even more.

'Then come down and talk to someone who would understand.' He ventured another step. 'Please, Emily. For everyone's sake – come down.'

The girl began to weep and cling more desperately to the pinnacle. It was as if she finally realised the implications of what she had intended to do. Suddenly, she lost her nerve and began to panic. Emily tried to turn back but her foot slipped and she lost her hold on the pinnacle. There was a gasp of horror from below as she teetered on the very brink of the parapet, then Colbeck darted forward to grab her and snatched her back to safety.

Emily Hawkshaw fainted in his arms.

After another tiring day in the boiler shop, Gregory Newman was eager to get home to Turton Street. As he came out of the railway works, however, he found Adam Hawkshaw waiting to speak to him.

'Good evening, Adam,' he said, cheerily.

'Can you come to the shop?' asked the other. 'Mother wants to talk to you as soon as possible.'

'Why – what's happened?'

'Emily tried to commit suicide.'

'Dear God!'

'She was going to throw herself off the church tower.'

'What on earth made her do that?'

'We don't know, Gregory.'

'Where is Emily now?'

'She's in bed. The doctor gave her something to make her sleep.'

'Did she change her mind at the last moment?'

'No,' said Hawkshaw with a tinge of resentment. 'That Inspector Colbeck went up the tower and brought her down again. We saw him catch her as she was about to fall. It's a miracle she's alive.'

'This is terrible news!' exclaimed Newman.

'Then you'll come?'

'Of course. Let me go home first to take care of my wife then I'll come straight away. How has Win taken it?'

'She's very upset.'

'Emily – of all people! You'd never have thought she'd do anything as desperate as this. Whatever could have provoked her?'

'She took fright when Inspector Colbeck wanted to question her.'

'And did he?'

'No, Emily ran away before he came back. She sneaked out when we weren't looking. We were searching for her when we heard this noise from the churchyard. We got there in time to see it all.'

Newman started walking. 'Tell Win I'll be there directly.'

'Thanks,' said Hawkshaw, falling in beside him.

'Did Emily really mean to go through with it?'

'She didn't say. When she was brought down from the tower, she was in a dead faint. She came out of it later but she refused to tell us anything. Emily just lay on the bed and cried.'

'The doctor was right to give her a sedative.'

'I'm worried, Gregory,' said Hawkshaw, showing a rare touch of sympathy for his stepsister.

'So am I.'

'What if Emily tries to do that again?'

The suicide attempt was also being discussed over a drink at the Saracen's Head. Victor Leeming was astonished by what he heard.

'Why did she do it, Inspector?' he asked.

'I'm hoping that that will emerge in time.'

'A young girl, throwing her life away like that – it's unthinkable.'

'Emily had come to the end of her tether.'

'She must have been in despair even to consider

suicide. I mean, it's the last resort. You're only driven to that when there seems to be absolutely no future for you.' He gave a shrug. 'Was she so attached to her stepfather that she couldn't live without him?'

'I don't know,' said Colbeck. 'What is clear, however, is that Emily Hawkshaw is consumed with guilt over something. She's nursing a secret that she's not even able to divulge to her mother.'

'Is there any chance she'll confide in you, sir?'

'I doubt it.'

'But you saved her life.'

'She may resent me for that. I brought her back to the very things she was running away from. We'll have to wait and see, Victor. However,' he went on, as Leeming drank some beer, 'tell me what you discovered. Did you find Constable Butterkiss at all helpful?'

'Very helpful.'

Putting his glass aside and referring to his notebook, Leeming described the people on the petition whom he considered to be potential suspects. Of the ten names that he had written down, six had acquired a tick from the Sergeant. All of the men lived in or near Ashford and had a close connection with Nathan Hawkshaw.

'Did you ask him about Angel?' said Colbeck.

'I did, Inspector, and there certainly is such a man.'

'Would he have been at that fair in Lenham?'

'Definitely.'

Leeming passed on the details given to him by George Butterkiss and argued that Angel had to be looked at as a potential suspect for the murder of Joseph Dykes. The man whose name had first been voiced by Gregory Newman had a long record of criminality. He had been in the right place at the right time to attack Dykes.

'But we come back to the old problem,' said Leeming. 'How could Angel have persuaded Dykes to go to such a quiet part of the wood?'

'He couldn't, Victor – and neither could Nathan Hawkshaw.'

'So how did the victim get there?'

'I can think of only one possible way.'

'What's that, Inspector?'

'Dykes had been drinking heavily,' said Colbeck, 'and probably looked to spend most of the day at the Red Lion. What was the one thing that could get him out of that pub?'

'A knife in his ribs.'

'There was a much easier way. A woman could have done it. When you returned from the scene of the crime, you told me that it was a place where young couples might have gone. I think that someone may have deliberately aroused Dykes's lust.'

'From what I hear, that wouldn't have taken much doing.'

'Once she had lured him to the wood, the killer could strike.'

'Yes,' said Leeming, warming to the notion. 'The woman was there to distract the victim. If that's what happened, it's just like those two murders on the train.'

'It's uncannily like them,' agreed Colbeck, 'and it raises a possibility that has never even crossed our minds before. Supposing that all three

283

murders were committed by the same man?'

'Angel?'

'Hardly.'

'Why not?'

'I can accept that he's a legitimate suspect for the murder of Dykes but he had no motive to kill the hangman or the prison chaplain. No, it must be someone else.'

'Well, it absolves Hawkshaw of the crime,' observed Leeming. 'If the same man is responsible for all three murders, Hawkshaw must have been innocent. He couldn't have killed two people after he was dead.'

'There's another fact we have to face,' said Colbeck, taking a sip of his drink as he meditated. 'This is pure speculation, of course, and we may well be wrong about this. But, assuming we're not, then the man who butchered Joseph Dykes in that wood allowed someone else to go to the gallows on his behalf.'

'Then why did he go on to commit those revenge murders?'

'Guilt, perhaps.'

'Remorse over the way that he let an innocent man be hanged?'

'Perhaps. He may be trying to make amends in some perverse way by killing the people whom he feels made Nathan Hawkshaw's last hour on earth more agonising than it need have been.'

'It doesn't add up, sir.'

'Not at the moment, Victor, but it opens up a whole new line of inquiry.' He glanced down at the petition. 'And it suggests that someone on this list needs to be caught very quickly indeed.'

'Yes, he could have killed *three* victims.'

'Four,' said Colbeck. 'You're forgetting Nathan Hawkshaw.'

'Of course. He had the most lingering death of all. He was made to take the blame for someone else's crime.'

'That's what it begins to look like.' He picked up the petition. 'We must make our first calls this evening. And if we have no success with this part of the list, we must work our way through the rest of it – and that includes the women.'

'Wait a moment, sir.'

'Yes?'

'Would someone who let Hawkshaw go on trial for a murder that he didn't commit then sign a petition for his release?'

'What better way to disguise his own guilt?'

'That's true. Who do we start with, sir?'

'Peter Stelling. He's an ironmonger. We can rely on him to have a ready supply of wire. We'll have to see if his stock contains anything resembling the murder weapon we found near Paddock Wood.'

'Does that mean we cross Angel off the list?'

'For the moment. From what you've told me about him, we'd have the devil's own job tracking him down.'

'We'd need Amos Lockyer to do that, Inspector.'

'Who?'

'He was a policeman here for years,' said Leeming, 'and he helped Constable Butterkiss a great deal. Lockyer was dismissed for being drunk on duty and carrying a loaded firearm. According to

Constable Butterkiss, he was a real bloodhound. He was the only person who ever managed to find Angel and arrest him.'

'Where is this man now?'

'Working on a farm near Charing, apparently. At least, that's what Butterkiss told me. He reveres the man though he was amazed to see his name on that petition.'

'I don't recall an Amos Lockyer there,' said Colbeck, studying the document closely. 'Where is he?'

'Right there,' said Leeming, pointing to the illegible squiggle in the first column. 'I couldn't read it either but that's definitely him. Lockyer's father used to be a watchman in the town. That's what got him interested in being a policeman.'

'You never mentioned him earlier.'

'That was because I'd crossed him off my list.'

'Simply because he was once a local constable?'

'No, sir. I'd need a better reason than that. We both know that there are bad apples in police uniform as everywhere else. I only crossed off Amos Lockyer when Butterkiss told me a little more about him.'

'Go on.'

'To start with,' said Leeming, 'he's no spring chicken. And he has a bad leg. A poacher he tried to arrest shot him in the thigh. I can't see him leaping out of a moving train, can you?'

'Yet you say he had great skill in finding people?'

'That's right. Lockyer was famed for it.'

Colbeck thought hard about what Madeleine Andrews had learned in Hoxton. Jacob Guttridge had been followed by an older man with a unusual rolling gait. It was too much of a coincidence.

'I'll speak to the ironmonger on my own,' he decided.

'What about me?'

'Go back to Constable Butterkiss and tell him that your need his services again.' Leeming pulled a face. 'Yes, I know that he's not your idea of a boon companion, Victor, but this is important.'

'Can't it wait until tomorrow?'

'No. Ask him to drive you to Charing at once.'

'Not another long journey with George Butter-kiss!'

'You need him to find the farm where this Amos Lockyer works. And when you do,' said Colbeck, 'I want you to bring the man back to Ashford immediately.'

'How is she now, Win?' asked Gregory Newman, his face pitted with concern. 'I was shocked when Adam told me what she tried to do.'

'We all were,' said Winifred Hawkshaw. 'It was terrifying to see her up on that church tower. Thank heaven she was saved! The doctor gave her some pills to make her sleep. Emily won't wake up until the morning.'

'Make sure that she doesn't slip out again.'

'I'll lock the door of her room. It's dreadful to treat my own daughter like a prisoner but it may be the only way to keep her alive.'

They were sitting in the room at the rear of the butcher's shop. Though he had been home to see to his wife, Newman had not bothered to change

287

out of his work clothes or to have a meal. The crisis required a swift response and he had run all the way to Middle Row. Winifred Hawkshaw was deeply grateful.

'Thank you, Gregory,' she said, reaching out to touch him. 'I knew that I could count on you.' She gave a pained smile. 'You must be so sick of this family.'

'Why?'

'We've brought you nothing but trouble.'

'Nonsense!'

'Think of all those arguments we had with Adam when he was younger. You were the one who stepped in and found him somewhere else to live. Then came Nathan's arrest and all the horror that followed it. And now we have Emily trying to kill herself.'

'Is that what she really did, Win?'

'What do you mean?'

'I'm wondering if she was just trying to frighten you.'

'Well, she certainly did that,' admitted Winifred. 'I was scared stiff when I saw her up there. And I do believe she meant to jump. Why else would she have climbed up on that ledge? It was so dangerous.'

'Do you have any idea what made her do it?'

'Only that she's been very unhappy for weeks – but, then, so have we all. Emily is no different to the rest of us.'

'Adam said that Inspector Colbeck wanted to question her.'

'That's right. He called here earlier for the second time today. I sent him away. I pretended that she was asleep so that I could warn her that she'd have to talk to a policeman from London.'

'What did she say to that?'

'Well, she wasn't very pleased,' replied Winifred. 'Emily seemed to be afraid of talking to anyone. Then I mentioned the petition again. When I asked her why she didn't sign it, she had this sudden fit. It was like the kind of seizure that my mother sometimes has.'

'Emily needs to be looked at properly by the doctor.'

'I know, Gregory. After I'd calmed her down, I told Emily that I couldn't let her go on like this any longer. But she begged me not to call in the doctor again.'

'Why not?'

'She wouldn't say. Emily just cried and cried.'

'It's been weeks since the execution now,' said Newman, running a hand through his beard. 'I'd have expected her to be over the worst. It's not as if she was actually there, after all.'

'No, I made her stay away.'

'How did she sneak out today?'

'Eventually,' she said, 'I went out to call the doctor and Adam was busy elsewhere. Emily must have picked her moment and gone. As soon as I realised she wasn't here, we went off in search of her. Then we heard all the noise coming from the churchyard.'

'It must have been dreadful for you,' he said, getting up to put an arm around her. 'To lose a child is bad enough for any parent, Win, but to lose one in that way would have been unbearable.'

'Yes,' she whispered, nestling against his body.

'I just can't believe it. Emily was always so trustworthy.'

'Not any more, Gregory.' She pulled back to look up at him. 'I'll be afraid to take my eyes off her from now on. I dread to think what might have happened if Inspector Colbeck hadn't gone up that tower after her.'

'What did he do exactly?' he said, standing away from her.

'He talked to her very quietly and made her change her mind. When she tried to get down again, she slipped and almost fell. Honestly, Gregory, my heart was in my mouth at that moment.'

'But the Inspector grabbed her just in time?' She nodded. 'We all owe him thanks for that. I could see that even Adam was upset and he's never got on well with his stepsister.' He resumed his seat. 'You said that Inspector Colbeck called earlier today.'

'Yes, he wanted to question Adam.'

'What about?'

'That murder the other night.'

'It had nothing to do with Adam,' he said, staunchly.

'I know but the stationmaster remembers someone who looked like him, taking a train to Paddock Wood that same night.'

'Lots of people look like Adam. There are two or three young men at the railway works who could be taken for his twin. Did the Inspector have anything else to say?'

'A great deal. He came in here to see me.'

'Why?'

'It was rather upsetting, Gregory,' she said,

wrapping her arms around her body as if she were cold. 'Out of the blue, he asked me what happened to my first husband. He wanted to know how Martin died.'

'That was an odd thing to ask.'

'He did apologise when I told him I didn't want to talk about that. So he turned to Emily instead. The Inspector was interested to know what she said to me after she was attacked by Joe Dykes.'

'But you weren't here at the time, were you?'

'No, I was over in Willesborough. She spoke to Nathan.'

'And – like any father – he went charging off after Joe. I remember him telling me about it afterwards,' said Newman. 'He said that this fierce anger built up inside him and he couldn't control himself. It was just as well that he didn't catch up with Joe that day.'

'But it helped to hang him all the same,' she said, grimly. 'Going off in a temper like that. There were half-a-dozen witnesses who couldn't wait to stand up in court and talk about the way they'd seen him running down the street with a cleaver.'

'I'd have done no different if Emily had been my daughter.'

'I suppose not.'

'Joe Dykes was a menace to any woman.' He sat back in his chair. 'So what did you tell Inspector Colbeck?'

'The truth – that Emily wouldn't talk to me about it.'

'She confided in Nathan.'

'Yes, and he told me what she said but it was

not the same. I wanted to hear it from my daughter's own lips. And there was another thing that worried me at the time, Gregory.'

'What was that?'

'Well,' she said, 'Nathan and I had always been very honest with each other. Yet when I tried to talk to him about Emily, and what she'd said when she came running back here that day, I had the feeling that he was holding something back. I only ever got part of the story.'

It took Colbeck less than two minutes to establish that Peter Stelling was not the killer. Since he had a business to run, and a wife and four children to look after, the ironmonger would not have had the necessary freedom of movement. In addition, Stelling was such a mild-mannered man that it was difficult to imagine him working himself up into the fury symbolised in the slaughter of Joseph Dykes. The second name on Colbeck's list did not keep him long either. As soon as he learned that Moses Haddon, a bricklayer, had been in bed for a week after falling from a ladder, he was able to remove his name from the list. In the case of both men, however, he took the trouble to ask if they could describe Amos Lockyer for him. Each man spoke well of the former policeman and said that he was short, stout and well into his fifties. They confirmed that the wound in his leg had left him with a rather comical waddle.

He owed a debt of gratitude to Madeleine Andrews for providing a possible link between Lockyer and Jacob Guttridge, and it gave him his first surge of optimism since they had arrived in Ashford. Relishing the memory of Madeleine's surprise visit to the town, he went on to question the next person, wearing a broad smile on his face.

She was in the kitchen when she heard the front door open and shut.

'Where have you *been*?' she asked, chastising her father with her tone of voice. 'Your dinner is getting cold.'

'I was held up, Maddy,' said Caleb Andrews, coming into the kitchen to give her a conciliatory kiss. 'We got talking about the murder of that prison chaplain and time just flew by.'

'Helped along by a couple of pints of beer no doubt.'

'A man is entitled to a few pleasures in life.'

Madeleine served the meal on to two plates and set them on the table. She sat opposite her father and passed him the salt. He shook a liberal quantity over his food.

'They all agreed with me, you know,' he said.

'You mean that they didn't dare to disagree.'

'The killer was someone who served time in Maidstone prison.'

'I'm not so sure, Father.'

'Well, I am,' he asserted, stabbing the air with his knife. 'For two pins, I'd give you the money to take a train to Ashford so that you can tell Inspector Colbeck what I said. He'd know where to look then.'

'Oh, I fancy that he can manage without your help.'

'I have this feeling in my bones, Maddy.'

'Save it for your workmates,' she advised. 'Robert is a trained detective. He knows how to lead an investigation and it's not by relying on suggestions from every Tom, Dick and Harry.'

'I'm not Tom, Dick or Harry,' he protested. 'I'm your father and, as such, I've got connections with this case. I told them all that Inspector Colbeck had come calling here.'

'Father!'

'Well, it's true, isn't it?'

'I don't want you and your friends gossiping about me.'

'What am I supposed to tell them – that you've taken the veil?'

'Don't be silly.'

'Then stop pretending that you and the Inspector are not close. You're like a locomotive and tender.' He swallowed a piece of meat. 'Well, maybe not *that* close.' He winked at her. 'Yet, anyway.'

Her gaze was steely. 'You're doing it again, aren't you?'

'It's only in fun, Maddy.'

'How would you like it if I stopped cooking your meals for you and told you it was only in fun?'

'That would be cruel!'

'At least, you'd know how I feel.'

'Maddy!' She picked at her own food and he watched her for a moment. 'Look, I'm sorry. I let my tongue run away with me sometimes. I won't say another word about him. I promise you.' He sliced up his beans. 'What have you been doing with yourself all day?'

'Oh, I had a very quiet time,' she said, determined to conceal from him where she had been. 'I cleaned the house then read for a while.'

'Did you work on the painting?'

'A little.'

'When are you going to give it to him?'

'When it's ready, Father. And,' she told him, pointedly, 'when you're not here to embarrass me.'

'I wouldn't embarrass you for the world.'

'You've done it already since you walked through that door.'

'Have I? What did I say?'

'I'd rather not repeat it. Let's talk about something else.'

'As you wish.' He racked his brain for a new subject. 'Oh, I know what I meant to tell you. When you read the paper this morning, did you see that Jake Guttridge was being buried today?'

'Really?'

'I bet he was there as well.'

'Who?'

'The killer. The man who strangled him on that excursion train. I'd bet anything that he turned up at the funeral just so that he could get in a good kick at the coffin. It's exactly the sort of thing that he'd do.'

Madeleine ate her dinner, not daring to say a word.

Because they had been asked to bring someone back with them, Victor Leeming and George Butterkiss travelled in the cart that had taken them to Lenham on their first journey together. This time it smelled in equal proportions of fish, animal dung and musty hay. The potholes made an even more concerted assault on the Sergeant's buttocks and he was glad when they finally reached Charing, a charming village on the road to Maidstone. His aches and pains increased in intensity when he learned that they had gone there in vain. The farmer for whom Amos Lockyer had worked told them that he had sacked the man months earlier for being drunk and unreliable.

Hearing a rumour that the Lockyer had taken a menial job on the staff at Leeds Castle, they rode on there, only to be met with another rebuff. After only a short time in service at the castle, Lockyer had failed to turn up for work and vanished from his lodging. Nobody had any idea where he could be. George Butterkiss drove his unhappy passenger back towards Ashford. The road seemed bumpier than ever.

'Why is the Inspector so keen to speak to Amos?' asked Butterkiss.

'I don't know,' said Leeming.

'Does he want him to help in the investigation?'

'Possibly.'

Butterkiss beamed. 'It will be wonderful to work alongside him once again,' he said. 'Amos Lockyer, me and two detectives from the Metropolitan Police. A quartet like that is a match for any villain.'

Conscious that he would have to listen to his zealous companion all the way back, Leeming gritted his teeth. When rain began to fall, he swore under his breath. It was the last straw.

'We'll be soaked to the skin,' he complained.

'I know what Amos would have done at a time like this,' said Butterkiss, remaining resolutely cheerful. 'Never let things get on top of you – that was his motto. If Amos was sitting where you are, Sergeant, do you know what he'd suggest?'

'What?'

'That we sing a song to keep up our spirits.'

'Don't you dare!' warned Leeming, turning on him. 'I don't want my spirits kept up after this wild goose chase. If you sing so much as a single note, Constable Butterkiss, you'll be walking all the way home.'

Adam Hawkshaw waited until it was quite dark before he opened the door of his lodging and peeped out. The rain was easing but it was still persistent enough to keep most people off the streets that evening. When he saw that nobody was about, he pulled down his hat, stepped on to the pavement and pulled the door shut behind him. Hands in his pockets, he walked swiftly off into the gloom.

Robert Colbeck was beginning to get worried. He had expected Leeming and Butterkiss to be back hours earlier with the man they had sought. Charing was no great distance from the town, miles closer than Lenham. Even if they had had to go to an outlying farm, they should have returned by now. The combination of rain and darkness would slow them down but not to that extent. Colbeck wondered if they had encountered

297

trouble of some sort. He sat near the window of his bedroom for what seemed like an age before he finally heard the rattle of a cart below.

Hoping that they had at last come back, he went downstairs and hurried to the door, ignoring the rain and stepping out from under the portico. By the light of the street lamps, to his relief, he saw a wet and disgruntled Victor Leeming, seated on the cart beside an equally sodden George Butterkiss. There was no third person with them. Before he could even greet them, however, Colbeck was aware of sudden movement in the shadows on the opposite side of the street. A pistol was fired with a loud bang. The noise frightened the horse and it bolted down the High Street with the driver trying desperately to control it. Taken by surprise, Leeming was almost flung from the cart.

Robert Colbeck, meanwhile, had fallen to the ground with a stifled cry and rolled over on to his back. Satisfied with his work, the man who had fired the shot fled the scene.

Chapter Eleven

It was ironic. Robert Colbeck, the assassin's intended target, suffered nothing more than a painful flesh wound in his upper arm whereas Victor Leeming, who just happened to be nearby at the time, collected a whole battery of cuts and bruises when he was hurled from the cart as it overturned. The Sergeant was justifiably upset.

'It's not fair,' he protested. 'All that I expected to do was to ride to Charing to pick someone up. Instead of that, I'm drenched by rain, bored stiff by Constable Butterkiss, beaten black and blue by that vicious cart of his, then flung to the ground like a sack of potatoes.'

'You have my sympathy, Victor.'

'And on top of all that, we came back empty-handed.'

'That was unfortunate,' said Colbeck.

They were in his room at the Saracen's Head, free at last from the inquisitive crowd that had rushed out into the street to see what had caused the commotion. Colbeck's injured arm had now been bandaged and the doctor had then treated Leeming's wounds. Back in dry clothing again, the Sergeant was puzzled.

'Why are you taking it so calmly, sir?' he asked.

'How should I be taking it?'

'If someone had fired at me, I'd be livid.'

'Well, I was annoyed at the damage he did to my frock coat,' said Colbeck, seriously. 'I doubt if it can be repaired. And the blood will have ruined my shirt beyond reclaim. No,' he continued, 'I prefer to look at the consolations involved.'

'I didn't know that there were any.'

'Three, at least.'

'What are they?'

'First of all, I'm alive with only a scratch on me. Luckily, the shot was off target. The man is clearly not as adept with a pistol as he is with a piece of wire.'

'You think that it was the killer?'

'Who else, Victor? He's frightened because we

299

are closing in on him. That's the second consolation. We've made more progress than we imagined. The man is right here in Ashford. He's given himself away.'

'What's the third consolation, sir?'

'He thinks that he killed me,' said Colbeck. 'That's why I fell to the ground and stayed there. Also, of course, I didn't want to give him the chance to aim at me again. Believing I was dead, he ran away. There was no point in trying to chase him because I had this searing pain in my arm. I'd never have been able to overpower him. Much better to give him the impression that his attempt on my life had been successful.'

'He's in for a nasty surprise.'

'Yes, but it does behove us to show additional caution in future.'

'I will,' said Leeming. 'I'll never ride on that blessed cart again!'

'I was talking about the killer. He's armed and ready to shoot.'

'You mentioned a pistol just now.'

'That's what it sounded like,' said Colbeck, 'though I couldn't be sure. It all happened in a split-second. One of the first things we need to do is to find the bullet. That will tell us what firearm was used.'

'We'll have to wait until daylight to do that.'

'Yes, Victor. In the meantime, we need to talk to Butterkiss.'

'Keep him away, Inspector! He almost did for me.'

'He tried his best to control that runaway horse.'

'But he still managed to overturn the cart,' said Leeming, ruefully. 'And while I hit the ground and took the impact, Constable Butterkiss simply landed on top of me. He wasn't really hurt at all.'

'Nevertheless, I'd like you to fetch him.'

'*Now*, sir?'

'If you feel well enough to go. His local knowledge is crucial to us. Give him my compliments and ask if he can spare us some time.'

'I don't need to ask that. If we're not very careful, he'd spare us twenty-four hours a day. The man is so blooming eager.'

'Eagerness is a good quality in a policeman.'

'Not if you have to ride beside him on a cart!' Leeming went to the door. 'Will you come down to meet him, sir?'

'No,' said Colbeck, glancing round, 'this room is more private. And nobody will be able to take a shot at me in here. Be careful how you go.'

'Yes, Inspector.'

'And you might ask him to bring needle and thread.'

'Why?'

'He was a tailor, wasn't he? Perhaps he can repair my coat.'

When the visitor called, George Butterkiss was regaling his wife with the story of how he had fought to control the galloping horse in the High Street. He broke off to answer the door and was delighted to hear the summons delivered by Victor Leeming.

'I'll get my coat at once, Sergeant,' he said.

'Talking of coats,' said the other, detaining him

with a hand, 'the Inspector has a problem. That bullet grazed his arm and left a hole in his sleeve. He's very particular about his clothing.'

'Inspector Colbeck would be a gift to any tailor.'

'Can you help him?'

'I'll need to see the damage first. A simple tear can be easily mended but, if the material has been shot away, it may be a question of sewing a new sleeve on to the coat.'

Butterkiss ran swiftly up the stairs. When he reappeared soon afterwards, he was back in police uniform even though he only had to walk thirty yards or so to the Saracen's Head. His enthusiasm was quite undiminished as they strolled along the pavement together. The Sergeant found it lowering.

'I haven't told you the good news,' said Butterkiss.

'Is there such a thing?'

'Yes, Sergeant. When I took the horse back and explained what had happened, the owner examined the animal carefully. It had no injuries at all. Isn't that a relief?'

'I'd have had it put down for what it did to me.'

'You can't blame the horse for bolting like that.'

'Well, I'm in no mood to congratulate it, I can tell you.'

'How do you feel now?'

'Vengeful.'

'I thought that we had a lucky escape.'

'What's lucky about being thrown headfirst from a moving cart?'

Butterkiss laughed. 'You will have your little

joke, Sergeant.'

They turned into the Saracen's Head and went up the stairs. When they were let into Colbeck's room, they were each offered a chair. The Inspector perched on the edge of the bed.

'Thank you for coming so promptly, Constable,' he said.

'Feel free to call on me at any hour of the day,' urged Butterkiss.

'We need your guidance.'

'It's yours for the asking, Inspector.'

'Then I'd like you to take another look at these names,' said Colbeck, handing him the petition. 'Are you ready, Victor?'

'Yes, sir,' said Leeming, taking his notebook dutifully from his pocket. 'I'll write down all the relevant details.'

'We drew a blank with the first batch of names. Can you take us slowly through the next dozen or so, please?'

'If I can read their handwriting,' said Butterkiss, poring over the document. 'There are one or two signatures that defy even me.'

'Do your best, Constable.'

'You can always count on me to do that.'

Taking a deep breath, he identified the first name and described the man in detail. As soon as he learned the age of the person, Colbeck interrupted and told him to move on to the next one. Leeming's pencil was busy, writing down names then crossing them out again. Of the fifteen people that Butterkiss recognised, only seven were deemed to be worth closer inspection.

'Thank you,' said Colbeck. 'Now turn to the

women, please.'

Butterkiss lifted an eyebrow. 'The women, sir?'

'As opposed to the men,' explained Leeming.

'But a woman couldn't possibly have committed those murders on the trains nor could one have fired that shot at you, Inspector.'

'You are mistaken about that,' said Colbeck. 'Earlier this year, the Sergeant and I arrested a woman in Deptford who had shot her husband with his army revolver. The bullet went straight through his body and wounded the young lady who was in bed with him at the time.'

'Dear me!' exclaimed Butterkiss.

'Never underestimate the power of the weaker sex, Constable.'

'No, sir.'

He addressed himself to the petition once more and picked out the female names that he recognised. Most were found to be very unlikely suspects but three names joined the Sergeant's list.

'Did you make a note of their details, Victor?' asked Colbeck.

'Yes, Inspector.'

'Good. You can talk to those three ladies tomorrow.'

'What about me?' said Butterkiss.

'I have two important tasks for you, Constable.'

'Just tell me what they are.'

'I want you to find Amos Lockyer for me.'

'I'll do it somehow,' vowed Butterkiss. 'What's the other task?'

Colbeck reached for his frock coat. 'I wonder if you could look at this sleeve for me?' he said.

'Tell me if it's beyond repair.'

Winifred Hawkshaw was on tenterhooks. Whenever she heard a sound from the adjoining bedroom, she feared that her daughter had woken up and was either trying to open the door or to escape through the window. After a sleepless night, she used her key to let herself into Emily's room and found her fast asleep. Putting a chair beside the bed, Winifred sat down and kept vigil. It was an hour before the girl's eyelids fluttered. Her mother took hold of her hand.

'Good morning,' she said, sweetly.

Emily was confused. 'Where am I?'

'In your own bed, dear.'

'Is that you, Mother?'

'Yes.' Winifred rubbed her hand. 'It's me, Emily.'

'I feel strange. What happened?'

'The doctor gave you something to make you sleep.'

'The doctor?' The news brought Emily fully awake. 'You let a doctor touch me?'

'You'd passed out, Emily. When the Inspector brought you down from that tower, you were in a dead faint.'

The girl needed a moment to assimilate the information. When she remembered what she had tried to do, she brought a hand up to her mouth. Her eyes darted nervously around the room. She felt trapped.

'We need to talk,' said Winifred, softly.

'I've nothing to say.'

'Emily!'

'I haven't, Mother. I meant to jump off that tower.'

'No, I can't believe that,' insisted her mother. 'Is your life so bad that you could even *think* of such a thing? It's sinful, Emily. It's so cruel and selfish and you're neither of those things. Don't hurt us any more.'

'I wasn't doing it to hurt you.'

'Then what made you go up there in the first place?'

'I was afraid.'

'Of what?'

'Everything.'

Emily began to sob quietly and her mother bent over to hug her. The embrace lasted a long time and it seemed to help the girl because it stemmed her tears. She became so quiet that Winifred wondered if she had fallen asleep again. When she drew back, however, she saw that Emily's eyes were wide open, staring up at the ceiling.

'Promise me that you won't do anything like this again,' said Winifred, solemnly. 'Give me your sacred word of honour.' A bleak silence ensued. 'Did you hear what I said, Emily?'

'Yes.'

'Then give me that promise.'

'I promise,' murmured the girl.

'Say it as if you mean it,' scolded Winifred. 'As it is, the whole town will know what happened yesterday and I'll have to face the shame of that. Don't make it any worse for me, Emily. We *love* you. Doesn't that mean anything to you?'

'Yes.'

'Then behave as if it does.'

'I will.'

Emily sat up in bed and reached out for her mother. Both of them were crying now, locked together, sharing their pain, trying to find a bond that had somehow been lost. At length, it was the daughter who pulled away. She wiped her eyes with the back of her hand and made an effort to control herself.

'You need more time,' said Winifred, watching her closely. 'You need more time to think about what you did and why you did it.'

'I do.'

'But I'll want the truth, Emily.'

'Yes, Mother.'

'I have a right to know. When something as wicked and terrible as this happens, I have a right to know why. And I'm not the only one, Emily,' she warned. 'The vicar will want to speak to you as well.'

'The vicar?'

'Taking your own life is an offence against God – and you made it worse by trying to do it from a church tower. The vicar says that it would have been an act of blasphemy. Is that what you meant to do?'

'No, no,' cried Emily.

'Suicide is evil.'

'I know.'

'We couldn't have buried you on consecrated ground.'

'I didn't think about that.'

'Well, you should have,' said Winifred, bitterly. 'I don't want two members of the family denied a Christian burial in the churchyard at St Mary's.

You could have ended up like your father, Emily. That would have broken my heart.'

Emily began to tremble violently and her mother feared that she was about to have another fit but the girl soon recovered. The experience she had been through was too frightful for her to contemplate yet. Her mind turned to more mundane concerns.

'I'm hungry,' she announced.

'Are you?' said her mother, laughing in relief at this sign of normality. 'I'll make you some breakfast at once. You need to be up and dressed before he calls.'

'Who?'

'Inspector Colbeck. He was the person who saved your life.'

A long sleep had revived Robert Colbeck and got him up early to face the new day. The stinging sensation in his wound had been replaced by a distant ache though his left arm was still rather stiff when he moved it. Before breakfast, he was outside the Saracen's Head, standing in the position that he had occupied the previous evening and trying to work out where the bullet might have gone. Deciding that it must have ricocheted off the wall, he searched the pavement and the road over a wide area. He eventually found it against the kerb on the opposite side of the High Street. Colbeck showed the bullet to Victor Leeming when the latter joined him for breakfast.

'It's from a revolver,' said the Inspector.

'How can you tell, sir? The end is bent out of shape.'

'That happened on impact with the wall. I'm going by the size of the bullet. My guess is that it came from a revolver designed by Robert Adams. I saw the weapon on display at the Great Exhibition last year.'

'Oh, yes,' said Leeming, enviously. 'Because we saved Crystal Palace from being destroyed, you were given two tickets by Prince Albert for the opening ceremony. You took Miss Andrews to the Exhibition.'

'I did, Victor, though it wasn't to see revolvers. Madeleine was much more interested in the locomotives on show, especially the *Lord of the Isles*. No,' he went on, 'it was on a second visit that I took the trouble to study the firearms because they were the weapons that we would be up against one day – and that day came sooner than I expected.'

'Who is this Robert Adams?'

'The only serious British rival to Samuel Colt. He did not want the American to steal all the glory so he developed his solid frame revolver in which the butt frame and barrel were forged as a single piece of metal.'

'And this was what they fired?' said Leeming, handing the bullet back to him. 'You thought that it came from a pistol.'

'A single-cocking pistol, Victor. Adams used a different firing mechanism from the Colt. I'm sufficiently patriotic to be grateful that it was a British weapon,' said Colbeck, pocketing the bullet. 'I'd hate to have been shot dead by an American revolver last night.'

'Who would own such a thing in Ashford?'

'A good point.'

'You were right to stay on the ground when you were hit, sir. If it was a revolver, it could have been fired again and again.'

'Adams designed it so that it would fire rapidly. What probably saved me was that the self-cocking lock needed a heavy pull on the trigger and that tends to upset your aim.'

'Unless you get close enough to the target.'

'We'll have to make sure that he doesn't do that, Victor.'

Having finished his breakfast, Colbeck sat back and wiped his lips with his napkin. Leeming ate the last of his meal then sipped his tea. He pulled a slip of paper from his pocket.

'You want me to talk to these three women, then?'

'Ask them why they signed that petition.'

'One of them lives in a farm near Wye.'

'Then I suggest that you don't go there by cart. Take a train from Ashford station. Wye is only one short stop down the line.'

'What will you be doing, sir?'

'Going back to source.'

'Source?'

'I'm going to have a long overdue talk with Emily Hawkshaw,' said Colbeck. 'This whole business began when she had that encounter with Joseph Dykes. It's high time that the girl confided in me. After what happened on the top of that church tower yesterday, I feel that Emily owes me something.'

Caleb Andrews had been driving trains for so

long that he knew exactly how long it took him to walk to Euston Station from Camden. He also knew how important punctuality was to a railway company. After a glance at the clock, he got up from the table and reached for his hat.

'I'm off, Maddy.'

'Goodbye,' she said, coming out of the kitchen to give him a kiss.

'What are you going to do today?'

'I hope to finish the painting.'

'One of these fine days,' he said, 'you must come down to Euston and do a painting of me on the footplate. I'd like that. We could hang it over the mantelpiece.'

'I've done dozens of drawings of you, Father.'

'I want to be in colour – like the *Lord of the Isles*.'

'You *are* the Lord of the Isles,' she said, fondly. 'At least, you think you are when you've had a few glasses of beer.'

Andrews laughed. 'You know your father too well.'

'Try not to be late this evening.'

'I will. By the way,' he said, 'you needn't bother to read the newspaper this morning. There's no mention at all of Inspector Colbeck. Without my help, he's obviously making no progress.'

'I think that he is. Robert prefers to hide certain things from the press. When he's working on a case, he hates having any reporters around him. They always expect quick results.'

'The Inspector had an extremely quick result. As soon as he got to Ashford, someone else was murdered on a train.'

311

'Father!'

'You can't be any quicker than that.'

'Go off to work,' she said, opening the door for him, 'and forget about Robert. He'll solve these murders very soon, I'm sure.'

'So am I, Maddy He's got a good reason to get a move on,' said Andrews with a cackle. 'The Inspector wants to get back here and have his painting of the *Lord of the Isles*.'

Robert Colbeck was pleased with the way that the sleeve of his frock coat had been replaced. George Butterkiss had done such an excellent job sewing on a new sleeve that Colbeck was able to wear the coat again. Looking as spruce as ever, he turned into Middle Row and raised his top hat to a woman who went past. Adam Hawkshaw was displaying joints of meat on the table outside the shop. The Inspector strolled up to him.

'Good morning,' he said, breezily.

'Oh.' The butcher looked up at him, visibly shocked.

'You seem surprised to see me, Mr Hawkshaw.'

'I heard that you'd been shot last night.'

'Who told you that?'

'Everyone was talking about it when I got here this morning.'

'As you can see,' said Colbeck, careful to give the impression that he was completely uninjured, 'reports of the incident were false.'

'Yes.'

'Might I ask where you were yesterday evening?'

'I was at my lodging,' said Hawkshaw. 'On my own.'

'So there's nobody who could confirm the fact?'

'Nobody at all.'

'How convenient!'

The butcher squared up to him. 'Are you accusing me?'

'I'm not accusing anybody, Mr Hawkshaw. I really came to see how Emily was after that unfortunate business at the church.'

'Emily is well.'

'Have you seen her this morning?'

'Not yet.'

'Then how do you know she is well?'

'Emily doesn't want you upsetting her, Inspector.'

'Your stepsister was upset long before I came here,' said Colbeck, firmly, 'and I intend to find out why.'

Before Hawkshaw could reply, the detective went past him into the shop and knocked on the door at the rear. It was opened immediately by Winifred Hawkshaw. She invited him in.

'I was expecting you to call,' she said.

'Really? You can't have heard the rumour then.'

'What rumour?'

'The one that your stepson managed to pick up somehow.'

'I haven't spoken to Adam yet. I've stayed close to Emily.'

'That's understandable,' said Colbeck. 'Yesterday evening, when I was standing outside the Saracen's Head, someone tried to shoot me.'

'Good gracious!'

'Being so close, you must surely have heard the bang.'

'Now that you mention it,' said Winifred, pushing back a wisp of stray hair, 'I did hear something. And there was the sound of a horse and cart, racing down the High Street. I was in Emily's room at the time, too afraid to leave her in case she woke up and tried to ... well, you know. I stayed there until I was exhausted then went to my own bed.'

'How is Emily?'

'She's still very delicate.'

'She would be after that experience.'

'Emily doesn't remember too much of what happened.'

'Then I won't remind her of the details,' said Colbeck. 'Some of them are best forgotten. Has the doctor been yet?'

'He promised to call later on – and so did the vicar. Emily is unwilling to see either of them, especially the doctor. She begged me to send him away.'

'What about me?'

'I can't pretend that she was keen to speak to you, Inspector, but I told her that she must. Emily needs to thank you.'

'I'm just grateful that I came along at the right time.'

'So are we,' said Winifred, still deeply perturbed by the incident. 'But what's this about a shot being fired at you, Inspector? Is it true?'

'I'm afraid so.'

'Someone tried to *kill* you? That's terrible.'

'I survived.'

'Do you have any idea who the man was?'

'Yes, Mrs Hawkshaw,' he replied, 'but let's not

314

worry about me at the moment. Emily is the person who deserves all the attention. Do you think that you could bring her down, please?'

'Of course.'

'Has she given you any idea why she went up that tower?'

'Emily said that she was afraid – of everything.'

Winifred went off upstairs and Colbeck anticipated a long wait as the mother tried to cajole her daughter into speaking to him. In fact, the girl made no protest at all. She came downstairs at once. When she entered the room, she looked sheepish. Winifred followed her and they sat beside each other. Colbeck took the chair opposite them. He gave the girl a kind smile.

'Hello, Emily,' he said.

'Hello.'

'How are you this morning?'

'Mother says I'm to thank you for what you did yesterday.'

'And what about you?' he asked, gently. 'Do you think I earned your thanks?'

'I don't know.'

'Emily!' reproved her mother.

'I'd rather her tell the truth, Mrs Hawkshaw,' said Colbeck. 'She's probably still bewildered by it all and that's only natural.' He looked at the girl. 'Do you feel hazy in your own mind, Emily?'

'Yes.'

'But you do recall what took you to the church?'

Emily glanced at her mother. 'Yes.'

'It was because you were so unhappy, wasn't it?'

315

'Yes, it was.'

'And because you miss your stepfather so very much.' The girl lowered her head. 'I'm not going to ask you any more about yesterday, Emily. I know you went up that tower to do something desperate but I think that you changed your mind when you actually got there. However,' he went on, 'what interests me more is what happened all those weeks earlier. You were attacked by a man named Joseph Dykes, weren't you?'

Emily looked anxiously at her mother but Winifred did not bail her out. She gave her daughter a look to indicate that she should answer the question. Emily licked her lips.

'Yes,' she said, 'but I don't want to talk about it.'

'Then tell me what happened afterwards,' invited Colbeck.

'Afterwards?'

'When you came running back here. Who was in the shop?'

'Father.'

'What about your stepbrother?'

'Adam had gone to Bybrook Farm to collect some meat.'

'So you only told your stepfather what happened?'

'Nathan was her father,' corrected Winifred. 'In every way that mattered, he was the only real father that Emily knew.'

'I accept that, Mrs Hawkshaw,' said Colbeck, 'and I can see why Emily should turn to him.' His eyes flicked back to the girl. 'What did your father say when you told him?'

'He was very angry,' she said.

'Did he run off immediately?'

'No, he stayed with me for a while.'

'Nathan said she was terrified,' explained the mother. 'He had to calm her down before he could go after Joe Dykes. By that time, of course, Joe had vanished.'

'Let me come back to your daughter,' said Colbeck, patiently. 'You were not to blame in any way, Emily. The chain of events that followed was not your doing. You were simply a victim and not a cause – do you understand what I'm saying?'

'I think so,' said the girl.

'You don't need to take any responsibility on to your shoulders.'

'That's what I told her,' said Winifred.

'But Emily didn't believe you – did you, Emily?'

'No,' muttered the girl.

'Why not?'

'I can't tell you.'

'Then answer me this,' said Colbeck, probing carefully. 'What happened afterwards?'

'Afterwards?'

'Yes, Emily. When your father got back to the shop after he'd failed to find the man who assaulted you. What happened then?'

A look came into her eyes that Colbeck had seen before. It was a look of sudden fear and helplessness that she had given when she felt that she was going to fall to her death from the church tower. The interview was over because Emily was unable to go on but Colbeck was content. He had learned much more than he had expected.

Notwithstanding his dislike of rail travel, Victor Leeming had to admit that it was quicker and safer than riding beside George Butterkiss on a rickety cart that gave off such pungent odours. The journey to Wye was so short that he barely had time to admire the landscape through the window of his carriage. It was his third call that morning. Having spoken to two of the women and satisfied himself that they could not have been implicated in the crimes, Leeming was on his way to meet the last person on his list.

Wye was a quaint village with a small railway station at its edge. It took him only ten minutes to walk to the address that Butterkiss had given him. Kathleen Brennan lived in a tied cottage on one of the farms. When he knocked on the door, all that the Sergeant knew about her was that she worked there and brought produce in to Ashford on market days. Butterkiss had not warned him how attractive she was.

When she opened the door to him, he discovered that Kathleen Brennan was a woman in her twenties with a raw beauty that was set off by her long red hair and a pair of startling green eyes. Even in her working dress, she looked shapely. She put her hands on her hips.

'Yes?' she asked with a soft Irish lilt.

'Miss Kathleen Brennan?'

'*Mrs* Brennan.'

'I beg your pardon. My name is Detective Sergeant Leeming,' he told her, showing her his warrant card, 'and I'd like to ask you a few questions, if I may.'

'Why?'

318

'It's in connection with the murder of Joseph Dykes. May I come in for a moment, please?'

'We can talk here,' she said, folding her arms.

'As you wish, Mrs Brennan. You signed a petition, I believe.'

'That's right.'

'Do you mind telling me why?'

'Because I knew that Nathan Hawkshaw was innocent.'

'How?'

'I just did,' she said as if insulted by the question. 'I met him a lot in Ashford. He was a nice man. Nathan was no killer.'

'Were you at that fair in Lenham, by any chance?'

'Yes, I was.'

'And did you witness the argument between the two men?'

'We all did,' she replied. 'It took place in the middle of the square. They might have come to blows if Gregory hadn't stopped them.'

'Gregory Newman?'

'He was Nathan's best friend. He pulled him away and tried to talk sense into him. Gregory told him to go home.'

'But he came back, didn't he?'

'So they say.'

'And he was seen very close to where the murder took place.'

'I know nothing of that, Sergeant,' she said, brusquely. 'But I still believe that they hanged the wrong man.'

'Have you any idea who the killer might be?'

'None at all.'

'But you were shocked when Hawkshaw was found guilty?'

'Yes, I was.'

'Did you go to the execution?'

'Why are you asking me that?' she challenged. 'And why did you come here in the first place? That case is over and done with.'

'If only it were, Mrs Brennan,' said Leeming, 'but it's had so many tragic consequences. That's why Inspector Colbeck and I are looking into it again. Your name came to our attention.'

'I can't help you,' she said, curtly.

'I get the feeling that you don't *want* to help me.'

Leeming met her gaze. Kathleen Brennan's manner verged on the hostile and he could not understand what provocation he had given her. Without quite knowing why, he was unsettled by her. There was something about the woman that made him feel, if not threatened, then a trifle disturbed. Leeming was glad that they were conversing in the open air and not in the privacy of her cottage.

'You haven't told me if you attended the execution.'

'And I'm not going to.'

'Are you ashamed that you went?'

'I didn't say that I did.'

'But you felt sorry for Nathan Hawkshaw?'

'We all did – that's why Gregory got the petition together.'

'Was he the person who asked you to sign?'

'No,' she said, 'it was Nathan's wife.'

'Did you simply put your name on that list out

of friendship?'

Anger showed in her face. 'No, I didn't! You've got no call to ask me that, Sergeant. I did what I believed was right and so did the others. We wanted to save Nathan.'

'Yet you had no actual proof that he was innocent.'

Kathleen Brennan's eyes glinted and she breathed hard through her nose. Leeming could see that his questions had inflamed her. She stepped forward and pulled the door shut behind her.

'I've got to go to work,' she said.

'Then I won't stop you, Mrs Brennan. Thank you for your help.'

'Nathan Hawkshaw was a good man, Sergeant.'

'That's what everyone says.'

'Try listening to them.'

She walked abruptly past him and headed across the field towards the farmhouse on the ridge. Leeming was nonplussed, unsure whether his visit had been pointless or whether he had stumbled on something of interest and significance. As he trudged back to the station, he wondered why Kathleen Brennan had made him so uneasy. It was only when, after a lengthy wait, he caught the return train to Ashford that he realised exactly what it was.

There was an additional surprise for him. As the train chugged merrily along the line, he looked absent-mindedly through the window and saw something that made him sit up and stare. A young woman was riding a horse along the road at a steady canter, her red hair blowing in the wind. The person who had told him that she had to go to work was now riding with some urgency towards Ashford.

Inspector Colbeck was so intrigued by what he had learned from his meeting with Emily Hawkshaw that he took himself to a wooden bench near St Mary's church and sat down to think. The square tower soared above him and he looked up at it with misgiving, certain that, if the girl really had committed suicide, then the full truth about the murder of Joseph Dykes would never be known. Emily was young, immature and in a fragile state but he could not excuse her on those grounds. In the light of what he had discovered, he simply had to talk to her again.

Winifred Hawkshaw was unhappy with the idea. When he returned to the shop after long cogitation, she became very protective.

'Emily needs to be left alone,' she claimed. 'It's the only way that she'll ever get over this.'

'I disagree, Mrs Hawkshaw,' said Colbeck. 'As long as she feels such a sense of guilt, there's always the possibility that she'll attempt to take her own life again – and I may not be on hand next time.'

'My daughter has nothing to feel guilty about, Inspector.'

'Is that what she's told you?'

'No,' admitted Winifred. 'She's told me precious little.'

'That in itself is an indication of guilt. If she's unable to confide in the person closest to her, what kind of secret is she hiding? Whatever it is, it won't let her rest. I simply must see her again,' insisted Colbeck, 'and this time, you must leave us alone together.'

'I couldn't do that.'

'I won't get the truth out of her with her mother there.'

'Why not?'

'Because I believe that it concerns you.'

Winifred Hawkshaw was discomfited. It took time to persuade her to summon her daughter but she eventually acceded to his request. There was an even longer delay as she argued with Emily then more or less forced her daughter to come downstairs. The girl was sullen and withdrawn when she came into the room. She refused to sit down.

'Very well,' said Colbeck, settling into a chair, 'you can stand up. I think that you know why I've come back again, don't you?'

'No.'

'I want the full story, Emily. And let me assure you of one thing. Whatever you tell me is in strictest confidence. I'm not going to pass it on to anyone – not even to your mother. She's the one person who must never know, isn't she? At least, that's what you think now.'

'I don't know what you're talking about.'

'I think you do, Emily. Did your father commit that murder?'

'No!' she retorted.

'Would you swear to that?'

'On the Bible.'

'But would you confess *why* you're so certain about it?' asked Colbeck, lowering his voice. 'No, you wouldn't, would you? Because you had a chance to do just that at the trial.' Emily's cheeks were drained of what little colour they possessed. 'The reason you know that he could not possibly have killed Joseph Dykes is that you were with your father at the time.'

'That's not true!' she cried.

'Except that you never saw him as your real father, did you? He was kind to you. He protected you from Adam. He was your friend.' The girl let out a gasp of horror at being found out. 'You loved him as a friend, didn't you, Emily? There's no question that he loved you. Nathan Hawkshaw went to the gallows rather than betray you.'

'Stop!' she implored.

'It has to come out, Emily,' he told her, getting up to stand beside the girl. 'The truth is a poison that must be sucked out of you before it kills you. I'm not here to judge you or to tell you that what you did was wrong. All I want to do is to find the man who did kill Joseph Dykes then went on to murder two other people. Did your mother tell you what happened yesterday evening?'

'No.'

'This man that we're after tried to shoot me, Emily.' She looked at him with dismay. 'Unless we catch him, there'll be other victims. You're in a position to help us. Do you want more people to be killed as a result of what happened that day at Lenham fair?' She shook her head. 'Then tell me the truth. You'll be helping yourself as much as me.'

Emily stared up at him with a fear that was

tempered with a wild hope. Colbeck could see that she was wrestling hard with her demons. The guilt that had been oppressing her for weeks was now bearing down like a ton weight.

'You won't tell Mother?' she whispered.

'That's something that only you should do, Emily.'

'I feel so ashamed.'

'I think that your father – your friend, I should say – deserved to bear the greater shame. You were too young to understand what was happening. He was much older – he knew.'

'I loved him.'

'And he loved you, Emily, but not in a way that a stepfather should. It cost him his life.' She shuddered. 'I'm sure that he repented at the last. He took the sin upon himself. You don't have to go through life with it hanging over you forever.'

'Yes, I do.'

'Why?'

Emily was not able to tell him yet. She was still shocked and frightened by the way that he seemed to have looked into her mind and discerned her secret. It was unnerving.

'How did you know?' she asked.

'There were clues,' he explained. 'When you were attacked by Dykes, you didn't turn to your mother for help. In fact, you pulled away from her. And, at the very time when you should have been drawn closer as you mourn together, you shut her out.'

'I had to, Inspector.'

'You lost the person you really loved and you felt that you couldn't live without him.'

325

'I caused him to die.'

'No, Emily.'

'If he hadn't been with me that day, he'd be alive now.'

'And what sort of life would it have been?' asked Colbeck. 'The two of you were lying to your mother and lying to each other. It could never have gone on like that, Emily. It was only a matter of time before you were found out. Think what would have happened then.'

'I hated all the lies and deceit,' she admitted.

'You went along with them out of love but it was never a love that you could show to the world. You asked me how I knew,' he went on, 'and it wasn't only because of the way you treated your mother. There was your fear of the doctor as well.' His inquiry was gentle. 'Are you with child, Emily?'

'I don't know – I may be.'

'If that's the case, then you tried to kill *two* people when you went up that church tower. That makes it even worse. You must have been in despair to do that.'

'I was. I still am.'

'No, Emily. We're drawing that poison out of you. It's going to hurt but you'll feel better for it in the end. You have to face up to what you did instead of trying to run away from it. Most important of all,' he stressed, 'you mustn't take all the blame on your own shoulders.'

'I can't help it, Inspector.'

'You were led astray by your stepfather.'

'That isn't how it was.'

'He admitted his guilt by giving his life to save yours.'

'It was not like that,' she told him, her eyes filling with tears. 'Joe Dykes did touch me in that lane but that was all he did. I only pretended that he did much more than that. Before I ran back here, I even tore my dress. I wanted Nathan to comfort me. That's how it all started,' she said with a sob in her voice. 'I just *wanted* him.'

By the time he got back to the inn, Victor Leeming had decided that his visit to Wye had not been in vain at all. He had something to report. To his disappointment, however, he did not find Colbeck at the Saracen's Head. In the Inspector's place were George Butterkiss and a complete stranger. The Constable leapt up at once from his chair and came across to Leeming.

'I found him, Sergeant,' he declared, as if expecting a reward.

'Who?'

'Amos Lockyer. Come and meet him.'

He took Leeming across to the table and introduced him to his friend. The two of them sat down opposite Lockyer, a short, fleshy man in his late fifties with an ugly face that was redeemed by a benign smile. His hand was curled around a pint of beer and, from the way he slurred his words, it was clearly not his first drink of the day.

'How did you track him down, Constable?' asked Leeming.

'I remembered the Romney Marshes.'

'Why?'

'Because I once told George that I'd like to retire there,' said Lockyer, taking up the story. 'I had an uncle who was on his last legs and he promised to leave his cottage to me. I got word of his death when I was working at Leeds castle. *That* was no job for me,' he told them with disgust. 'I wasn't born to fetch and carry for my betters because I don't believe that they were any better than me.' He gave a throaty chuckle. 'So, after I'd buried Uncle Sidney, I decided to retire.'

'That's where I found him,' said Butterkiss. 'At his new home.'

'You did well,' conceded Leeming.

'Thank you, Sergeant. But how have you got on?'

'The first two ladies on that list could be discounted at once, but I'm not so sure about the third. What can you tell me about Kathleen Brennan from Wye?'

'Nothing beyond what I told you before.'

'There was something very odd about Mrs Brennan.'

'You should have asked *me* about her,' said Lockyer, helpfully. 'What's odd about Mrs Brennan is that she's the only woman I know who wears a wedding ring without having been anywhere near a husband.' He grinned amiably. 'A husband of her own, that is.'

'She's not married?'

'No, Sergeant, and never has been.'

'How do you know her?'

'From the time when she used to serve beer at the Fountain,' recalled the older man. 'This was before your time, George, so you won't remember Kathy Brennan. She was very popular with the customers.'

'That was the feeling I had about her,' said

328

Leeming. 'She was too knowing. As if she was no better than she ought to be.'

'Oh, I don't condemn a woman for making the most of her charms and Kathy certainly had those. They were good enough to start charging money for, which was how she and I crossed swords.'

'You mean that she was a prostitute?' asked Butterkiss.

'Of sorts,' said Lockyer, indulgently. 'And only for a short time until she saw the dangers of it. I liked the woman. She always struck me as someone who wanted a man to love her enough to stay by her but she couldn't find one in Ashford. What made her change her ways was that business with Joe Dykes.'

'I don't remember that,' said Butterkiss.

'What happened?' prompted Leeming.

'Joe was in the Fountain one night,' said Lockyer, 'and he took a fancy to Kathy. So off they go to that lane behind the Corn Exchange. Only she's heard about his reputation for having his fun then running off without paying, so she asked for some cash beforehand.'

'Did he give it?'

'Yes, Sergeant. But as soon as Joe had had his money's worth up against a wall, he attacked the poor woman and took his money back from her. Kathy came crying to me but, as usual, Joe had made himself scarce. He was cruel.'

'In other words,' said Leeming, realising that he had just been given a valuable piece of information, 'Kathleen Brennan had a good reason to hate Dykes.'

'Hate him? She'd have scratched his eyes out.'

It was at that point that Robert Colbeck returned to the inn. Seeing the three of them, he came across to their table. As soon as he had been introduced to Lockyer, he took over the questioning.

'Did you follow Jacob Guttridge to his home?'

'Yes,' replied Lockyer, uncomfortably.

'Then you are an accessory to his murder.'

'No, Inspector!'

'Amos didn't even know that he was dead,' said Butterkiss, trying to defend his former colleague. 'The first he heard about the murder – and that of the prison chaplain – was when I told him about them.'

'It's true,' added Lockyer, earnestly. 'I was stuck on a farm, miles from anywhere. You don't get to read a newspaper when you're digging up turnips all day. When George told me what's been going on, I was shaken to the core.'

'Yet you admit that you followed Guttridge,' noted Colbeck.

'That's what I'm good at – finding where people live.' He took a long sip of his beer. 'I knew he'd lie low in Maidstone prison after the execution so I stayed the night there and waited at the station early next morning. Mr Guttridge caught the first train to Paddock Wood then took the train to London from there. Unknown to him, I was right behind him all the way.'

'Like a shadow,' said Butterkiss, admiringly

'Not exactly, George, because he walked much faster than me. This old injury slows me right down,' he said, slapping his thigh. 'He almost

330

gave me the slip in Hoxton. I saw the Street he went down but I didn't know which house was his. So I waited on the corner until he came out again and I followed him all the way to Bethnal Green.'

'To the Seven Stars,' said Colbeck.

'That's right, Inspector. How did you know?'

Leeming was bitter. 'We know all about the Seven Stars,' he said. 'If you went there, you must have discovered that Guttridge was going to be on that excursion train to watch the big fight.'

'It was the only thing that people were talking about,' explained Lockyer. 'The landlord was making a list of all those who were going to support the Bargeman. Jake Guttridge was one of the first to put himself forward, though he gave a different name. I don't blame him. The Seven Stars wasn't the place to own up to being a hangman.'

'What happened afterwards?'

'I trailed him back to Hoxton. The trouble was that he spotted me and broke into a run. I had a job to keep up with him but at least I got the number of his house this time. I earned my money.'

'From whom?'

'The person who paid me to find his address.'

'And who was that?'

'Inspector,' pleaded Lockyer, 'I had no idea that he intended to kill Guttridge. I swear it. He said that he just wanted to scare him. If I'd known what I know now, I'd never have taken on the job.'

'Give me his name, Mr Lockyer.'

'I was a policeman. I'd never willingly break the law.'

'His *name*,' demanded Colbeck.

'Adam Hawkshaw.'

Inspector Colbeck took no chances. Aware that Hawkshaw was a strong young man in a shop that was filled with weaponry, he stationed Leeming and Butterkiss at either end of Middle Row to prevent any attempt at escape. When he confronted the butcher in the empty shop, Colbeck was given a sneer of contempt.

'What have you come for *this* time?' said Hawkshaw.

'You.'

'Eh?'

'I'm placing you under arrest for the murders of Jacob Guttridge and Narcissus Jones,' said Colbeck, producing a pair of handcuffs from beneath his coat, 'and for the attempted murder of a police officer.'

'I never murdered anybody!' protested the other.

'Then why did you pay Amos Lockyer to find the hangman's address for you?' Hawkshaw's mouth fell open. 'I don't think it was to send him your greetings, was it? What you sent him was a death threat.'

'No,' said Hawkshaw, defiantly.

'You'll have to come with me.'

'But I'm innocent, Inspector.'

'Then how do you explain your interest in Jacob Guttridge's whereabouts?' asked Colbeck, snapping the handcuffs on his wrists. 'How do you account for the fact that you were seen taking a train to Paddock Wood on the night of the chaplain's murder?'

'I can't tell you that.'

'No, and you probably can't tell me where you were yesterday evening, can you? Because I don't believe that you were in your lodging. You were cowering in a doorway opposite the Saracen's Head, waiting for me to come out so that you could shoot me.'

'That's not true,' said Hawkshaw, struggling to get out of the handcuffs. 'Take these things off me!'

'Not until you're safely behind bars.'

'I had nothing to do with the murders!'

'Prove it.'

The butcher looked shamefaced. Biting his lip, he grappled with his conscience for a long time. Eventually, he blurted out his confession.

'On the night of the chaplain's murder, I did take a train to Paddock Wood,' he said, the words coming out slowly and with obvious embarrassment, 'but it was not to go after him. I went to see someone and I took the train over there again last night.'

'Can this person vouch for you?'

'Yes, Inspector, but I'd rather you didn't ask her.'

'A lady, then – a young lady, I expect. What was her name?'

'I can't tell you that.'

'Is that because you just invented her?' pressed Colbeck.

'No,' rejoined the other, 'Jenny is real.'

'I'll believe that when I see her, Mr Hawkshaw. Meanwhile, I'm going to make your mother aware of your arrest then take you back to London.'

'Wait!' said Hawkshaw in desperation. 'There's no need for this.' He swallowed hard. 'Her name is Jenny Skillen.'

'Why couldn't you tell me that before?'

'She's married.'

'Ah.'

'Her husband is coming back today.'

Colbeck knew that he was telling the truth. If he had a witness who could absolve him of the murder of Narcissus Jones then he could not be responsible for the other killings.

'Why did you pay Amos Lockyer to find that address?' he asked.

'I wanted revenge,' admitted Hawkshaw. 'When I saw the way that he made my father suffer on the scaffold, I just wanted to tear out his heart. I didn't say that to Amos. I told him that I just wanted to give the man a fright. He agreed to find his address for me, that was all. When he came back, he told me that Guttridge would be at a prizefight in a few weeks' time.'

'So you decided to go on the same excursion train?'

'No, Inspector – I give you my word. If I'm honest, I *thought* about it. I even planned what I'd do when I caught up with him. But I don't think I could have gone through with it.'

'Did you discuss this with anyone else?'

'Yes,' said Hawkshaw, 'and he talked me out of it. He told me that I couldn't bring back my father by killing the man who hanged him. He made me see how wrong it would have been and got me to promise that I'd forget all about it. He stopped me.'

'Who did?'

'Gregory – Gregory Newman.'

There were tears in his eyes as he stood beside the bed and looked down at his wife. Meg Newman had not woken all day. She lay in a sleep so deep that it was almost a coma. On the rare occasions when she did open her eyes for any length of time, she inhabited a twilight world of her own in which she could neither speak, move nor do anything for herself. Her husband gazed down at her with a mixture of love and resignation. Then he bent down to give her a farewell kiss that she never even felt.

'You once begged me to do this,' he said, 'and I didn't have courage to put you out of your pain and misery. I have to do it now, Meg. Please forgive me.'

Gregory Newman put the pillow over her face and pressed down hard. It was not long before his wife stopped breathing.

Having released his prisoner, Colbeck went marching off to the railway works with Leeming and Butterkiss. As a precaution, he deployed them at the two exits from the boiler shop before he went in. When he found the foreman, he had to shout above the incessant din.

'I've come to see Gregory Newman again,' he yelled.

'You're too late, Inspector.'

'What do you mean?'

'He left half-an-hour ago,' replied the foreman. 'Someone brought word that his wife had taken a turn for the worse. I let him go home.'

'Who brought the message?'

'A young woman.'

Colbeck thanked him then hurried outside to collect the others. When he heard what had happened, Leeming was able to identify the bearer of the message.

'Kathleen Brennan,' he said. 'I think she came to warn him.'

'Let's go to his house,' ordered Colbeck.

They hurried to Turton Street and found the door of the house wide open. The blind had been drawn on the downstairs front window. Colbeck went quickly inside and looked into the front room. Weeping quietly, Mrs Sheen was pulling the sheet over the face of Meg Newman. She looked up in surprise at Colbeck.

'Forgive this intrusion,' he said, removing his hat. 'We're looking for Mr Newman. Is he here?'

'Not any more, sir. He told me Meg had passed on and he left.'

'Where did he go?'

'I don't know,' said Mrs Sheen, 'but he had a bag with him.'

'Thank you. Please excuse me.'

Colbeck came back out into the street again. Butterkiss was keen.

'What can I do, Inspector?' he volunteered.

'Nothing at all. He's made a run for it.'

'I just can't believe that Gregory is involved in all this. He's such a kind and considerate man.

336

Look at the way he cared for his sick wife.'

'He won't care for her anymore.'

'I think I know where he may have gone,' said Leeming.

'Where's that, Victor?'

'To the place where his female accomplice lives.'

'Who is she?'

'Kathleen Brennan. We need to get to Wye straight away.'

'How do you know that this woman is his accomplice?'

'Because I saw her riding towards Ashford earlier on,' said Leeming, 'and now I realise why. I never expected to hear myself say this, Inspector, but I think that we should take a train.'

Kathleen Brennan bustled around the tiny bedroom and gathered up her belongings. She put them in a large wicker basket, threw her clothes over her arm then went down the bare wooden stairs. Gregory Newman was sitting in a chair, brooding on what he had done. Putting everything down on the table, Kathleen went over to comfort him.

'It had to be done,' she said, 'and it was what your wife wanted.'

'I know, Kathy, but it still hurt me.' He gave a mirthless laugh. 'Strange, isn't it? I killed three people I hated and all I felt was pleasure and satisfaction. It's only when I smother someone I loved that I feel like a murderer.'

'It was no life for her, Gregory. It was a blessed release.'

'For Meg, maybe – but not for me.'

'Why do you say that?'

'Because I feel so *guilty*.'

He put his head in his hands. Kneeling beside him, Kathleen coiled an arm around his shoulders and kissed him on the temple. After a while, he looked up and tried to shake off his feelings of remorse. He pulled her on to his lap and embraced her warmly.

'Thank you, Kathy,' he said.

'This is what we both wanted, isn't it?'

'Yes.'

'You always said that we'd be together one day and now we are.'

'I didn't expect it to happen like this,' he said. 'I thought that Meg would have died long ago but she clung on and on. It would have been so much easier if she could have passed away by now.'

'I had to warn you,' she insisted. 'Sergeant Leeming frightened me with his questions. How on earth did he know that I was involved?'

'He didn't but he found his way out here somehow. That was a danger signal, Kathy. You were right to come to me.'

'He mentioned an Inspector Colbeck.'

'Damn the man!' said Newman. 'He's behind all this. He dug away until he unearthed things that I never thought he'd find. Because he was getting closer all the time, I shot him last night. I hoped I'd killed him.'

'It didn't sound like it.'

'Then we must get far away from here, Kathy. It's only a matter of time before they work out that I murdered Joe Dykes and the others.'

'Joe got his deserts for what he did to me,' she said, harshly.

'If you'd given me that cleaver, I'd have killed him myself.' She grinned. 'You should have seen the look in his eye when I brought him out of the Red Lion. By the time we got to the wood, he was panting for me.'

'Making him undress like that made such a difference,' he recalled. 'All that I had to do was to carve him up.' He kissed her full on the lips. 'I couldn't have done it without you, Kathy.'

'Or without Nathan.'

'He was just where we needed him.'

'When I saw what he was doing, I had no qualms about letting him take the blame. I looked on her as my own daughter and Nathan was–'

'Yes, yes,' she interrupted. 'You paid him back.'

'I paid them all back,' he said, proudly

'And now we can be together at last.'

As they hugged each other again, Robert Colbeck opened the door. He doffed his hat and he stepped into the room. They sprang apart.

'You shouldn't leave the windows open,' warned Colbeck. 'It only encourages eavesdropping.'

'What are *you* doing here?' gasped Newman, getting to his feet.

'I've come to arrest the pair of you.'

'I thought that I shot you.'

'You tried to, Mr Newman, but your aim was poor. You'll pardon me if I don't turn my back and let you have a second attempt with a piece of wire. I know that's your preferred method.' He looked at Kathleen. 'My name is Inspector Colbeck. I believe that you met my Sergeant earlier.'

'Kathy is nothing to do with this,' insisted Newman.

'Then why did she ride to Ashford to warn you?' asked Colbeck. 'Sergeant Leeming saw her from the train. Your foreman told me that a young woman with red hair came for you in the boiler shop.' He saw Newman eyeing the open door. 'And before you decide to bolt again, I should warn you that the Sergeant is outside with Constable Butterkiss.'

Kathleen was dazed. 'How did you get here so quickly?'

'By train.'

'And you heard us through the window?'

'I'd worked out some of it out beforehand,' said Colbeck. 'Once I knew that Nathan Hawkshaw could not possibly have committed that crime, it narrowed the search down. The one thing I would like clarified is what happened to Hawkshaw's coat.'

'Gregory stole it,' said Kathleen.

'Be quiet!' he snapped.

'I think I can guess the circumstances in which it was taken,' said Colbeck, seizing on the detail. 'It was lying there with the rest of his clothing, wasn't it – and with the meat cleaver that he'd brought?'

'How did you know about that?' asked Kathleen, open-mouthed.

'I think you'll be surprised what we know, Miss Brennan.' He produced the handcuffs again. 'We'll spare you the indignity of these,' he said,

340

'but Mr Newman is another matter. Shall we, sir?'

Gregory Newman heaved a massive sigh and held out his wrists. As soon as Colbeck tried to put the handcuffs on him, however, he pushed the Inspector away, grabbed Kathleen by the hand and ran through the door. Constable Butterkiss tried to stop him but was buffeted aside by a powerful arm. Newman ran to his cart and lifted Kathleen up into the seat, intending to whip the horse into a gallop and get free. But he became aware of an insurmountable problem.

'We took the liberty of taking your horse out of the shafts,' said Colbeck, pointing to where the animal was grazing happily, 'in case you tried to escape.' Newman leaned over to grab his bag from the back of the cart and thrust his hand into it. 'I also took the precaution of removing this,' said Colbeck, taking out the revolver from beneath his coat. 'Unlike you, I know how to fire it properly.' Newman slumped forward in his seat. 'Are you ready for these handcuffs now, sir?'

They had never seen Superintendent Tallis in such an euphoric mood. He normally smoked cigars in times of stress but this time he reached for one by way of celebration. Colbeck and Leeming stood in his office at Scotland Yard and basked in his approval for once. Cigar smoke curled around their heads like a pair of haloes.

'It was a triumph, gentlemen,' he said. 'You not only solved two murders that occurred on trains, you exonerated Nathan Hawkshaw from a crime that he didn't commit.'

341

'Too late in the day,' said Leeming. 'He'd already been hanged.'

'That fact has caused considerable embarrassment to the parties involved and I applaud that. Where a miscarriage of justice has taken place, it deserves to be exposed. It will be a different matter for that monster, Gregory Newman.'

'Yes, sir. He's as guilty as sin.'

'So is that she-devil who helped him,' said Tallis, thrusting the cigar back between his teeth. 'They may have disposed of one hangman but there'll be another to make them dance at the end of a rope. When I was a boy,' he went, nostalgically, 'over two hundred offences bore the death penalty and it frightened people into a more law-abiding attitude. Only traitors and killers can be executed now. I maintain that the shadow of the noose should hang over more crimes.'

'I disagree, Superintendent,' said Colbeck. 'To hang someone for stealing a loaf of bread because his family is starving is barbaric in my view. It breeds hatred of the law instead of respect. Newman and his accomplice deserve to hang. Common thieves do not.'

Tallis was almost jovial. 'I'll not argue with you, Inspector,' he said, 'especially on a day like this. I know that you'll win any debate like the silver-tongued barrister you once were. But I hold to my point. To impose order and discipline, we must be ruthless.'

'I prefer a combination of firmness and discretion, sir.'

'That's the way we solved the railway murders,' said Leeming.

'Yes,' said Colbeck with amusement. 'Victor was firm and I was discreet. We made an effective team.'

Colbeck's discretion had been shown in abundance. He tried to protect those who would be hurt by certain revelations. Though he told the Sergeant about his long interview with Emily Hawkshaw, he had suppressed the facts that he knew would scandalise him. Edward Tallis had been told nothing about the relationship between the girl and her late stepfather. Colbeck had not deemed it necessary. The evidence to convict Gregory Newman and Kathleen Brennan was irresistible. There was no need to release intimate details that would be seized on by the press and turn an already unhappy home into an unendurable one.

'How did the widow receive the news?' asked Tallis.

'Mrs Hawkshaw was in a state of confusion, sir,' said Colbeck. 'She was delighted that her husband's name had been cleared but she was shocked that Gregory Newman was unmasked as the killer and the man who sent those death threats. She had trusted him so completely.'

'He must have hated her to let her husband die in his place.'

'I think that he loved her, sir, and felt that Hawkshaw was unworthy of her. In his own twisted way, he thought that he could please her by killing two of the people who had inflicted needless pain on her husband. Yes,' he said, anticipating an interruption, 'I know that there's a contradiction there. How can a man allow someone to go to the gallows in his stead and then avenge him? But it was not a contradiction that troubled Gregory Newman.'

'His life was full of contradictions,' said Leeming. 'He pretends to care for his wife and yet he goes off to see Kathleen Brennan whenever he can. What kind of marriage is that?'

'One that imposed immense strain on him, Victor.'

'You're surely not excusing him, are you?' asked Tallis. 'I'm no proponent of marriage, as you know, but I do place great emphasis on sexual propriety. In my opinion, Newman's relationship with his scarlet women is in itself worthy of hanging.'

'Then there'd be daily executions held in every town,' said Colbeck, bluntly, 'for there must be thousands of men who enjoy such liaisons. If you make adultery a capital offence, sir, you'd reduce the population of London quite markedly.' Tallis bridled. 'No, the problem with Gregory Newman was that he had too much love inside him.'

'Love! Is that what you call it, Inspector?'

'Yes. He was a man of deep passion. When his young wife was taken so tragically ill, that passion was stifled until it began to turn sour. We saw it again in his strange devotion to Win Hawkshaw. We did, Superintendent,' he went on as Tallis scowled. 'He cared for her enough to want to rescue her from an undeserving husband even if it meant sending that husband to the scaffold. Love turned sour is like a disease.'

'It infected him and his doxy,' said Tallis. 'If I had my way, she'd be paraded through the streets

344

so that all could see her shame. The woman deserves to be tarred and feathered.'

Colbeck was glad that he had not confided details of the more serious irregularity that he had uncovered. The Superintendent would have been outraged, insisting on the arrest of Emily Hawkshaw on a charge of withholding vital evidence at the trial of her stepfather. Colbeck saw no gain in such an action. The girl had already punished herself far more than the law would be able to do. Before he left Ashford, she had confided one piece of reassuring news to Colbeck. She was not pregnant. No child would come forth from her illicit union to make her shame public. Colbeck had left the girl to work out her own salvation. Thoroughly chastened by all that had happened, she seemed ready to take a more positive attitude to past misdemeanours.

'The rest,' declared Tallis, 'we can safely leave to the court.'

'That's what everyone felt at Hawkshaw's trial,' said Leeming.

'Don't be impertinent, Sergeant.'

'No, sir.'

'Our work is done and – thanks to you, gentlemen – it was done extremely well. I congratulate you both and will commend you in my report to the Commissioners. You have cleansed Ashford of its fiends.'

'We did get some assistance from Constable Butterkiss,' remarked Leeming, ready to give the man his due. 'He found Amos Lockyer for us.'

'That reflects well on him.'

'Yes,' said Colbeck, smiling inwardly as he

thought of Madeleine Andrews, 'our success is not solely due to our own efforts, sir. We had invaluable help from other sources.'

The last bit of paint was still drying on the paper when she heard the sound of the Hansom cab in the street outside. Madeleine Andrews was flustered. Certain that Robert Colbeck had come to see her, she was upset to be caught in her old clothes and with paint all over her fingers. She grabbed the painting and hid it quickly in the kitchen, swilling her hands in a bucket of water and wiping them in an old cloth. There was a knock on the front door. After adjusting her hair in the mirror, Madeleine opened the door to her visitor. He was holding a posy of flowers.

'Robert!' she said, pretending surprise.

'Hello, Madeleine,' he said, 'I just wanted to thank you for the help that you gave us and to offer this small token of my gratitude.'

'They're beautiful!' she said, taking the posy and sniffing the petals. 'Thank you so much.'

'You deserve a whole garden of flowers for what you did.'

'I'm so glad that I could help. But you are the only true Railway Detective. You are on the front page of the newspaper once again.'

'Yes, Superintendent Tallis was pleased with that. He feels that our success should be given wide publicity to deter other criminals.'

'He's right.'

'I have my doubts, Madeleine. It only serves to warn them to be more careful in future. If we reveal too much about our methods of detection in newspaper articles, we are actually helping the underworld.'

'Be that as it may,' she said, 'won't you come in?'

'Only for a moment.' He stepped into the house and she closed the door behind them. 'I'm on my way to Bethnal Green to honour a promise I made to Victor Leeming.'

'Oh, yes. You told me that he was set upon at the Seven Stars.'

'That's why I'm letting him lead the raid. I'll only be there in a nominal capacity. We're going to close the place down for a time by revoking the landlord's licence.'

'On what grounds?'

'Serving under-age customers, harbouring fugitives, running a disorderly house. We'll think up plenty of reasons to close the doors on the Seven Stars. And however random they may seem,' he went on, 'I can assure you that those reasons will all have a solid foundation. In his brief and bruising visit there, Victor noticed a number of violations of the licensing laws.'

'And that's where Jacob Guttridge used to go?'

'Only when disguised under a false name.'

'Who was the man who followed him that night?'

'Amos Lockyer,' he replied. 'A policeman from Ashford who was dismissed for being drunk on duty and who took on the commission to make some money. In fairness to him, it never crossed his mind that such dire consequences would result from his work.'

'I'm thrilled that I was able to help you.'

'It will encourage me to call on you again, perhaps.'

Madeleine beamed. 'I'm at your service, Inspector,' she said. 'But while you're here, I have a present for you – though it isn't quite dry yet.'

'A present for me?'

'Close your eyes, Robert.'

'You're the one who deserves a present,' he said, closing his eyes and wondering what she going to give him. 'How long must I wait?'

'Only a moment.' She took the posy into the kitchen and returned with the painting. Madeleine held it up in front of him. 'You can look now, Robert.'

'Good heavens! It's the *Lord of the Isles*.'

'I knew that you'd recognise it.'

'There are two things you can rely on me to recognise, Madeleine. One is a famous locomotive in all its glory.'

'What's the other?'

'Artistic merit,' he said, scrutinising every detail. 'This really is a fine piece of work. Quite the best thing you've ever done.'

'Then you'll accept it?'

'I'll do more than that, Madeleine. I'll have it framed and hung over the desk in my study. Then I'll invite you and your father to come to tea one Sunday and view it in position.'

'That would be wonderful!'

Madeleine had never been to Colbeck's house before and she felt that the invitation marked a step forward in their relationship. He had been careful to include her father but she knew that he was giving her a small but important signal. Her own signal was contained in the painting and he could not have been more appreciative.

'Thank you, thank you,' he said, unable to take his eyes off the gift. 'It's quite inspiring.'

'Father was very critical,' she said.

'He is inclined to be censorious. I find no fault in it at all.'

'It was my choice of locomotive that upset him. Mr Gooch built the *Lord of the Isles* for the Great Western Railway. Since he works for another railway company, Father thinks that I should have done a painting of one of their locomotives.'

'Mr Crampton's *Liverpool*, for instance? A splendid steam engine. That was built for the London and North Western Railway.'

'*Lord of the Isles* has a special place in my heart,' she said. 'As I was painting it, I recalled that magical day we spent together at the Great Exhibition. That's when I first saw it on display.'

'I, too, have the fondest memories of that occasion,' he told her, looking across at her with affection. 'When the painting has been hung, bring your father to take a second look at it.' He gave her a warm smile. 'Perhaps we can persuade him that you did make the right choice.'

It was the clearest signal of all. Madeleine laughed with joy.

The publishers hope that this book has given you enjoyable reading. Large Print Books are especially designed to be as easy to see and hold as possible. If you wish a complete list of our books please ask at your local library or write directly to:

Magna Large Print Books
Magna House, Long Preston,
Skipton, North Yorkshire.
BD23 4ND

This Large Print Book for the partially sighted, who cannot read normal print, is published under the auspices of

THE ULVERSCROFT FOUNDATION